Books by A.Z.A Clarke

Battalions of Oblivion

Dream Guy

I0663149

Dream Guy

ISBN # 978-1-78651-367-0

©Copyright A.Z.A Clarke 2016

Cover Art by Posh Gosh ©Copyright 2016

Interior text design by Claire Siemaszkiewicz

Finch Books

Published in 2016 by Finch Books, Newland House, The Point, Weaver Road, Lincoln, LN6 3QN, United Kingdom.

Finch Books is a subsidiary of Totally Entwined Group Limited.

Battalions of Oblivion

DREAM GUY

A.Z.A CLARKE

Dedication

For Hugo who may read it,
Sebastian who suggested it
and Peter who has read it.

Chapter One

Fishpeople

A late lesson on a damp November afternoon... Joe had already had sports and maths, psychology, English and French. He was shattered, especially after having walked away from so much aggro from bloody Charlie Meek during break and lunch. His classroom was dark and sweaty. There was no need for blinds — none of which worked anyway — but the windows were moist with condensation, and the room was quiet, apart from the hum of the projector and numerous teenage jaws masticating chunks of gum.

Joe was trying to stay awake. He liked looking at Mr. Crosbie's pictures, and these were strange — full of intense, somber colors. There were snowy scenes marred by the blood of children being killed against sunsets gleaming through bare branches, crucifixions with crowds of blokes looking as though they'd come from the pub after a heavy Saturday night then contorted bodies surrounded by flying fish and walking rats with hats and curled mustachios. That couldn't be right. He squinted, but the familiar heaviness of his head and eyelids assailed him. He pinched himself to stay awake, but the heat was too much. Even the discomfort of the creaking plastic chair couldn't stop him from drifting away from the classroom and into the deepest sleep.

Then he opened his eyes. Something had woken him. He looked around and recoiled. Every student in the class had a fish head — wispy catfish whiskers over suckery open mouths, barracuda jaws, weird mola mola fins where their hair ought to be, a couple of trout with delicate little teeth and tongues. They all had those glassy eyes, just like it said in recipe books — bright, moist, black eyes. They were breathing air. Then it seemed to occur to them that they were breathing air and that, technically, they couldn't.

Their sucky mouths gaped, fishy lips opening and closing faster and faster. They began bumping into one another, blundering about, their bodies still human but their brains too small to govern those bodies. Then they revolved with the swirl and drive of a shoal of mackerel in the sea, no longer threshing, now turning on Joe with glazed stares — glares that turned from accusation into threat. They were an exact copy of the fish in that slide of Crosbie's.

Joe scrambled out of his seat and stood by the door. One of the fish-people stepped forward, then another, and they came at him. He raised his hands to fend them off then the first one reached him. He felt its fishy lips puckering and flapping against his palm. It was real. He wrestled with the door handle then fell into the corridor, slamming the door as he left the room, only to hear the sodden thump of a fishy nose against the wood. He slumped against the wall. The fluorescent lights were bright, and there was a chilly draft from the fire escape that had been left open by someone making a break for freedom after period seven. An English teacher was approaching, but he took forever to reach Joe because with every step, the corridor got longer.

"Joe Knightley, isn't it? What are you doing out here?" Mr. Tucker's voice was distant. "You look as green as this wall. Hey, Joe, are you all right? Joe, grab my hand, quick."

But Joe didn't have time to take Mr. Tucker's hand, because he'd been absorbed into the wall and was now trapped in the layer of mesh and plaster, gasping like the fish in Mr. Crosbie's room. The teacher was running his hands over the wall, calling his name over and over. Then Joe disintegrated and melted right through it, back into the classroom that was full of water like the fish tank at the fishmongers where they kept lobsters. Now the classroom was awash and the fish people were swimming around and around and around, their bodies still in their school uniforms, all of them chasing after one another until they became a shoal like in a documentary — swooping, splitting, dipping and recombining. Joe swam to the window to check his reflection. He had a human head, which meant he would drown if he stayed in the fish tank.

Mr. Crosbie was there, still showing slide after slide, but he was wearing scuba gear, apparently unfazed by the transformation of his habitat. Joe swam to a window and wrestled with it. He pushed up the lever handle then took hold of the catch to ease it open. Water started gushing out, and Joe pushed his head free, taking long gulps of cold air. He turned around as water cascaded around him. The fish-people pressed up against the window and tried to flap it shut, but the volume of water was too great, pouring out and out and out onto the ground. Fortunately for Joe, fins weren't equipped to close windows. Mr. Crosbie waded through the water, still thigh-high in the classroom, and he flicked on the light. Everyone turned to look at him. They shook their heads in bafflement and in the whir of movement, one by one, they regained their normal heads, although these were now soaked, causing some dismay among those who'd used gel or mousse to maintain their favored hairstyle.

"Joe, I know Hieronymus Bosch can seem a bit strange, but he doesn't normally cause my students to chunder out of the window. Have you quite finished?" Mr. Crosbie took off his aqualung and diving mask.

"I wasn't being sick, sir. It was the water." *How can I explain? It started as a dream...then somehow I made my dream actually come true. They're going to think I've gone bonkers. I think I've gone bonkers, but it did happen. It really happened. My dream came true. No way I can say that out loud.*

"Give him a detention, sir," urged several girls, their hair hanging in limp rats-tails. "Go on. He pinched the condoms from last time and used 'em to make water bombs. It was him. We saw."

His friend Smokey spoke up. "How can you have seen anything? Anyway, look around you. There isn't any evidence." Smokey's tone was customarily derisory. "Witless bimbos."

The girls turned as one on Smokey. "Give *him* a detention an' all, sir. Go on. He's abusing us. That's bullying that is, calling us bimbos. Go on, sir. Give him one."

"Smokey, Joe, get out of here before the lynch mob gets you. And Joe, try not to nod off in next week's lesson." Mr. Crosbie nodded at the boys. As they left, Joe heard him address the hyena-like hoydens surrounding him. "Now, girls, where's your sense of humor? What sort of fish did you turn into, Kaylee? A monkfish, I think—not particularly attractive but very tasty grilled with a saffron sauce."

As they came out, Mr. Tucker was waiting outside the classroom with the school nurse, pointing at the wall and saying, "Look. He was standing here, then the wall just sucked him up." The teacher closed his eyes and leaned his forehead against the wall, as if fighting off tears.

The nurse looked understanding and patted him on the shoulder. "I think you should see someone about this, Mark. Really I do. Look. Here's Joe Knightley now. Everything all right, Joe?"

"Yeah, fine, Mrs. Naismith."

"You see, Mark? Joe's absolutely fine. He's been in Mr. Crosbie's classroom all this time. Learn anything useful in PSHE this week then, Joe?"

"Not really." Joe burrowed into his rucksack for the brochure Crosbie had handed out. It was sodden and disintegrating. He offered it to the nurse. "Here. It's about how to be a town councilor, I think."

"Off you go then, Joe. And is that Silas with you?"

No one was meant to call Smokey by his given name, but Joe could see that he was too keen to ask Joe what the hell was going on to make a big issue of Mrs. Naismith's slip. Joe let Smokey hustle him down the corridor and out of the building before anyone else could interrupt.

"So?" Smokey stopped as they rounded the corner of Ashgate Way and sat down on someone's garden wall.

Joe bit his lip. "So what?"

Smokey reached into his jacket for his cigarettes and lighter. With disgust, he took one sodden fag out of the packet then scrunched up the whole squelchy mess and tossed it into the garden behind him. "Four quid down the drain. So why did we all grow fish heads, and you didn't? If it hadn't been for you, we'd all have been swimming around there for the next week without anyone noticing. Mind you, it was quite cool being a piranha. I was just about to give Lisa a little nibble, then you came along and opened the window."

"I don't know. I don't understand anything." Joe shook his head. A flurry of movement caught his eye, and he hauled Smokey away as an irate woman emerged from the house on whose garden wall they were sitting. She yelled at them, snatched up Smokey's crumpled cigarettes and hurled the pack after them with a force that should have earned her a place on the Olympic javelin team.

"Don't do that again, you little sods!"

Smokey made to turn around so he could tell her to eff off, but Joe was still tugging at his sleeve, determined not to let things get out of hand. Smokey shrugged then went back to the fishy business.

"What do you mean, you don't understand?"

"I was asleep. I just woke up, and it'd happened. Wasn't Tucker looking sick as a parrot? That was worth it. Weird though. Could you breathe? What was it like when the water came in?"

"Crosbie made it happen. He just whipped out his scuba kit from somewhere and turned a stopcock and the whole place filled with water really quickly. Remember when we went on that trip to the battlefields in Belgium?"

"Yeah. Flanders field trip. What about it?"

"Remember that weird fountain outside Ypres? The tap standing in the middle of nowhere and just pouring out water?"

Immediately Joe recalled the huge blue tap with water gushing out of it, suspended in the air on a little roundabout on the way into Ypres.

"Well, it was like that," continued Smokey. "Just a big tap with loads of water filling the place up in seconds. It was a relief, speaking as a fish, I can tell you. We were all lying around flapping our gills until then."

"Why was the projector still working? When I came back in the room, it still had that weird picture up on the wall, but you guys were all swimming around, all going in the same direction. Did you know you were a fish, or were you just in a fish state?"

"I had conscious thoughts, like how fat and juicy Lisa's legs looked, but I didn't think, 'Hey, man, how did I get to be a fish?' That seemed natural." Smokey paused. "Do you think you made it happen when you fell asleep or something?"

"Don't be daft. How could I do anything like that?"

"You're bonkers, you are. Look. I'm going to be late back. I'd better get home."

Smokey nodded and thumped Joe on the back before loping off into the darkness. Joe adjusted his backpack and walked on toward his house. He felt damp and increasingly cold, so he quickened his pace and was almost running by the time he reached the path. The lights were on in the front and upstairs, which meant that Mum was home.

After his shower, he came downstairs in shorts and a T-shirt. His parents might nag about money, but at least they kept the house at a decent temperature, despite moaning nonstop about heating a drafty Edwardian barrack. Joe still remembered going around the house the first time six years before. They'd left Liesel, then three, with Gran, but both Ben and Joe had wanted to see the house. High ceilings, weirdly shaped rooms, the old-fashioned bathroom and the open-plan kitchen leading into the walled garden with an apple tree and a mass of rhododendrons... They'd all loved it. It had been way too expensive, but somehow his parents had scraped together the deposit. Joe had been eight when they'd moved in. First he'd shared with Ben, but when it came to Ben's GCSE year, they'd moved Joe upstairs to the third-story loft, which had been converted into two bedrooms and a shower room.

Susan Knightley was in the kitchen, leaning over the table where Liesel was slumped over some homework. They both looked up as Joe came in, still rubbing his hair dry with the towel.

"Good day?" asked his mother.

"All right. You know."

"See if you can help Liesel with this stuff, will you? Then I can get on with making supper."

Joe sighed. "I don't know why you can't be just like everyone else and get us stuff to microwave."

"A, because it's expensive. B, because it's bad for you. C, because I want us to sit down and talk to one another occasionally instead of living like strangers occupying the same space, and D, because I like cooking. How many times do we have to go over this one, Joe? I'm never going to be 'like everyone else', and you might as well accept it."

Her voice was beginning to sound plaintive, so Joe rushed to help Liesel to avoid any further discussion. He just couldn't seem to say anything to her these days without getting some ratty answer. Liesel shifted her book away as Joe sat next to her.

"Joe's no good. I'm better at maths than he is. I'll wait for Ben."

Joe rolled his eyes and curled his lip at her. Ben was best at everything. Ben was the one everyone wanted to wait for. Ben was the reason girls like Becky Sutton and Chloe Hance even spoke to Joe. It wasn't exactly original to hate your own brother, but increasingly, Joe found himself unable to resist loathing Ben — Mr. Perfect. He wished that girls liked him for himself, not because his brother was the best-looking boy in year twelve. And if they found out the truth about Ben—which they would any day now that Charlie Meek had seen him coming out of the Rainbow Hacienda down in Brighton entwined with his boyfriend, snotty Zahid—they'd think Joe was gay too. Bloody Ben.

Chapter Two

Home

"That's not very fair," said Mrs. Knightley to Liesel, as Joe lumbered off to slump on the sofa and mess with the remote. "Joe is actually quite good at maths, and you were really mean."

"So?" Liesel thumped her books into a pile and stood, the wooden chair legs screeching against the tiled floor.

"Liesel, how many times have I told you not to do that?"

"You shouldn't have put in your soppy old quarry tiles then. Dad wanted to put lino down, and it would have been miles better — and cheaper," Liesel answered.

Before Mrs. Knightley could say any more, Liesel had flounced out. Joe peered over the sofa and saw his mum pursing her lips in frustration. Instead of following Liesel, his mum began dicing onions like a fiend. Ben would be back soon. He would smooth things over.

In the sitting room, Joe checked out the PS4 but all the games seemed lame. He flicked through the channels on the telly. Every channel was showing hours and hours of stuff that had been on a hundred times before. It was like supper being nothing but leftovers. He flicked to *The Simpsons*. It was one he'd seen before, but it was still better than all the other rubbish sitcoms.

So what exactly happened in Crosbie's class? So bizarre, the bright colors of the fish, the slop of the water, the graininess of the plaster. There had been a moment between wakefulness and sleep when something had tipped him out of the solid world he had known, a shiver of awareness like the moment you know when you've made the wrong move in a computer game, and it's too late to back off. He'd lied to Smokey. Well, he hadn't denied it point-blank, but he certainly hadn't told the truth, because he'd known that he *had* made the dream happen. He just wasn't sure how.

By now, Joe was lying full stretch along the sofa, his feet propped on the armrest at the other end. He gazed at his feet distractedly as his eyes drooped closed, trying to work out the exact sequence of events and simultaneously thinking that his feet seemed outrageously enormous. They reminded him more and more of those pictures drawn by Elizabethan explorers of the one-footed tribesmen who used their feet as umbrellas to protect themselves from the heat of the sun. His eyes snapped open, but his feet were up there, entirely the right size. Big, as Mum never tired of pointing out, but not bizarrely huge.

He closed his eyes again then heard the scrape of a key in the lock, and he sat up quickly, adjusting his T-shirt and crossing his arms as Ben came in. Joe listened as his brother took off his coat, hung it on the rack in the hall and went through to the kitchen, where he exchanged effusive kisses and hugs with his mother. Liesel came running downstairs and joined in, her earlier grump forgotten. Joe idled on the sofa, his gaze fixed on the patterns in the carpet.

Liesel showed Ben the maths homework. While sniffing at the pot of whatever stuff Mum had on the stove and agreeing with her disquisition on which herbs to use to bring out the flavor of beef, Ben also managed to give Liesel a tutorial in long division. He was such a suck-up. Then he came through to the sitting room.

"What's up, mate?" Ben sat on the arm of the sofa and clapped a hand on Joe's shoulder, nearly knocking him off. Joe shrugged his hand away.

"Nothing much. You know. Just school."

"I heard something weird happened in Crosbie's class. You must have done something pretty amazing to freak Tucker out. He was gibbering like a chimp in the nurse's room." Ben threw himself into the big armchair, plonked his feet onto the coffee table and looked at Joe, who averted his gaze.

"It was nothing. He was just imagining stuff. He probably picked up one of those weird pills that Charlie Meek is punting around the place. He's such a dodgy geezer, Meeky." Joe leaned forward, picked up the *Radio Times* on the table and stared at it as though Jane Asher's recipe for a stress-free dinner party was massively gripping. But Ben wasn't about to be diverted onto the topic of Charlie Meek.

"I heard something about tons of water coming out of the room and everyone's heads going weird, except yours."

"Where'd you hear that?"

"Michaela Potts. You know. Big hair, thinks she's God's gift to Terpsichore. She's in your class, isn't she? She's always hanging about, but she doesn't usually say much. A bit different today."

Ben's dance classes...*argh*. "It's embarrassing you doing dancing."

"You know why I do the dance class. It's good for balance, and it's given me upper body strength, hoicking all those girls around." Ben's pained expression reminded Joe of the way their mother had reacted to him over the dinner business.

"It's poufy. People laugh at you." He sounded strident — and stupid.

"They don't any more. Not since they worked out it's a great way to pull in girls — and you get to cop a feel." Ben smirked. "In fact, we've had a few new recruits. I'm getting a bit less of a workout these days."

"Well, you're hardly interested in feeling up girls, are you?"

"Oh, don't flog that old horse again, Joe. It's dead already." Ben stood up. "If you don't want to talk about the fish thing, that's cool with me. You just have to say."

Before Joe could reply, Ben called into the kitchen, "I'll be there to help in about an hour, Mum, but I've got work to do now, okay?"

"That's fine, darling. Joe, homework. Go on. Hop to it."

Joe stood, yawned and trudged upstairs. There was some reading to do for English and for psychology. He had to draw some triangles for maths and a rain gauge for geography. It was a worthless collection of activities. Teachers were either cynical bastards, deliberately concocting useless tasks, or even sadder, that they were pathetic tossers who genuinely believed that the work they set had a purpose.

He turned on the bedside light and the desk lamp, unpacked his bag and stacked his books on his desk. He sat in his swivel chair and twirled around. Dad and he had painted the room last summer. Now it was white with black gloss skirting boards and woodwork. They had whitewashed the floorboards, and Mum had found him black bed linen and a rug that looked like a Mondrian painting, with big red and white panels crossed by thick black lines. Three of the four walls were covered in whitewashed corkboard, and these were pinned with layer after layer of drawings.

Joe could track his progress through the drawings. Through chinks, you could see copies of Tintin and Snowy, Thompson and Thomson, Captain Haddock, Dennis the Menace, Gnasher, Desperate Dan. There had been an Asterix phase, but Joe had really only been interested in scenes of Roman-bashing, along with some of the more familiar comic book heroes — Batman and his 'Pow! Thwack!', Spiderman swinging through the streets of New York, a brief X-Men phase. That had been succeeded by the Matt Groening phase, not so much the Simpsons as Abdullah and the sad rabbit of School and Love being Hell. And the Sandman. He couldn't work out which of the artists who had worked on the Sandman he liked best, but his favorite pictures were always the ones of Morpheus himself. Punk, eyes shaded, speech bubbles reversed so that his words were white in a black puddle, like a whisper from the dark. Mum had thought he had been too young for the books, but Dad had said he was mature enough and had given him the first three.

This year, for the first time since he'd been a little kid, he'd begun his own strip. It was based on his family, but the pictures weren't on display. They were carefully stowed in the portfolio chest that Mum had found in a secondhand shop and restored for his birthday. He went over and pulled the third drawer open, where he knew that no one would look—not Gloria the cleaner, not Mum, not Liesel on her snooping expeditions. He slid across to his draftsman's table and switched on the halogen desk lamp, pulled at the tapes fastening the folder and leafed through the sheets of A3 cartridge paper on which he'd started to record his family's peculiarities. He hadn't had a chance to show them to Dad, not yet. The way things were going, he wondered if he ever would. He tied the folder up again, hid it away and reached for a fresh sheet of paper.

First he taped it to the table surface, portrait layout.

Then he drew up a series of boxes—a large box along the whole width of the paper at the top, three medium-sized boxes evenly spaced in the center then a pair of boxes at the bottom, the left-hand one slightly larger than the right, and a zigzag margin interlocking the two, in a stylized tearing of the page. He took a pencil and sketched in the outlines of his characters—Liesel, Mum, Ben, himself—but this time they were animals. He gave Mum a sheep's head. Liesel was depicted as a little weasel with mean, darting eyes and he'd drawn himself as a donkey. But Ben's head was normal—a little vulpine around the mouth, otherwise as gorgeous as always. There they were in frame one, ready for inking.

Next came the lettering. He'd named his series the Knormal Knightleys. And this time, the final box had a picture of Donkey Joe giving Ben an almighty kick and sending him flying through the window into the moonlit garden.

As usual, once Joe was absorbed into the world of his strip, he lost all sense of time and place. Nothing intruded on his concentration. All his fears for his father, all his irritation with his mother, all his loathing of his sister and brother poured onto the page. At last, rubbing his eyes, he covered his drawing board with innocuous sketches and bits of tracing paper. He stood, stretched and ambled downstairs, feeling altogether better.

Downstairs, Ben and Liesel were watching MTV, arguing about who was the prettiest member of the boy band polluting the screen. Mum was finishing off the cooking while listening to some comedy program on Radio Four. Joe went to the dresser and got out the cutlery.

"Got everything done, love?" asked Mrs. Knightley.

"Pretty much. Have you heard from Dad today?"

"Yeah, he sent an email. There's one just for you, as well."

"Do I have time to check it before we eat?"

"Yes, I suppose so. Go on then." Joe heard resignation in her voice.

Joe sat down at the computer in the corner of the kitchen and logged on. The only good thing about Dad's current job was that he'd gotten his company to pay for the installation of a broadband connection at home. There was the email in the family's postbox. Dad had written to Ben and Liesel too, but Joe noticed that his email was longer than theirs, which was a pathetic thing to notice, he knew, but it made him happy anyway.

Dear Joe,

How's tricks, old man? It's dull as ever out here in the desert, but the job does seem to be moving on a bit, which is good news after all the delays we've had recently. The thing I wanted to write to you about is a book that one of the guys here showed me, all about a mag published in the 1980s that was all comics, called Raw, and I wondered if you'd heard of it. If not, I'll try to get one of the Americans out here to get hold of it for you next time they go home.

Also, I got your latest copies, and it made me think it was probably time you did stuff of your own again, wouldn't you say? I don't think I told you, but when I packed to come out here, I put in the book you made when you were seven. When I look at it, it takes me right back to when you were all kids, just after we'd moved. Ben was eleven and mad about skateboards and nothing else, Liesel was just three. You were the only one I could have a sensible conversation with that didn't involve cuddly toys or ball bearings and Tony Hawk. You stuck so many things in that notebook. Of course, there were the monsters and the robots and the stuff that seven-year-olds like – Godzilla, some superhero cartoon off the box. But you also did those really funny drawings of the family. I was wondering if you'd ever thought about doing anything like that again. You could scan them in and email them to me. Even snail mail seems to work – although none of us expected it to – if you don't want to leave your work on the computer for the others to see.

The thing is, it looks like with all the delays so far that my contract will last longer than we'd thought. And if you could do a strip for me and send it out, maybe home wouldn't feel quite so far away.

What about it? I've put this in a separate email from the others because if you did it, you probably wouldn't want the rest of the family to find out about it. And I wouldn't really want them to know either. Just a secret for the two of us, because then you'll be able to draw and write exactly what you want.

I miss you all so much.
Love, Dad.

Joe swallowed hard. He could just hear his father's voice, faintly, like an echo. He'd been away for two and a half months now. His company had offered him a pretty stark choice – the reconstruction contract or redundancy. And the money they'd offered if he'd take the contract had been too good to miss. Mum and Dad were going to be able to pay off the mortgage and fork out for Ben's university course so he wouldn't have to take out a loan.

"Are you ready, Joe?" Susan Knightley didn't take her eyes off Joe as he closed the email and came to the table.

"What's this about Dad's contract?"

"They want him for a year. He can come home at Christmas

and Easter, but basically, he's out there until next October."

Joe sat, his elbows on the table, his fingers plunged deep into the dense thicket of his hair, massaging his skull. "That sucks." He could tell by the tone of her voice that she hadn't been happy with the news either, although financially it was a miraculous break from the continual teetering on a tightrope between solvency and debt. They'd have no money worries at all at the rates Dad was getting paid. They might even have savings.

Liesel and Ben soon filled the silence with gossip and chatter about school and teachers and the endless negotiations about whom Mum would ferry where and when. Joe could stay at home alone. He didn't play any instruments or sports that needed lessons or practice or concerts or matches. Maybe that was the reason Liesel and Ben got on so much better with each other than with Joe — hours spent in the car together and pretty much the same obsessions with music and sport. It had always been that way, almost since Liesel was born.

Joe made good his escape as soon as he'd finished shoveling up the last of his stew.

"Don't you want any pudding?"

"I'm all right, Mum. Honest."

The other two smiled uneasily and said good night in chorus before returning to their conversation. Joe went back upstairs.

Chapter Three

Lamborghini Gallardo

Nirvana on the iPod, a sole halogen light over the drawing board… First the blue pencil for the rough outline then the heavy pencil. Then the color and finally, the ink. And there it was, the dream—voluptuous curves, steel hubcaps, cruel grills, a shade somewhere between gold and cadmium lemon, black leather upholstery with yellow stitching, six-gear transmission and, lurking in the center of the car, the V10 engine that delivered five hundred horsepower at seventy-eight hundred revolutions.

If only… It wasn't as if he were greedy. He wasn't aiming as high as the Murciélago, but even the smallest Lambo was as expensive as a house. Money was a weird thing. If you said it fast, one hundred and forty thousand pounds didn't sound like so very much, not when the radio bombarded you with all those boring statistics about how many billions the National Health Service cost or how much credit card debt had been run up in the last six months. But in real life, where you had to take the rubbish out and make sure you did your share of the ironing before Mum would part with a tenner, where next year, a job at McDonalds or at the local Tesco's on minimum wage was going to be the only way to get any spare cash, the price of a Lamborghini was a crazy number, like the number of matches it would take to build a scale replica of the Houses of Parliament—seventy-eight million three hundred thirty-three thousand six hundred twenty-five—or the number of elephants it would take to stretch between earth and the moon—give or take about fifty-two million five hundred eighty. Unfortunately, there weren't enough elephants in the world to run that particular experiment, although it would be interesting to design a spacesuit for an elephant.

Joe went to the bathroom to brush his teeth and check his pimple status before turning out the light. The thing was, if he could make people turn into fish, why couldn't he make a drawing turn into a real car? It would be inconvenient, though, to have a full-sized car in his room. So perhaps, if he put the drawing outside in the drive, it would be there, ready for the morning.

Joe slipped on a pair of combats and his hoodie. Then he dug around his desk for a plastic wallet and slipped his drawing into it. He quietly eased his door open. He clung to the wall, taking each step one at a time. Now was not the time for an interrogation from Mum or Ben. But it was dark downstairs, all the lights switched off in the living room and the hall. A dull orange glow from the streetlight shone through the stained glass in the front door. Joe eased back the bolts then carefully pulled at the lever on the lock. He put it on the latch and went into the front garden. There was a pile of bricks tucked below the front wall, left over from the last lot of repairs. Joe took one to anchor down the drawing, hoping that a Lamborghini had sufficient clearance for a brick. He positioned the car so that it was facing out of the drive. He could almost imagine it there. Almost, but not quite.

After locking up properly, he went to the kitchen and poured himself some mineral water from the fridge. A light flicked on at the top of the stairs.

"Joe, is that you, love?" Susan Knightley sounded sleepy and a little hesitant.

"Yeah, Mum."

"What are you doing skulking about in the dark?" Relief sharpened her voice. "Honestly, I thought we were being burgled."

"I couldn't get to sleep. I just thought I'd get some water."

"Fine. Go to bed, sweetheart. It's past midnight."

Which reminded Joe that he had done absolutely no homework. He could blag the reading, but he knew he had better do the drawings for maths and geography. It didn't take long, twenty minutes or so with a protractor and a set square, and both assignments were done. He repacked his school bag and climbed into bed, turning his alarm clock on before taking one last look at the picture of the Gallardo, which he had taken from a brochure and stuck on the wall. Then he switched off the light.

* * * *

The next thing Joe knew was his mum ruffling his hair and stroking his cheek.

"Come on, love. I don't know what you were doing up half the night, but it's time for breakfast. You'll be late if you don't get up now."

He shoved her hand away, then jackknifed up, his eyes bleary. "Okay, Mum. I'll be down in a sec." He waited and she backed away. She was wearing her power suit. No wonder she had come up. She had one of her meetings with senior management. She'd be chewing the carpet if they weren't out of the house promptly this morning.

"See you downstairs then." She turned and went, closing the door with a businesslike click behind her. Joe had the quickest shower ever, threw on his uniform and clattered down the stairs three at a time. He wrenched the front door open and looked in the driveway. There she was — golden, glowing in the dull November dawn. She had been reversed into the drive and the first thing that Joe could see was the twin exhausts, one on each side of the car's rear, positioned in the grill, and above, the neat cursive signature confirming that it was a Lamborghini. The first surprise was how small it was — low, with sweeping curves and a voracious, snub-nosed front. The second surprise was that the car had no number plates.

Neither at the front nor at the back. He wondered where those should go and how to get them. But for now, he was content to walk around the extraordinary beast in the driveway—wondering, worshipful, awed. It did not take him long to start touching the metal, running his hands over the roof and the bonnet. He walked around again. It was left-hand drive.

Presumably it was legal to use left-hand drive cars in the UK. Tourists from Europe did it all the time. But it must be a little weird. He stood by the driver's door. He didn't have a key, but there was no visible lock anyway. Presumably it was one of those flash electronic plip keys. He hadn't thought about keys last night. He hadn't thought about anything practical, because who would? He reached down and pushed at the latch. The handle made a solid, substantial sound, and the door eased open a little way then rose into the air. The scent of leather wafted upward and he gazed at the bucket seats with stitching, the bizarre seventies-style swirly carpeting, the handbrake and the range of dials—rev counter, tachometer, speedometer, temperature gauge, fuel gauge, altitude, latitude, longitude. The car seemed to have it all, but he'd have to climb in and check.

He stretched his right leg in then folded himself up and levered his left leg in afterward. He'd have to practice so the maneuver was smooth and natural, a little less like an ostrich taking a seat. He closed the door. It gave a thick, dark clunk. He was enveloped in the black interior, adjusting his posture in the hard seat, stretching his arms out to grasp the wheel, seeking out the pedals with his feet. There were three.

Accelerator, brake and clutch, he assumed. There was no key in the ignition. There was no gearstick either, just some weird additional levers sticking out from the steering column, which must be the famous robotized e-gear. There were buttons everywhere, a satellite positioning system, a CD sound system and really that was it. Not much more than Dad's standard executive VW. Not even much more than Mum's old Golf.

The glove compartment was locked. He reached round the edge of the seats and under the carpets, but there was no sign of a key. Then the dream ended and the nightmare began, because Mrs. Knightley opened the door of the beautiful machine then leaning one hand on the roof of the Gallardo, said with quiet menace, "Joe, where the hell did this come from?"

He looked up at her. She did not seem surprised or amazed or awed, just suspicious, verging on furious. He noticed her skinny eyes with wrinkles radiating along clearly defined paths, and she had a lipless mouth, like a lizard's poised to eat a fly. This wasn't just a morning mood. She was about two seconds away from a Grade-A tantrum.

"I won it. I won it in that prize draw I entered at the airport when we went to Tenerife in the summer."

"You can't have. You had to be eighteen to enter that. And you had to pay twenty quid. You didn't have twenty quid."

"Ben entered it for me and I paid him back."

"Ben's not eighteen either."

"He said he was."

"For God's sake, Joe, we were in an airport. They were checking people's passports. And they just drove it here in the middle of the night and left it for you, I suppose?"

"We just said that our group leader had all the passports, and they didn't care. They just wanted the money."

"So they just thought they'd drop the car off with no warning — no phone call, no letter, nothing?"

"I guess not."

"So how did they verify your identity?"

"What do you mean, Mum?"

"They're not going to hand over a car worth the price of a flat to some snotty-nosed fourteen-year-old, Joe. Give me a break." She pushed back from the car and stood, hands on hips, elbows out in classic 'impatient mother' stance.

"I just found it here, Mum. I just assumed." He had a feeling that the innocent tone in his voice was wearing thin.

He could see where she was going and decided to forestall her. "I don't have the leaflet anymore. I chucked it ages ago."

"So you think that you may have won this car in a dodgy raffle designed to fleece fools in the airport. Well, you'd better get out of there, give me the key and let me get it out of the way and into the garage so I can get my car out and take it to work…where I will then waste half my morning by phoning around, trying to work out how to give the damned thing back."

"You can't give it back! It's a prize. It's *my* prize." Apart from the fact that he had no idea who she could give it back to.

"You won it under false pretenses, Joe. You can't drive it. I won't drive it. We can't afford to insure it, and they won't think it good publicity when they discover that it was handed over under fraudulent circumstances to a couple of daft schoolboys."

Joe had no answer to this tirade. He just sat there, looking up at his mother. Her hands were shoved deep in her pockets as though she were preventing herself from taking a swipe at him.

"Get out of the car, Joe. And give me the key."

He clambered out. It wasn't comfortable or dignified getting out of the car in front of an unsympathetic witness. It was better once he was standing up and able to look down on his mother. "There's no key."

"What!"

Although she didn't swear out loud, her silence was eloquent. Joe took a step back. "I can't find a key. I thought they would have left it in the car, but it doesn't seem to be there. Maybe they dropped it through the letterbox."

"If there is no key, Joseph Knightley, you will be mincemeat. I will turn you into meatloaf for your brother and sister to eat for supper tonight and if there are any leftovers, I will feed you to the cat and the hamster and the goldfish." Mrs. Knightley turned and walked back toward the door where Ben appeared. Joe didn't think it was a good time to remind her that the cat was dead and buried in the garden.

"Holy sh…ugar!" He managed to cut off the expletive as he caught his mother's glare. "Where did *that* come from?"

"You should know, Ben. You helped Joe lumber us with it."

"What do you mean?" He looked entirely blank. Joe winced and closed his eyes.

"You pretended you were eighteen and you paid the money he needed to enter this stupid draw. Didn't you?"

Ben caught Joe's eye and uneasily rubbed his chin. "Yeah, that's right. Yeah, it's coming back to me." He came over to Joe and gave him a big hug. "Hey, man, congratulations! I can't believe it!"

"Nor can I," said Susan. "Did you see an envelope as you were coming out of the door, Ben?"

"No, nothing. Why?"

"This car has just appeared here in our driveway, without a key. So my car is trapped in the garage and we have this thing cluttering up the front garden."

Ben came up with a solution at once. Susan could sit in the car, release the handbrake then the two boys could roll the car a short way down the drive, which would provide enough room to drive the Golf onto the lawn. Then they could push the Lamborghini back into the garage, where it would be safe until the prize draw company came to collect it. It was workable, even when one of the Golf's wheels ended up in a flowerbed and needed to be levered onto a plank so that Susan could get it back onto the tarmac. She couldn't wait and had to leave with Liesel still sobbing with laughter at the sight of her two brothers covered in mud, ensuring that at least the females in the Knightley family reached school and work on time.

Ben and Joe waved them off then went back inside. They'd missed the bus for school and walking there would make them even later. There was no real rush. They'd both make it in time for the second lesson. It wasn't as if they were habitual absentees.

"Do you want the first shower, Joe?"

"No, you go ahead." He avoided Ben's eyes.

"So what was all that about me paying for your prize draw ticket?"

"Thanks for covering for me, Ben." He made to run upstairs, but Ben caught his arm and Joe turned to look at his brother.

"Seriously, Joe, where'd you get that car?"

"You wouldn't believe me if I told you. But I didn't nick it."

"Of course you didn't. First of all, where would you find a car like that around here? And second, if you'd nicked it, I don't think you'd be such a complete tosser as to park it in our front drive." Joe smiled and Ben let go of his arm abruptly. "Okay. It's your secret. But Joe, if you need my help, you just have to ask."

"Yeah. I know. Give me a shout when you're out of the shower."

Joe would rather apply for a place on the X-Factor than get any help from Ben. He clumped upstairs to his bedroom, stripped off his muddy uniform then jumped into the shower and whispered, "I'm a racing car passing by like Lady Godiva." As the water pulsed down, he played air guitar and sang, "Don't stop me now, don't stop me, don't stop me, don't stop me now..."

Chapter Four

The Key

Ben and Joe walked to school in their customary uneasy silence. The gates were closed when they arrived, and they had to show passes to the security guard in his little hut. The big security drive seemed stupid and unnecessary, like most school rules, but since a boy who had been kicked out had come back and tried to stab the receptionists as well as his form teacher, the place was harder to get into than the Queen's knickers.

Which meant any skiving was also quickly picked up. As they crossed the forecourt to the main classroom block, Ben spoke.

"Do you want me to come and explain to Elphick?"

"Nah. I'll do it myself. It's all right. Thanks."

"Okay. See you later then." Ben headed off toward the sixth form block.

Joe crossed the lobby to Elphick's office. The door was open, which meant she was there. No escaping it then. He knocked and waited in the doorway.

"Come in." Elphick, the youngest-ever deputy head of Cosham High School and extremely up herself as a result, was abrupt.

"It's me, Mrs. Elphick. I'm late this morning. I've missed first period."

"So I see. Oversleeping isn't a common complaint in the Knightley household. Do you have an explanation?" Elphick leaned back in her chair, her arms crossed.

"I do, but it's a bit complicated. We got a new car, and it

was parked in the drive, but we couldn't find the key, so we had to move it by hand then get my mum's other car out of the garage for her, and by then, me and Ben—"

"Ben and I." She'd been head of English until her promotion the previous year.

"Ben and I had missed the bus. My mum didn't have time to write a note in my diary, but she said you could phone her to check."

"Thank you, Joe. I might do that, have a little chat about your recent contretemps in the canteen, perhaps. Or discuss the narcolepsy that seems to be plaguing you in lessons. I don't suppose you have that problem at home."

Joe was tempted to give an equally sarcastic response, but he knew that would rile her, and now she was just toying with him like a cat with a beetle. There were plenty of mice for her to sink her teeth into. He just had to wait for her to be distracted by one and accept that she was going to bat him about a bit from paw to paw.

When she saw he wasn't going to rise, she turned back to her computer and said, "I appreciate your dropping in, Joe. Off to your classes now."

He was in time for the second half of double geography. He shook himself into an apologetic posture before knocking and entering.

"Sorry I'm late, Mr. Green. I've just been to Mrs. Elphick."

"Fine, Joe. Got your rain gauge?"

Joe had to take a seat near the front, next to Nell Brennan. He found his folder and handed over the work, accepted the worksheet that everyone was theoretically completing and sat down by Nell. She had finished and was curled over the textbook, reading ahead. He was tempted to swipe her completed worksheet and copy it, but he knew the Nell of old, and she'd kick up a bleeding big stink if he tried anything like that. Some girls would have been fine with it or would even have handed their work over as a matter of course, but Nell was afflicted with a competitive streak, combined with general hatred of the opposite sex. She was flinching from him now, hunching farther away, if that were possible.

Joe focused on isobars and wind speeds. The worksheet was straightforward to anyone with half a brain. It took only minutes to fill it in. He looked around. As far as he could see, everyone had finished, but Green was deep in some marking and hadn't noticed that Donna Pettigrew was texting *War and Peace* to her mate, Liesha Atkins, or that Warren had one hand up the back of Vikki Watt's blouse and was struggling to unclasp her bra while she sat apparently unconcerned.

Joe dug in his book bag for his sketchpad. He flicked it to a fresh page and began doodling. He penciled a quick line drawing of the Gallardo from various angles. Then Green stood up, stretched and cleared his throat. The class snapped to attention, although it took Vikki a little undignified groping about to resecure her assets.

"Right. Let's go through the worksheet then. Nell, will you start us off with the answer to number one?"

Of course, she obliged. Of course, she had the answer right, and of course, she had to explain her method to the rest of the class since over half of them had no clue what to do, still less how to do it. *The school should just give in and appoint her to teach,* thought Joe. *She does it better than most of the staff.* Greeno set the class to redoing the worksheet.

"Joe, check your answers against Nell's. You've probably grasped the principle at work here, but if either of you finds any discrepancies, I'm sure you can sort out your differences."

Nell shoved her sheet at Joe without meeting his gaze before turning back to her book and studiously ignoring him. Unfortunately, their answers matched entirely so there was no chance of irritating her by forcing her to explain her thinking on any of the questions. He wondered what her solution to his key dilemma would be. He drew the Lamborghini bull then a key fob around it. Then it came to him. He simply had to draw the key and dream about it, just like he had with the car. If he could set up the dream, he would be able to get the key. Then maybe Mum would calm down enough to let them keep the car.

The first thing was to track down an image of the key. There was one more lesson before break, maths. If he could make a quick getaway, he might reach the IT room before the geeks colonized it. There was bound to be an image of the key on the Internet.

Nell was watching him doodle. He didn't look her directly in the eye, but he was aware of her glance. He knew exactly which buttons to press. He began with a rough outline but soon had the sweep of arms, hips, thighs and the high, rounded breasts in place. Then he started on the detail—the micro-mini of fur, the little leather bikini bra, the long, tousled hair, the pouting lips, the huge cow eyes with eyelashes owing more to Maybelline than nature.

Nell muttered a scornful, "Typical!" and turned so that she didn't have to gaze any longer on the pneumatic cavegirl Joe had drawn on the back of…oh, Nell's worksheet.

Ouch. The thing was, winding Nell up wasn't a plan. He'd never started out the day thinking 'Hmm, must needle Nell until she's in a complete fury', but if she provided him with an opportunity, he always took it. Because now, the only time she ever seemed to realize he existed was when he aggravated her. Three years ago, they had shared everything. Now they couldn't share a desk without provoking each other.

Joe glanced at his watch. The bell was about to go. He packed up surreptitiously. Green was one of those teachers who had succumbed to the illusion that his lessons were interesting and took it as a mortal insult if anyone appeared to want to leave the classroom too early. The bell went. Joe waited until Green nodded absently. He was first out of the door and the first into his maths class. He took the desk right under McKechnie's nose. She gave him a skeptical look, which soon dissipated as the rest of the class came in, and she prepared to grapple with today's subject, factorization.

Ibrahim Majeed came in. Zahid's brother. He saw Joe and gave him a filthy look and headed to the back of the class. Ibrahim hated all the Knightleys. Zahid said that it was because Ib was devout and blamed the Knightleys, thought they had corrupted him into falling for Ben. Even though every other member of the Majeed family seemed to be totally cool with it.

McKechnie cleared her throat. She was the only teacher Joe had any time for at all. She had been at the school longer than most other teachers, but she didn't look any specific age. She was in some limbo between thirty and sixty. Her basic uniform was a navy pleated skirt and a matching sleeveless sweater.

The days of the week depended on her shirt color. If it was lemon, it was Monday. Mint must mean Tuesday. Wednesday was always duck-egg blue, Thursday a sort of cream of mushroom and Fridays were pale pink. She had short, wiry hair, a nose like a ski jump, protuberant blue eyes and dark, heavy eyebrows that made her skin seem all the more colorless.

Other teachers might go off on a tangent, but the only tangent McKechnie knew was the trigonometric one, and she made damn sure that all her higher tier students understood all there was to know about that tangent too. Every day, she left the school in her navy coat, carrying her navy satchel and her navy handbag, climbed into her navy car and disappeared to some navy paradise. That was all anyone knew about her.

She only took top sets and no one ever messed about in her classes. She did occasionally have weak students who only achieved a B, but mostly, her students were drilled into A and A-plus grades. No time was ever wasted, no exercise was ever pointless and no idle interpersonal chitchat was permitted to interfere with the McKechnie Machine. Hers was the only lesson in which Joe had never been able to get away with a swift snooze.

Nell stood over Joe, who had taken her usual seat. He

looked at her blankly, determined not to react to her Medusa glare. It was only McKechnie's dry voice that ended their silent combat.

"Miss Brennan, if you'll take a seat – any seat – we can get started."

Nell's mouth tightened and Joe knew that another negative piece of data had been entered into her processor, just to add to the already item-heavy folder that Nell was storing on him. She went to the only empty seat in the class by sweaty Sonia Riding and sat there, simmering because Joe had made her appear petty.

As McKechnie led the class through the intricacies of the topic, there was no time to dwell on slights, intended or otherwise, and the bell came as a shock to all twenty-eight kids entwined in their problems. Joe stuffed his books into his backpack and was out of the door the second McKechnie dismissed them. He walked briskly, itching to run but determined to give no teacher any cause to haul him up for hurtling too fast down the stairs and into the IT space. His timing was good and by the time the usual rush for monitors started, he was already exploring Lamborghini images on Google. Then there it was, a fob with the Lamborghini bull and two keys, one folded up on itself, the other fully extended, complete with plip buttons. He hit Print, checked to see that it was coming out, logged off and went to pay the technician monitoring the room fifteen pence for the copy. Once he'd collected the picture, he was at a loss. He needed somewhere quiet to draw and snooze. He had twelve minutes left before the end of break. All the classrooms would be locked. There was nowhere quiet to go apart from the library, but it was more than five minutes' walk from the classroom block. By the time he'd reached it, he'd have to head back again.

The English classrooms were all on the top floor, though, and that was generally quiet at break. There were a couple of chairs outside the English office where parents could wait if they had been hauled in to see a teacher. It would seem a bit odd, but he could go there. He logged off, pushed his chair back from the desk and bumped into Ibrahim, who muttered "Kaffir," under his breath. Joe did say sorry but didn't hang around.

But before he reached the top floor, Joe had to navigate the main hall, which was where he encountered Charlie Meek with Dylan Spriggs and Damien Bewbush. They were leaning against a wall, juggling with their baseball caps and eating crisps. When they saw him, they maneuvered themselves into the middle of the corridor and blocked his way. Charlie looked at him, his eyes slitted and suspicious.

"What were you doing in Elphick's room this morning?"

Joe considered the 'none of your business' line but couldn't be bothered with the aggravation it would cause.

"I was late. I had to explain why. That's all."

"So why was you late?" Charlie was not yet ready to let it go.

"Family stuff." Joe's gaze and voice were steady. It was funny realizing that he was taller than Charlie now. Meeky had always been the biggest boy in the class, but this year, Joe had topped him. Dylan and Damien were shorter still, although Damien did have the physique of a side of beef. Both acolytes munched their crisps with menace. But their packets were nearly empty and the effect was less impressive with crumbs.

"Bumboy stuff with your bumboy brother." Charlie turned away.

"Like you with your bumboy mates, you mean." It escaped before Joe could master his unruly tongue. Charlie whipped around and brandished his fist under Joe's chin.

"I'll get you for that. Elphick's on me case, otherwise I'd do it now, but I'll get you, you little sod. You and your shirt-lifter brother. Poofs." He hawked and spat. His timing was impeccable. It landed inches away from a pair of black patent leather stilettos in which Mrs. Elphick's feet were firmly planted.

"Charles, how pleasant of you to demonstrate your

charming manners to the rest of us. Fortunately, I have paper towels in my office, so you will come with me while I ring your mother to comment on this episode, and you will then clear up your phlegm. And did I hear you use homophobic language? I believe I did. I think our school code of conduct has something to say about that too. Shall we discuss the next few days of your schooling while you tidy up the mess?"

"What about Joe? He called my friends bumboys. That's ho-mo-pho-bick."

"Really, Charlie? And who threw the first insult in this edifying conversation? Damien, perhaps you can assist me in my inquiries. Who first used the term *bumboy*, Charlie or Joe?"

Damien stuttered and stammered. Dylan rolled his eyes and said, "Charlie, Mrs. Elphick. Charlie said it first." He gave Charlie a weary look. "I've had enough of this, Charlie. My mum is going to go mental if I get in trouble again, and every time I hang out with you, I do."

Charlie was so astonished by this defection that for once, he was silent.

"Thank you for corroborating my suspicions, Dylan. You may go to your next class, as should the two of you." She nodded in dismissal and Joe, Dylan and Damien melted away.

The first bell for the end of break clanged through the building and Joe ran up the stairs. At least now he'd be able to get into the classroom, and provided he got one of the side places toward the back of the room, Mr. Thomas was unlikely to notice if he dozed off during the class.

He'd counted on it without considering Smokey, though. It was the only other class they shared, and Smokey regarded it as an extension of his break. Mr. Thomas had neither the power nor the will to alter things, and where Smokey led, the rest of the class—particularly the girls—followed in unquestioning obedience. Mr. Thomas was always wringing his hands and pleading for coursework, but none of his students ever really heard him, perhaps because his laments were muffled by his unfortunate beard. It was meant to be an elegant Balbo-type beard – the cheeks bare, just a tidy, trimmed patch of moustache and chin coverage – but he couldn't shave straight and had wiggles and cuts. He had discovered when he first experimented with facial hair that there was no consistent color. The beard and moustache came out in different tints of gray and ginger, giving his chin the air of a kitten with mange. So he took the unfortunate step of dying it to a uniform tint identified by the hair experts in the class as Autumn Leaves. Despite the fact that his beard now clashed with the rest of his hair, Mr. Thomas did not take the dye experiment further, although he did maintain the upkeep on his chin with a six-weekly top-up of Autumn Leaves.

It wasn't that Smokey hated English or Mr. Thomas. He was easily bored, though, and the immediate reward of baiting Mr. Thomas far outweighed the ultimate goal of actually getting a GCSE in English. This particular morning was no exception.

Smokey sauntered into class just after the second bell had jangled through the classroom, his timing impeccable. Mr. Thomas hadn't yet taken the register. However much he might wish to put Smokey down as late, he couldn't, since unfortunately Silas Murphy was present as the register was being called. Flustered, not entirely sure what he wanted to teach, he asked Lindsay Morgan to recap on the reading homework. She was busy excavating her handbag in search of a certain shade of lip gloss for Keisha Taylor. She jumped as Thomas called her name a third time and asked whether she'd actually read Chapter Fourteen of *To Kill a Mockingbird*, as set for homework the day before yesterday.

"You soppy or something? I ain't read it. What do I wanna read *that* for?"

"Because it's your main examination text, Lindsay." Thomas took the patient but weary path, wasted on Lindsay.

"Look, I'll go and get them notes from Smiths before the

exams. I don't have to read your stupid book."

"Shall we read it together? Lindsay, perhaps you'd start."

"I don't have no book."

"Then you can share with your neighbor. Keisha, perhaps you'd be so kind as to let Lindsay glance over your shoulder at the book."

Smokey put up his hand. Mr. Thomas tried to ignore it, going over to the desk where Lindsay was sitting to draw the book to her attention.

"Sir, why you making Lindsay read? She can't read. She's rubbish."

"You what! Did you hear that, sir? He's disrespecting me. He's saying I can't read. I can read, sir, can't I? I just don't want to. That's all," protested Lindsay.

Joe wanted to kick Smokey under the table to get him to stop, but he was intent on creating mayhem and warded off Joe's probing foot.

"Don't want to? You can't. That's all there is to it. You got your cousin to take your tests for you last year, otherwise you'd be in the special class where you belong."

"Silas, that is a highly insulting comment. Apologize to Lindsay at once."

"For what, sir?" Smokey's smile, false as Britney Spears' breasts, deepened. "Telling the truth? I'm not apologizing. She should apologize for wasting our time."

"Silas, am I going to have to send you to see Mrs. Elphick?"

"Yeah, I think you are going to have to send me to see Mrs. Elphick. Then I can tell her how you want some illiterate bimbo to read to us." Smokey rose and his smile broadened further. "Do you want to write out a note for me, sir?"

Mr. Thomas' cat's-bottom mouth tightened as he returned to his desk, pulled out the blue slip that had to accompany any student sent out of a class, then filled it in. Smokey hovered over him, waiting to be excluded from the lesson. Without looking Smokey in the eye, Mr. Thomas thrust the chit into his waiting hand then held the door open. Joe winced. Smokey had an uncanny gift of escalating every confrontation, and Elphick had already been onto him and his parents about it. But Thomas was so thin-skinned and such a jerk.

The door closed behind Smokey, and Joe sighed, hoping at last to be able to get his head down. But Mr. Thomas had given up on Lindsay and now glanced in Joe's direction.

"Start us off, would you, Joe? From the beginning of +++, if you wouldn't mind."

So Joe read at a steady drone, doing his best to kill off Scout's characteristic individuality, desperate to be left to his own devices. Mr. Thomas soon tired of his monotone and took over the job, throwing himself into the reading, perhaps in the hope that Harper Lee's prose would transport him elsewhere. At last, Joe was able to find a fresh page in the sketchbook he always carried with him. He placed the drawing he'd made from the photo of the Gallardo fob and keys beside it and started copying. It didn't take long. Fortunately, Mr. Thomas was by now so immersed in his own performance that he did not notice as Joe's head drooped and settled against the wall, his hand on the drawing he'd just completed.

The problem was that Mr. Thomas' voice kept intruding into Joe's dream, particularly when he put on a strange accent to play the part of Dill, who'd run away from home, reached the Finch house and hidden under Scout's bed. Then there was a knock at the door and in slouched Smokey, followed by an implacable Mrs. Elphick, who was neither prepared to babysit on behalf of her colleague, nor willing to put up with Smokey's continual taunting of his teacher. Joe shook his head to clear the sleep away.

"Silas, I believe you have something to say to Mr. Thomas and the rest of this class."

Smokey turned slightly, caught her eye and wheeled back to the rest of the room.

"I apolo—" But as he began speaking, a small child in shorts held up by braces, a grubby white shirt and a pale-blue bow tie plowed past both Mrs. Elphick and Smokey.

He paused, saw the vacant seat by Joe and sat himself down.

"Boy, am I glad I found you. You wanted this, didn't you?" His voice was high, like someone on helium, but there was an unmistakable Southern drawl to it. Joe looked at him then closed his eyes and mouthed, "Holy shit." Dill surreptitiously handed over the Lamborghini keys and sat back in his chair, his feet dangling.

"Young man," demanded Mrs. Elphick, "just who do you think you are and what on earth are you doing in this classroom?"

"Why, I'm Charles Baker Harris, ma'am, but everyone calls me Dill." The boy looked around him for the first time, perplexity furrowing his brow. "I don't rightly know what I'm doing here, ma'am, 'cept I had to give something to Joe Knightley here."

By this time, the whole class was alert, an extraordinary break with the tradition of Thomas' groups. As one, they gazed at the boy, uncertain whether they could believe that this was truly Dill Harris or whether this was some bizarre stunt that Thomas had resorted to in yet another attempt to engage their evanescent interest.

"Where are you from?" Mrs. Elphick suddenly switched her attention to Mr. Thomas. "Do you have a budget to hire child actors, Mr. Thomas, or have you prevailed on someone to dress up for free? I know it's been suggested that you liven up your approach, but this seems a little extreme."

"I don't know where he's come from. He's nothing to do with me."

"Guv," added Mrs. Elphick crushingly, "no doubt it's more than your job's worth." She swiveled away from Thomas and turned her laser glance on Dill. "So you had to give something to Joe Knightley. Is that right, young man?"

"Yes, ma'am. I guess I can go back now. Back to Alabama. Ain't I in Alabama anymore?"

"No, young man, we are *not* in Alabama. And how we are to get you there is beyond me. I suppose I'd better get onto social services. How is it, Joe, that recently you have become the epicenter of any confusion in this building? It comes back to me now. We owe Mr. Tucker's temporary absence to your apparently being sucked into a wall. And there's the state of Mr. Crosbie's room, which reeks of fish and seems to have been flooded."

Joe looked at Mrs. Elphick and shook his head. "I don't understand that, Mrs. Elphick, but Dill is staying with us. He's meant to be shadowing Liesel, my little sister. If it's okay, can I keep him with me until the end of this lesson? Then I'll take him over to her on my lunch break?"

"Take him back now. I'll sign you out. Come with me. You, Silas, will return to your seat and cause no further trouble. I will see you this afternoon at three-thirty-five for your detention." She beckoned at Joe and Dill to follow her, turned as precisely as a drill sergeant and stalked down the corridor, expecting the boys to tag faithfully behind her. She was not disappointed. Meekly, Dill slipped his little paw into Joe's hand and trotted beside him as Elphick's kitten heels tapped along the corridor.

Chapter Five

Ditching Dill

At the secretary's office, Mrs. Elphick signed the form allowing Joe to leave the school premises for no more than fifty-five minutes, which should be enough to walk the mile to Liesel's school, deposit the child and return before the end of the lunch hour.

It was not warm, and Dill wore only a lightweight shirt. Joe took off his fleece and handed it to him. It swamped Dill, making him look as though he were wearing a fluffy red dress. Joe helped Dill roll up the sleeves then zipped himself in his jacket and put on his backpack before leading the kid out of the school gate.

"What happened exactly? How did it feel?"

"Coming here? Well, I was hid under Scout's bed, so it was dark anyway. I kept my eyes closed. She was just coming in the room, and I reached my hand out. She squealed and ran to get Jem. I thought she'd be along any time, but I closed my eyes again, and when I opened them, I was holding this key, just outside this schoolroom. I knew exactly what to do. But this ain't part of the book, is it?"

"No. We should check the book, see whether it carries on as normal."

"Ya think it won't? Say, how'm I goin' to get back?"

Joe paused. He wasn't sure. It was all very well saying he could dream Dill back into the book, but Joe had now twigged that the consequences of his dreams could be a touch unpredictable. By this time, they had reached a bus shelter between the two schools. They both sat down on the bench and Joe dug in his book bag for the tattered copy of *To Kill a Mockingbird* he had inherited from Ben. He leafed to Chapter Fourteen and began scanning the text.

"Boy, you sure do read fast. What's it say?"

"Nothing. Jem checks under the bed and there's nothing there. There's no mention of you at all."

"Do I come back later?"

Joe continued scanning the book. He knew it reasonably well by now, for he had pinched it two years ago when Ben was studying it in class and had reread it this term. But now, there was no trace of Dill after Chapter Fourteen.

"I have to get you back into the book somehow. The thing is, I have to go to sleep. I just don't think there's time. I need somewhere to go to sleep as well."

Dill didn't seem to think this at all odd. Something else had struck him. "Say, there were blacks in your class. You have black people in your school?"

Joe nodded. "You're in England. We don't have segregation and stuff. And I don't think it happens any more in the States either. Look, I'll take you to my sister's class. You stick with her. Everyone in her class is nine or ten. I hope that doesn't worry you. But the thing is, you don't look more than nine. You'll find it easier in the primary school, and if you just keep your head down until school is over, I'll come and get you. Then once we're home, I can try to put you back in the book." Joe tried to sound calm, since any anxiety might alarm Dill.

"Sure. What's your sister like? Is she anything like Scout?" Dill hopped off the bench, totally sanguine about events and eager to get going.

Joe shook his head at the idea. "No. Unfortunately, she's nothing like Scout. She isn't a tomboy. In fact, she hates boys, and she's a mouthy little cow." He stood up and slung on his backpack, leading the way as Dill took two or three steps to keep pace with him.

"Scout can be one of them too — a mouthy little cow." Dill enunciated the words, striving to imitate Joe's diction. Joe grinned in response.

"Look, don't let on I called her that. She'll pay me back, and she's mean."

"Oh, I understand mean. Is she prissy?"

"Yup. She's really prissy. She's always neat and tidy and her hair never gets in a mess and she looks after all her stuff. She's a girly girl. She's into anything pink and fluffy. Have you met anyone like that?"

"Not that I remember. The only people I remember are the Finches and my mother and her new guy."

"Don't you go to school with girls like that?"

"I don't know that I go to school. I'm always in Maycomb for the summer. I don't exactly know what happens when I'm not there."

Joe finally clicked on what he had to do. When a character wasn't mentioned in the book, they existed in some sort of fictional waiting zone, a limbo. It wasn't clear if Dill went to school, because no scenes showing Dill in school were in the book.

"I don't know what you'll make of school, but see if you can stick it out for the rest of the day. I'll be along in three hours or so for you and Liesel. Just don't talk too much. And don't stick your hand up, even if you know the answers."

From what Joe had gleaned of Dill's personality, his last two requests were unlikely to be met. By this time, they had reached Liesel's school. Joe recognized the lady at the desk, trying to talk on two phones at once, placating one anxious parent while giving a rocket to an intransigent one. When she saw Joe, she rolled her eyes. She clearly remembered this Knightley, even if it had been over three years since he'd last crossed the doorstep. The boys waited until she'd finished her conversations.

"What can I do for you?" Mrs. Cartwright did not sound as though she was inclined to do anything for Joe.

"I'm sorry to disturb you, Mrs. C, but Dill here is staying with us and he's meant to be shadowing Liesel today. My mum asked me to bring him around to the school and check that everything was okay."

"We've had no notice of it. She didn't think to send us a note, I suppose. We're not a babysitting service, you know."

"She was really, really sorry, but she's in a big rush, and Dill's parents had an emergency with their documents." Joe avoided Dill's admiring glance as he spun his tale.

Mrs. Cartwright harrumphed like an agitated walrus and tapped at her computer.

"Liesel's in art just now. You'll have to check with Miss Donohoe. You remember her, I daresay. I'm sure she'll remember you, Joe. You know where the classroom is, just where it's always been."

It was weird to be back in a place that had been his whole universe not so long ago. Except that three years seemed more distant than the Cretaceous period to Joe, and he kept noticing changes, like the carpet tiles that had been renewed and the walls that had been repainted primrose and were hung with different pictures from the ones Joe had known. He led Dill down the corridors and up a flight of stairs and toward a door that had not changed. It still said *Year Four, Miss Donohoe*, and still had a big rainbow sticker beneath the sign. Joe waited for a second or two, listening to see if Donny was having one of her rages or if all was calm. He heard her harsh voice through the wood, instructing year four to tidy up now. It was clean-up time, all brushes to the sink, and William Monks was going to wash the brushes, this time without getting any paint on the carpet. Shrill and aggravating as a corncrake, she rattled on and on, failing to hear Joe's initial soft knocks. Dill took over, pounding the wood with his fist. The door suddenly opened, then Dill lost his balance.

"Who on earth is making that dreadful racket?" bellowed Miss Donohoe, gazing down at the crumpled boy at her feet. Dill hopped up and her eyes rose to take in Joe's looming figure. He was taller than she was now but she managed to reduce him back to a quivering four-footer with her gimlet gaze.

"Joseph Knightley. Come back to visit us, have you?"

"No, Miss Donohoe. That is, I've been sent with Dill here." Joe launched into his bizarre tale of lost passports and American houseguests with a degree less vigor than he had used with Mrs. Cartwright. He prayed that Liesel would back him up.

Miss Donohoe turned and summoned Liesel from a small table at the back of the classroom. Joe swiftly helped Dill out of the fleece.

"Liesel, come and sort out your houseguest. He'll need some paper and a pencil. We've got some numeracy skills to work on. You are still collecting them both at the regular time, aren't you, Joe? Tuesday is one of your days to collect Liesel, isn't it?"

"Yes, Miss Donohoe."

"Good. Then off you go."

Joe turned and left, relieved that Liesel had been given no chance to wreck his shaky story. As he left Liesel's school, he checked the time and began running. Unless he went full pelt, he'd never make it back for afternoon lessons. He'd just made it back to school by his deadline and sat panting and hungry through a psychology class, most of which passed entirely over his head, an occurrence that the teacher noticed.

"Feeling all right, Joe?"

Joe was about to say, "Fine, sir," when it occurred to him that here was the perfect solution to his problems. "No, sir. As a matter of fact, I think I'm going to be sick."

The teacher gave Joe a second look. "You do look a bit peaky. Do you really think you're going to throw up?"

Joe didn't say anything, just cradled his stomach and put one hand to his mouth, nodding. The teacher began to look panicked and hastily filled in an excuse note.

Mrs. Naismith was suspicious when Joe turned up at her door, but he managed a convincing retch and she hurried him to her inner sanctum where she had a couch and a bucket for him, returning almost immediately to her paperwork.

Joe closed his eyes and recalled the events of Chapter Fourteen of *To Kill a Mockingbird*. He went over them again and again, determined that this dream would not run out of his control. But Joe could not summon sleep. Morpheus would not come. To Joe's astonishment, his body took charge and he was sick, copiously and biliously into the bucket. When he was finally done with throwing up, Joe sat shakily and went over to the washbasin and rinsed out his mouth, shivering a little. He lurched back to the couch and lay there, and this time, he did fall asleep, curved toward the wall, away from the room and all the troubles that awaited him in the outside world.

This time, he was flying, flying high above a town. He could hear wind rushing in his ears. He was going fast, perhaps thirty or forty miles an hour, but he was not falling. He stretched out his arms and found that angling them slowed him down and allowed him to steer himself. He descended a little, looking at the woods around the town, trying to work out from the layout of the streets where he could be. It didn't look like a British town. The gardens were big, the houses were made of clapboard and the streets were wide. There were scarcely any cars, and those that he could see were old-fashioned, cars from a black-and-white movie with long bonnets and huge sweeping wheel arches and running boards. There were a few imposing brick buildings in the center of the town, one with a cupola and a statue of a blindfolded woman bearing scales outside and an American flag on top — the Stars and Stripes.

Joe racked his brain. Thomas had made them work out the layout of Maycomb using directions and descriptions from the book as a guide. Then someone had found a map in a study guide and they had all cribbed it, except for Joe, who had wanted to see if he could get it right. And he had, drawing a fuller and more detailed map, marked with quotations to back up his decisions. He felt vindicated when he saw that his drawing was closer to the town than the study guide's, until he remembered that this was his dream and consequently much more likely to correspond to his view.

There was a very fine garden and next door, a more functional yard, with a swing and an American football lying on the lawn. Joe circled what he believed to be the Finch property. He landed and walked up the steps onto the porch where there was a swinging wooden seat for two. He knocked at the door but no one came. There was a screen door and an inner door. He tried them both and they were open. In he walked. He called out a hello, but there was no response. He walked through the hall, past the doors opening onto a sitting room, a dining room and a study with a desk piled high with papers. He went in and looked at the walls lined with bookshelves. Behind the desk the wall was lined with law books. Joe left the study and just as he was about to go through to the kitchen, two children clattered down the stairs and raced past him through the swinging door to the back of the house. They had not seen him, though he stood right in front of them.

Once again, Joe was stymied. He couldn't work out how he was to get Dill back here, not now that Dill was safely practicing multiplication in Miss Donohoe's class, nor could he say anything to the Finch children. But then he turned, and there was Dill, right behind him, wearing a school smock and covered in yellow paint.

"How did you get so grubby? I thought you were doing maths?"

"I finished real quick. The sums were easy as pie, so Miss Donohoe said I should help that William kid clean up, but we just messed around, and he squelched yellow paint all over me. It was better than anything. We don't have paint so good back home."

"Quick, let's go upstairs and wash all that stuff off. I'll take the smock back."

It did not occur to Joe that a 1930s bathroom in deepest Alabama might not be quite what he expected.

"There won't be any water up there. The kitchen is the only place with a pump."

"Then just give me the smock and go and hide under the bed. Quickly, before they all come back in." Joe was convinced that a Finch of some sort would come in much too early and spoil the story once again.

"Okay. Say, that class was fun. I wouldn't mind doing something like that again. If you ever remember me." Dill's gaze was wistful. Joe steeled himself.

"It's been a pleasure to meet you, Dill, but I'm going to try not to do that again."

"I figured." Dill waved without looking back and ran up the stairs. Joe stood still, but was feeling dizzier and dizzier, everything around him shimmering. He reached out for a banister, but his hand passed through it then through the step behind it, and he was falling into darkness.

Mrs. Naismith was standing over him, tugging at his shoulders. "Wake up, Joe. Wake up. It's time for you to go home now. The bell's about to go."

He sat up and the bile rose again, but he did not retch this time. He screwed up his eyes and rubbed his temples.

"Would you like me to call your mother to fetch you? I know you've got to go down to the junior school to get your sister, but if you're not sure you can manage, I can always track down Ben."

Joe stood up and waited for his mind to clear a little more.

"It's all right. I can go. Thanks for looking after me, Mrs. Naismith."

"Just doing my job, Joe. You look pretty ropey still. Are you sure you don't want me to call Ben or your mum?"

"I'll be fine."

But of course, when he was back down at the gate of Liesel's school, he was anything but fine. The kids were streaming out, and usually Liesel was with her mates, but this time, she was being frogmarched across the playground by Miss Donohoe.

"Joe Knightley, where's that little boy you left me with

this morning?"

Joe tried to buy time. "What do you mean, Miss Donohoe?"

"You lumber me with an extra child, then the minute I turn my back, he's vanished into thin air. No record of any parents coming to collect him, or you, or your family. He's just gone. Disappeared. Evaporated."

Liesel was standing beside Miss Donohoe, looking as irritated and irritable as her teacher, her arms crossed, her nose in the air, her bunches swinging.

"Didn't Liesel see him go?"

"No, I didn't. We've searched the whole school and he's just not there."

"I'm sure he's somewhere around here. Maybe he panicked and ran away. Let me just call Mum and see if she's heard anything."

"I've spoken to your mother already. She seemed to know nothing about your houseguests, Joe. Nothing at all." Miss Donohoe gave a menacing grimace, like a chimpanzee about to eat its offspring. "So perhaps you could explain to me just where this boy came from and exactly where he has gone?"

"He came from America, just like I said, Miss Donohoe. And I think he's gone back there. There was some problem with his papers, and we just had to take care of him temporarily."

"He's gone back to America. Between half past twelve and half past three, he's returned to America. You are aware, I suppose, that the only means of reaching the US in three hours hasn't flown for several years now, apart from the fact that a nine-year-old child is unlikely to have a ticket for Concorde stuffed up his jumper, not that young Mr. Harris appeared to have a jumper."

"I can promise you, Miss Donohoe, Dill is safe and in good hands. Excellent hands. He is visiting the Finch family of Maycomb, Alabama."

Miss Donohoe gave Joe a suspicious look and released Liesel into his care. "I'm still not sure I shouldn't call the police and report this boy as missing."

"He's not missing, Miss Donohoe. He's exactly where he ought to be." Or so Joe hoped. He hadn't had time to check the book yet.

Liesel sighed and waved goodbye to her teacher, her face lapsing into a sulky pout with which Joe was too familiar.

"What was all that about? And why couldn't you look after that boy all afternoon? He was closer to your age than mine."

"Elphick thought he was junior school age. I couldn't argue with her, Dill didn't exactly have his birth certificate on him. Anyway, it didn't matter to him. He'd never been to school before, so it was all new and hanging with your class was a lot more exciting than psychology. Does it matter?"

"Only that Donohoe made me go into every toilet in the whole school to look for him—boys as well as girls."

Joe grinned. Liesel would have hated that. They stopped at the bus stop and waited there. Donohoe's interrogation had made them miss their regular bus. Joe dug in his backpack and found his copy of *Mockingbird*, then flicked to Chapter Fourteen. He read as fast as he could, and heaved a sigh of relief as Scout spotted what she thought was a snake under her bed, fetched Jem and extracted Dill from his hiding place. There was no mention of yellow paint. Perhaps he had managed to get it off, or perhaps it was just a detail that the book skimmed over. The action seemed to unfold as before, as far as Joe could remember. He stuffed the book back in his bag and rummaged again. This time he pulled out his bus pass and the Lamborghini key. Liesel was deep in the latest Jacqueline Wilson book. He examined the key closely. He could hardly wait to get home.

It was strange not to be on the usual school bus with all the other kids. It was after the main rush and before the people who had detentions could escape. The bus was quiet and there was a gentle murmur of pensioners muttering about the price of gammon and comparing blood pressure medication. Liesel kept reading while Joe clutched his key and watched the world out of the window. They were passing through an estate of ugly houses. They looked mean and poky, their windows too small, their brick drab, and even if they were well-maintained, they had no character, just box after brick box, each with the same little patch of lawn outside. Then the character of the streets changed, the houses got larger, the cars a little newer and finally they were at their stop.

They walked up the road and turned left into their street, past the other Victorian and Edwardian houses.

Unusually, Mrs. Knightley's car was in the drive. "Mum's home. That's weird," said Liesel.

There was also a dark-blue Fiat outside the house. Joe began to feel uneasy. They went in, and the door was on the latch. Mrs. Knightley emerged from the living room and watched Joe and Liesel come in.

"Liesel, up to your room to do your homework. Joe, you come in here. There are some gentlemen who would like a word with you."

Liesel was so delighted that Joe was in serious trouble that she skipped upstairs without a single moan in response to their mother's peremptory tone. Joe dumped his book bag and reached into his pocket to check that the Lamborghini key was still there.

Chapter Six

Carpeted

Joe's mother ushered him into the living room then carefully closed the door. She folded her arms and stood, as Joe glanced at the two men lurking by the fireplace.

They were corporate twins, wearing expensive-looking suits and identical purple shirts, one with a tie that had toning lavender and wisteria checks, the other with a mauve diagonal stripe. Both had short brown hair—but not too short—and regular features with square jaws, like models for posh watches. As the door opened and Joe sidled in, both turned to look at him, their faces neutral, their eyes cool.

"Take a seat, Joe." The taller one spoke as though used to being obeyed. Joe looked at him for a long moment before moving around to sit on the arm of the leather club chair at the far side of the room. Perching there, he felt less vulnerable than if he were to sink into its depths.

"My name is Christopher Taylor-West, and this is my colleague, Rudy Moss. We hear you've got a new Lamborghini Gallardo."

Joe said nothing in the lengthening silence. Rudy Moss took up the patter. He had a slight American accent.

"When your mother rang us this morning, we were a touch surprised to hear about your prize draw success." He drummed his fingers on the mantelpiece.

"Yes," said Taylor-West.

"Because we don't allow Lamborghinis to be used for that kind of promotion, you see. We don't need that kind of publicity. There's a waiting list for a Lamborghini."

"Exclusive, you see," said Taylor-West.

Still Joe said nothing, just kept his hand clenched around the key.

"In fact, there's no record of any Gallardo going out of the showrooms in the UK at all." Rudy Moss sounded baffled rather than aggressive. But Joe did not relax.

Taylor-West took over the talking. "We're planning to take a look at the car, as we've discussed with your mother." Taylor-West began to bluster a little. "But what we'd like to know is how a schoolboy comes to have a Gallardo in his drive when we have no record of any purchase, or even theft, associated with any of our cars."

"If you can assist us with our inquiry, Joe, it would be very helpful." Moss' voice was not at all flustered, more threatening.

"I'm afraid I can't help you, really."

"And I believe there's no key. Is that correct?"

Joe gave a vague shrug and went "Mmm." So he wasn't lying, strictly speaking. After all, there was no way of knowing that the key in his possession was the key for his Lamborghini. And if they really wanted to get the engine running, he assumed they would have some way of bypassing the ignition system, which would be useful to know. Besides, producing the key would only provoke further interrogation, and Joe wanted to get the examination of the car over with.

Moss and Taylor-West exchanged a dissatisfied glance.

They moved as one, suggesting that somewhere there was a factory that churned out men like them — bland, uniform and following orders with unquestioning obedience.

"Okay, let's take a look at this baby." Moss walked over to the door and turned. "I assume you'll want to accompany us, Joe. It is your car, after all."

"Yes," said Joe. Sue Knightley looked grim. He could see that she wasn't happy that her son had been as good as accused of stealing a car. She wasn't happy that he even had a car, and she certainly wasn't happy about watching them gawp at the car in question. Silently, she followed them into the garage.

The Gallardo appeared as beautiful as ever. It sat in the midst of all the usual clutter of a family of five, almost glowing in the ugly fluorescent lighting, making everything else in the garage — the bikes, the lawn mower, Dad's array of DIY tools, the chunks of wood and half-built shelves — seem stark, ugly and cheap.

Silently, thoroughly, Moss and Taylor-West opened up the car. Taylor-West took a smartphone out of an inner pocket and began tapping at it as Moss pulled out a Maglite torch and started an inventory of the car.

First he walked around the car. "No registration." Then he climbed into the driver's seat. "No apparent mileage." He hauled himself out and examined the doorways of the car. "No chassis number or VIN." He went to the back of the car where the engine cover was open. He shone the torch all around the engine. "No engine number." He looked at Taylor-West. "No sign of wear or tear." They were both looking uneasy.

"We don't understand. This has to be a counterfeit. We need to impound this vehicle immediately and subject it to further tests," said Moss.

"Impound? I don't think so. I'm quite happy to ask the police or get my solicitor into this, but I think taking the car away is out of the question just at present." Sue Knightley spoke quietly but firmly. Joe watched her morph into a figure almost as formidable as Elphick.

"We'd...um...give you a receipt," hedged Taylor-West.

"A receipt? You must be joking!" Mrs. Knightley made it abundantly clear that she was running out of patience with the Lamborghini men. They exchanged a glance. Moss shrugged.

Taylor-West said, "We could...er...buy it...from you?"

"That will be Joe's decision, following advice from our solicitor and discussion with my husband, who is currently away on business. But we are in regular email contact with him and will, of course, draw this to his attention."

"Errm, uh, how long before you make a decision? We need to make a report as soon as possible, you see." Taylor-West was beginning to wilt, although the garage was not warm.

"You can make an initial report, and I will get back to you by the end of the week. Friday lunchtime. In the meantime, you'd better think this through carefully. I know exactly what this car is worth, and I have quotes from several insurers, one of which I will be taking up as soon as I've said goodbye to you. If anything happens to this car, I'll be very quick to give your name to the insurers."

"Now, there's no need to be so mistrustful, Mrs. Knightley." Moss gave a little laugh with no mirth in it at all. "Your caution is understandable, but if you can assure us that this car will be kept safely in your garage for the next few days, I'm sure we can be patient."

"You'll have to be patient. Is that all, gentlemen?" It was quite clear that Sue Knightley did not think her visitors were remotely gentlemanly. Joe watched her with renewed respect as she opened up the garage door and watched them go into the street. She stood in the driveway, arms folded, and watched as they drove away. Then she came back into the garage where Joe was standing.

"You were amazing, Mum."

She rolled her eyes. "Bloody suits. Give them an Armani label and they think they can get away with anything. Tossers. But I'm not happy about you getting us into this."

"I've got a key, Mum." Joe was bewildered by his own confession. He reached into his pocket and took out the keys, placing them in her outstretched hand. She held them up, examining them as she might one of the older pots of leftovers from the fridge, considering whether to chuck the contents.

"Where did they come from, Joe?"

"A messenger delivered them to the school."

56

"Why didn't you say anything to Laurel and Hardy there?"

"It didn't feel right. They didn't seem right." He met his mother's eyes, which softened. She came over to him and ruffled his hair.

"Right. Let's see what this baby does, then." Joe was startled by the look of anticipation on his mother's face. She climbed into the driver's seat and called up to him, "Aren't you getting in too?"

"Yes." He went around to the passenger seat and got in. She waited until he'd closed the door then slid the key into the ignition. Joe tried to relax but was cracking his knuckles. She checked the car was in Neutral, then she turned the key. The throaty rumble of the engine covered Joe's swift exhalation of relief as the car came to life. Mrs. Knightley revved the engine and the roar echoed around the garage.

"Shall we take her for a spin?" she asked.

"It's got no number plates, Mum. Won't we be pulled over?"

"Let's do it tonight—later on, when the roads are quiet. How about it?" She switched off the engine and pulled out the key, then inhaled deeply, taking in great lungfuls of leather.

Then she started fiddling with the rearview mirror and examining the dials and buttons on the console.

"Mum! I don't believe you. You just told those men we were going to keep it in the garage."

"I didn't tell them anything of the sort. They made a suggestion, which I am entitled to ignore. I just told them they'd have to be patient."

"You're a lawyer, Mum. You can't drive a car with no registration or insurance."

"Actually, Joe, I've registered the car and I just need to confirm my acceptance of the insurance proposal over the Internet. Once that's done, we can drive this baby all over Europe if we feel like it."

"When did you register the car?"

"After I spoke to the Lamborghini people and discovered they were snotty gits. They were horrified by the whole idea of the prize draw. I rang up the Vehicle Licensing office in Wales and explained the situation. They told me to go to a post office and register the vehicle directly, so I did. Then I got plates for the car from a garage. This car has taken all bloody day to sort out and it's going to cost us a fortune. But it is a beauty."

"We don't have to sell it?"

"I don't know. We'll have to wait and see what Dad says, but knowing him, he'll want to hang on to it, at least until he's had a go in it. The thing is, those guys will be coming back now that they think the car is some sort of knockoff."

She levered herself out of the car, then waited until Joe had emerged and closed his door. She pressed the plip button and the car flashed its lights and beeped at them. Then she went over and hauled the garage door down, checking the lock carefully.

"We can have a takeaway tonight. I have a feeling that sorting out the insurance proposal will take a while. What do you feel like?"

"Indian."

"Indian it is. Liesel will moan, but she always does, unless Ben suggests it first." She grinned at Joe. "So we'll just say he wants Indian, and there we go, a moan-free zone."

"In your dreams." It occurred to Joe that he could do something to Liesel in his dreams. It would be cool to have a moan-free Liesel. Very tempting indeed. But he wasn't quite sure of his control just yet. It was something to work toward, though.

But Liesel didn't moan, and Ben was delighted to have takeaway, as it was his night for the washing-up. They were all excited by the car, even though the thousands it would cost to insure made them all gulp. They listened to old Disney songs as they ate their dopiaza and rogan josh, cracked the poppadums and teased Liesel for emptying three quarters of a jar of mango chutney over everything she ate.

They took turns to email Dad then they sat companionably on the sofa to roast the candidates participating in some terrible reality contest.

Joe discovered how tired he was only when Ben nudged him awake. "Hey, sleepyhead, if you're so knackered, shouldn't you go to bed?"

He started up and said, "Knackered?"

Three pairs of fond eyes looked at him and Liesel said, "You've been nodding off for the past fifteen minutes. Didn't you sleep last night?"

"Not too well." Joe extracted himself from the sofa. "I'll go up. 'Night." He bent to kiss his mother and found himself kissing the other two as well, something he hadn't done since he was nine or ten. They were wrangling over the judges' decisions before he closed the door.

Too tired to think, Joe got ready for bed on automatic pilot. He remembered to check that his alarm clock was set before he fell back into his bed and was asleep. It was just after nine-fifteen.

The rise and fall of voices woke him. He was facing the wall. He could tell from the glow that the room was filled with sunlight. He turned over and saw five turbaned men on a golden carpet sitting in the middle of his room. The biggest guy was wearing a lavender robe over a fuchsia tunic and clutching a book in his left hand. To his right sat a smaller man, hunched over, but with a seriously crazy beard. His robe was green with silk embroidery, and his tunic was purple. To the left of the large man were three men, one fat dude in purple and violet who was writing something onto parchment, and to his right, two smaller men kneeling, holding scrolls and wearing red robes. These two looked like servants.

Green Bushy Beard spoke first.

"Our esteemed Ahmed Karabashi is, I believe, correct in his view that the provenance of the basin is immaterial. What matters is the pleasure one derives from gazing at the object, not its authenticity."

One of the men in red replied, "While we respect a scholar so venerated as Ahmed Karabashi and a writer so famed as yourself, Seyyid Lokman, as craftsmen we must assert that authenticity is more important than appearance. If I buy a bowl from a merchant who tells me it is crafted by the great artist Wu Xianyang of China, I expect to pay a far greater price than I would pay for the work of a potter from Iznik. I would be enraged to discover that the basin I had been admiring, and for which I paid so many piastres, was an item sold in bazaars all over the empire."

The large man in lavender spoke. "Here is the situation. This basin has been purchased for the sultan under the impression that it was Chinese, and a consequently inflated price was paid out of his coffers for the piece. Now we know that the basin is not Chinese, and no one is willing to admit that they were fooled into purchasing the bowl. Everyone is terrified of telling the sultan, first of all, how much it cost and, second of all, that it is not as valuable as it has been made out to be. But what is the right thing to do?"

Joe watched as Lokman and Karabashi waited for the scribe and the two craftsmen to respond. But the three small men would not meet the eyes of the scholar or the writer, and they seemed to have lost the power of speech.

"What would happen if you told the sultan the truth?" Joe asked. All the men looked up at him in astonishment.

"Who is this infidel?" asked the scribe. He seemed relieved by the distraction from the question of the basin.

"Where has he come from?" asked one of the painters. "How did he enter our chamber?"

Then the men whirled round and noticed that they were not in their chamber.

"Where are we?" they all asked. Karabashi and Lokman asked with amusement, but the scribe and his two red-robed companions were uneasy and unamused.

"You're in England."

"England? What strange place is this? What sorcery has transported us here?"

"I am afraid I dreamed you, although I have no idea how. If you are all quiet, I can probably dream you back home. Where do you come from?"

"We serve the sultan and we should be in Istanbul. We should be in the scriptorium at the Imperial Palace." Karabashi stood up, and Joe was impressed to see his turban graze the ceiling. "Are we in our own time or in another?"

"I think another. Who are you?"

Karabashi introduced himself then his companions. "I am Ahmed Karabashi, scholar. This is my friend, the great chronicler, Seyyid Lokman Ashuri. Here is the scribe Ilyas and the two painters Osman and Ali."

Joe, feeling underdressed in his usual sleeping gear of boxers and T-shirt, reached for his toweling dressing gown that had fallen off the bed. Lokman reached over and handed it to him. He pulled it on and stood up. He came up to Karabashi's shoulder. He wasn't sure whether to bow or not, but since they had invaded his room, he thought not.

"I'm Joe Knightley. I am a draftsman." That sounded like a term they might understand. "So what are you going to do about this bowl thingy?"

"Should we find ourselves once more in the Imperial Palace, I myself shall place the object before the sultan and tell him that it came in truth not from China but from Iznik. If he chooses to punish me for speaking the truth, so be it. My argument will then be disproved, in which case I should merit punishment." Karabashi shrugged and sat down again. Osman, Ali and the stout scribe looked shocked, their eyes now as round as their little white faces. Joe went over to his desk and sat in his chair.

"You could always point out that it's pretty amazing that your own craftsmen can now produce bowls that are as good as the Chinese ones," he mused. "So good that this one fooled all the experts at the palace."

The little men gasped and applauded Joe's notion while Lokman and Karabashi raised their eyebrows at each other.

"A natural courtier. The ability to deliver unpalatable

truths is a gift."

"You'd better wait until you've seen how the sultan takes it." He bowed at this point. "Now I'd better try to return you where you belong."

He climbed back into bed. As he turned over and pulled the duvet over his head, the light in the room seemed to fade. It was the last thing he was conscious of before the alarm started beeping at him relentlessly. He sat up, switched on the light, bashed the clock to turn off the alarm and looked at the floor of his room where the five men had sat last night. They had left their golden carpet behind.

Chapter Seven

Friendship

Joe folded up the golden carpet woven from silken threads and tucked it away in his cupboard. He remembered that Mum was doing her best to hang on to the Lamborghini and that he had safely returned not just Dill, but also those weird Ottoman scholars to their various homes, which meant that he was possibly learning how to control some of his dreams. He just had to experiment a little, but not at school. He didn't want any more dreams at school. Elphick was already much too interested in him, and the essential thing at school was to avoid Meek and his henchboys.

Smokey was waiting just inside the school gate for Joe to arrive. He was curious about Dill, he was still probing the issue of the fish and he wanted to know how Joe had gotten out of most of his lessons the previous day. Joe protested that he had been sick, but Smokey was suspicious. "It's like you don't trust me, man."

Joe laughed and lied. "I'd trust you with my life. Honest, Smokey." Which Smokey seemed to accept for the moment. Fortunately, the first bell for registration went. Joe watched Smokey lope away and turned to go upstairs to his own form room. He didn't trust Smokey at all, even though they'd been friends since they were six. But there was less and less to say. Joe wanted to get his exams. Smokey didn't. Joe hated cigarettes and didn't much like the taste of booze. Smokey was a committed twenty-cigs-a-day man, although where he got a fiver or more for fags was anybody's guess, which was another thing Joe didn't want to get tangled up in. Smokey was hanging with people who were dealing in all sorts of stuff.

He'd offered Joe some fake perfume for Mum's birthday, but since Joe had carefully saved up and knew exactly what he was going to get her, he'd passed on the offer of a knockoff that smelled to him like cat's pee. It was only a matter of time before Smokey got really dodgy.

About three weeks into term, it had become obvious that Smokey was not taking school remotely seriously. They had been hanging about on the edge of the sports field at lunchtime, watching a five-a-side match. Smokey had run into the middle of the field, snaffled the ball and taken it all the way down to the opposite goal where he scored, then ran off the field with the ten players he'd ticked off streaming after him, hurling abuse in his general direction and threatening worse for later.

"Why do you get such a kick out of pissing people off?" Joe had asked.

"Why do you get such a kick out of being an arse-licker?"

Joe didn't react. He just turned his back on Smokey and walked away. Later Smokey had sidled up to him and said, "No hard feelings, mate. Just having a laugh." But Joe knew it wasn't just a laugh. Smokey thought he was a stuck-up swot, and he thought Smokey was a total waste of space. But they masked their feelings and still made the same jokes they'd always made, hanging out more from force of habit than friendship. Once Joe had tried to ask what Smokey really wanted out of life. He'd given a glib answer.

"Packet of fags, nice evening down the boozer and a bit of tail now and again. Have you noticed Sharon Beasely's knockers? Wouldn't mind a bit of that."

The thing that Joe didn't understand was that Smokey came from just as bland a middle-class family as he did.

Smokey was the third of four kids. His dad ran his own print business and his mum was an accountant. They had a nice house, and they occasionally socialized with the Knightley parents. Smokey's pointless and somewhat feeble impression of the Hard Man of Azalea Drive was a pose. It had certainly escaped the notice of most of their peers, including Charlie Meek, who had it in for Smokey as much as he did for Joe.

Still, Joe felt bad about lying to Smokey. He ought to make it up to him somehow. The ideal way would be a night on the town, wearing sharp suits, boozing, clubbing, picking up pretty girls, dancing and generally pretending to take part in a cheesy ad for an alcopop. Joe had no worries about creating such a night out. If he'd managed to dream a posse of Ottoman Empire geezers into his room and out again, he could certainly manage a night on the razzle.

Back home, Joe got all his homework out of the way.

Ben and Liesel were safely at dance class until seven p.m. Then he worked on a sketch for his father. Before long, Mrs. Knightley was calling up the stairs for Joe to come for a ride in his extraordinary prize. They were fully insured, the number plates had been delivered and as soon as she had screwed them into position, she was going to take the car for a spin.

It was glorious. Mum took the car gingerly down the road then onto the dual carriageway, heading for the airport. She went in a loop round a section of the motorway then home via the backstreets. The car growled and purred and crooned as they drove around, and it almost seemed disappointed to be heading back into the garage. The drive left Joe and his mother equally exhilarated.

"I'm surprised we haven't seen Silas around here. Haven't you told anyone at school about this?" Mrs. Knightley pulled the garage door down and double-checked the lock.

"Nah, not until we know whether we can keep it."

"We're keeping it, sweetheart. If they want to run tests, they can come here and run them. They can't impound the car. I've checked."

"You're brilliant, Mum."

She kissed Joe's cheek as he brushed past her into the house. "Cheeky so and so. You're only saying that because you've got exactly what you want. We'd be on much safer ground if you could find that lottery ticket, kiddo. In the meantime, I can wangle it so that possession is nine-tenths of the law."

Liesel and Ben were waiting for their supper. Joe scarcely noticed what he was eating, eager to get back to his current drawing then to bed.

Once he'd switched the light off, he lay back and thought about what kind of night out Smokey would find memorable.

A fast car was essential. Flash suits, pretty girls, clubs. Things that teenagers thought about and grown-ups got to do — or at least expensive ads gave the impression that they got to do them. He imagined getting ready with Smokey for a night on the town. Smokey would wear aftershave — lots — and garish colors, a yellow shirt with a purple suit. Joe would look quieter — a black suit with a Nehru collar and a black shirt. Their wallets would be full. They'd have money to burn, maybe three or four hundred quid. They'd arrive at a club in a black limousine. As they got out, they'd be waved in past the queue of punters, then they'd be inside, and it would be sleek and smart, with girls who looked like models but with a bit more flesh on them.

And there they were. Smokey turned to Joe and clapped him on the shoulder.

"This is the business, mate."

Joe smiled back, then Smokey swaggered up to the bar. "Red Bull and vodka please. Twice," he shouted over the music.

Joe shook his head. "It's okay, I'll get my own. You go and find someone to chat up."

Smokey threw himself into the crowd that was pulsating to the Chemical Brothers. Joe turned back and ordered himself some water. He caught glimpses of Smokey — an arm, a leg, a gyrating shoulder or the back of his head. He watched the other people. The music hurt his head, so he turned the volume down — not for the clubbers, just for himself, as though he were using an iPod that delivered silence instead of tracks. The dancers throbbed and punched the air, people swarmed about—upstairs, into dark crannies. Lights swirled and flashed, a smoke machine pumped out a mist in which Joe spotted hands groping for thighs or breasts, hips pumping together, feet tangling. A girl in a trance swayed by the side of the dance floor, her arms up, her eyes closed, defenseless and carried somewhere else by the beat.

Joe sipped his water and saw a man reaching into a handbag and extracting a mobile phone, which he pocketed. Then the thief moved on to another table and another, snaffling change, wallets, a stray earring. It seemed so obvious, but the people behind the bar were too busy to notice and the punters were lost in their world of rhythm and flirtation. The thing was, there were bouncers. They wouldn't want the club to get the reputation of being a place where you got ripped off. Joe slipped from his barstool and headed to the corridor where more and more people were jammed in their effort to be seen at the right place.

He reached the door and the night air was a relief after the dense sweatiness of the actual club. He tapped a bouncer on the arm.

"Excuse me. There's a guy in there cleaning out people's bags and pockets."

The bouncer turned to Joe, frowning, his eyes old. "What's he look like?"

"Twenties, brown hair in a sort of quiff, big nose, dark suit, dark shirt, stringy red tie, black and white shoes."

"If we pick him up, will you hang around long enough to identify him?"

It occurred to Joe that if this ended up in a police statement, he'd have some talking to do. Explaining what a fourteen year old had been doing getting into a club intended for over-eighteens, for starters. Explaining what he was doing in a club when he was meant to be safely in bed. Explaining where he'd gotten a pocket full of cash. But Joe shrugged and agreed to identify the guy. The bouncer summoned two other men with bald bullet heads, tuxedos and bow ties. They cleared their way down the corridor and back into the main club. They fanned out across the dance floor, looking out for the guy Joe had described.

One found him. The others took him in a pincer movement, hustled him out of the place and into a small back room. Then they called Joe. By the time he got into the office, they'd stripped the guy down and his haul for the night was on the table — three mobile phones, a couple of wallets, the single pearl-and-diamond earring, a lot of loose change and a fistful of notes. The man shrugged, as though he got caught quite regularly. But he watched Joe with chilly curiosity that made them all uneasy. A bouncer got Joe to write down his name and address then took him back into the main club. He led Joe to the bar.

"Get this guy a bottle of champagne on the house, will you?"

Smokey came up, each arm around the waist of a girl. One was dark, with heavy eyeliner and a full mouth and the other had auburn hair in a sleek French knot and wore a long, flowery skirt, a matching top and had a brown leather belt resting on her hips.

She was very pretty, but she shoved Smokey's arm away as though his fingers stung. She was about to turn away in a strop when Joe held out a flute of champagne.

"I like your style," said Smokey, reaching out for a glass. "This is my mate, Joe. Right, mate?" The Red Bull and vodka mix had gone straight to Smokey's head, and he slurred his words. The dark-haired girl giggled as though he were Matt Lucas and David Walliams rolled into one. She was drunk or stoned or both. "This is Denise, isn't it?" She nodded and held out her hand for a glass as well. Joe passed her his own. He hadn't taken a drink from it, and they'd only given him three glasses, but he didn't care.

"And this is Angela. That's right, isn't it? Angela."

Angela with the auburn hair gave him a defensive grin

that failed to reach her eyes. She swigged from the glass. "Denise, I'm out of here. Do you want to get a taxi with me or not?"

"Not. See you, Ange."

"See you. Don't do anything too stupid." Her glance drifted to Smokey, her lip curled and her eyes hardened. She turned and left. Denise threw her arms around Smokey's neck and nuzzled him. She whispered in his ear. Joe felt uncomfortable.

"I'm going home, Smokey. Hope you don't mind."

"Send the limo back, yeah?"

"Limo?" shrieked Denise. "You got a limo?"

Smokey nodded and she tightened her grip on him. Joe was not sure what would happen if he and Smokey separated, but he'd had enough of the nightclub. He didn't want to drink. He was intimidated by the women and he felt uneasy about the way the thief had stared at him in the small office.

"If I can, I will. Have a good night."

As Joe walked outside, he saw Angela waiting for a taxi. The limousine pulled up. The chauffeur opened the door. Angela stared in disbelief.

"Can we give you a lift?" Joe waited at the open door. She glanced at the chauffeur, a man with a grandfatherly face. Then she looked at Joe. He met her eyes, and she turned away first, then she climbed in. She huddled in the far corner of the car.

"Where to then?" asked the driver.

The girl leaned forward and gave the name of her street.

It wasn't far from Joe's home. The car rolled away, and she sat back, still tense. Joe started an idle conversation with her about how often she went clubbing, but she bit out monosyllabic answers so he left it. What was the point in trying to get to know a person he'd never see again? Soon enough they reached her front door. She gave a perfunctory thank you and rushed out of the car.

"Back home then?"

Joe nodded and found himself dozing off.

The next thing he knew, the alarm was ringing. He was back in bed, and it was morning. Dazed, he dressed, went downstairs, ate, left for school and met Smokey in the same place as yesterday.

Smokey looked absolutely shell-shocked.

"Did the limo make it back then?" Joe asked.

"I don't know. She took me back to hers. It was weird. I was there, and we were snogging away, then I conked out and when I woke up, I was trying to snog my pillow at home."

"Really?" Joe could just see his friend trying to make out with a pillow.

"Yeah, really, no suit, no dosh, no limo, no slapper in the bed next to me."

"She *was* a slapper."

"I know. She looked good in the club though. Good body, great arse." Smokey cocked his head. "So what's going on, Joe? How'd we get there? It was like a dream, going into some club and everyone treating us as if we were over eighteen."

Joe hesitated. "I can't really explain it."

"I think you can. What I don't get is why you did it. You hate discos and loud music and boozing. What was in it for you?"

"I wanted to see whether I could make it happen."

"And you did, didn't you? Just like the fish. I knew you made that happen, no matter what you said."

Both boys were silent. Joe wasn't comfortable with Smokey knowing about this. There'd be pressure. It had been stupid to give way to misplaced guilt and a desire to show off. Now that Smokey knew, there'd be requests and hassles, sure enough.

"I'll tell you what. Next time we go out for a night on the town, at least let me get a little bit further. I want a bit more than a snog next time."

"I thought you said you'd slept with Kelly Reynolds," Joe

70

commented.

Smokey mumbled and shuffled.

"What did you say?" Joe pressed.

"I didn't think you'd ever ask me right out, and I knew you wouldn't ask her. But as it happens, no, we...er... didn't get that far."

"She dumped you, didn't she?"

"No need to go into details." Smokey went on the offensive. "So how d'you do this stuff then?"

"I can't really explain. It hasn't happened that often yet. I'm still getting used to it. It's basically when I fall asleep."

"You could do anything. Win the lottery. Fly. Leap tall buildings in a single bound. How long has this been going on?"

"Not long, just a couple of days. I don't know how it works yet. I told you. I'm still getting used to it." The bell went, but Smokey wanted more information.

"So does it happen whenever you go to sleep? Every time? The things you dream come true? That's what that little kid was doing, wasn't it? What did he give you?"

"It's a long story, Smokey, and I've got to go to registration. So have you."

"I'll meet you after school and you can tell me then. I'll have thought of something really cool by then."

"I can't. I meet Liesel today, remember? Tuesdays and Thursdays I take Liesel home. I can't talk about it in front of her. And I've got tons of work to do. Coursework. You remember, for your GCSEs?"

"Lunchtime. That'll be enough time for me to tell you, and you can go home and fall asleep in your textbooks, which is what's going to happen anyway, so I might as well give you something worthwhile to get out of it."

Joe shook his head and ran off to his form room. At least he got there just before the second bell, so he couldn't be registered as late. That didn't dispel the feeling that taking Smokey into his dreams had been a major mistake.

Chapter Eight

Fiasco

At lunch, instead of going to the canteen, Joe headed for the football field, confident that it was the last place Smokey would look for him. Unfortunately, with the instinct of a terrier chasing a rat, Smokey tracked Joe down in minutes.

They sloped to the smoker's hangout near the undergrowth at the edge of the sports field. Smokey slumped against the chain-link fence and lit up. Joe remained standing.

"It's going to take me a bit of time to explain exactly what I want here."

Joe looked down at the baseball hat that concealed Smokey's face. It wasn't worth explaining to Smokey that there was no guarantee that anything would happen at all.

Smokey looked up, his eyes creased against the light. "I've worked it out, see? We get two girls—you know, slappers—and you dream us up a Learjet with a pilot and we can take 'em up and join the Mile High Club."

"What slappers? Do you mean girls from school?"

"No. Girls from a club. Like whatshername from last night."

"Denise?"

"Whatever. We go and pick up a pair, then we go out to the airport in the limo, into the jet and there we go."

"I am not interested."

Smokey looked up at Joe. He calculated for a second or two. "More interested in boys, like our Ben?"

"Don't talk to me about Ben. This has got nothing to do with Ben. This has got to do with your stupid fantasies.

I don't know if I can make my own fantasies happen, let alone yours."

"What is wrong with you? You were the one who got me into that place last night. Now you want to pull out just as we could have some serious fun?"

"I didn't have any fun last night. It was stupid. I hate dancing."

"So why'd you set it up?"

Joe shook his head and mumbled.

Smokey stood up. "What did you say?"

"I don't know how it happened. It was a mistake. It won't happen again."

"That's so unfair. You can't do that one night and say it's never going to happen again. You're so fucked up, Joe."

"Maybe I am." He walked away.

Smokey took a final drag of his cigarette, then threw away the butt.

It was beginning to rain again, and Joe's pace lengthened as he neared the school buildings.

"Okay," said Smokey, jogging to keep up with him. "Just take me along whatever you do next. How about it? No pressure."

"What's it got to do with you?"

"I'm your mate, aren't I?"

Joe turned suddenly and looked into Smokey's liquid blue eyes. "Are you?"

"What's that supposed to mean?"

"Nothing."

"Nothing? You're saying I'm not your friend. We've been mates since we were six, Joe. I know everything about you, including this little secret of yours. I don't understand why you give something one minute then take it away the next."

Joe didn't know which way to go. He could go inside the school building now, which would end the conversation automatically and probably his friendship with Smokey. Or he could let Smokey talk him around and give in to this stupid fantasy. The next thing he knew he'd be providing hot tubs and Malibu cribs for Smokey, who ultimately wanted nothing less than the lifestyle of a major R&B artist, as vividly depicted in countless identical videos on MTV, complete with gyrating, bikini-clad girls with acres of undulating skin, customized cars and bling. Joe could see where Smokey was heading, and it was a direction that just didn't interest him.

Except that flying in a private jet would be cool. It would be different. It would be useful to have the experience. Boffing a series of vacuous girls? Not so much. So he crossed his arms and said, "I'll think about it."

Which meant that he found Smokey accompanying him down the road to Liesel's school at the end of the day, trying to persuade him that this particular idea was worth trying.

Smokey's persistence was exasperating. Finally, Joe shut him up by saying that if Smokey said one word about any of this in front of Liesel, Joe would dream him into a one-to-one meeting with Elphick. Smokey backed off, but Joe could tell he hadn't heard the last of it.

It was not the first time that Smokey had come down with Joe to Liesel's school, or the first time that he'd come home with them on the bus. But it hadn't happened in a while and Liesel inevitably noticed.

"Funny you coming home now, just as Joe's got this stupid new car."

Of course, Smokey started asking questions and in her throwaway fashion, Liesel revealed the existence of the Lamborghini.

"Sweet," said Smokey. "Can't wait for a ride in that. Babe magnet or what?"

Ben was already home and at work on the computer in the kitchen, halfway through an essay. He stood up as they all came in. "Been a while, kiddo."

Smokey grunted. He hated being called kiddo, but it was Ben's established name for him. Silas' transition into Smokey had arisen on moving up to secondary school, and Ben couldn't say it without sniggering. Sometimes Ben had the right instincts. He got up and switched the kettle on.

"Here to see the famous wheels, I suppose."

Smokey nodded. Joe led him out to the garage. Despite his blasé façade, Smokey could not conceal his admiration for the car, involuntarily emitting small swooning cries like a mating pigeon. Ben joined them, bringing their cups of tea. He stood on the step into the garage, leaning against the doorway. "She's a beauty, isn't she? Shame Joe can't drive her for another eleven years. You can't be insured to drive something like this if you're under twenty-five."

Smokey laughed and went around the far side of the car.

Ben gave Joe a cautious look. "So now Mum's out of the way, you can tell me exactly where this car came from."

Joe shook his head. Smokey hadn't heard, absorbed by the car's clean lines and heady scent of leather.

"I can't say. It wasn't illegal, though." He drank some tea. Ben wouldn't let go.

"What's the big secret, Joe?"

"I can't talk about it." Joe hid his nose in the mug of tea again. Ben shrugged and turned away, leaving Joe to Smokey.

"If you can dream up one of these, why can't you dream up a flight on a Learjet with a couple of beautiful babes?"

Joe had no answer to that other than the simple fact that he didn't want to, but Smokey was persistent. "Come on. We can go up to your room now and before we know it, we'll be sitting up there at ten thousand feet, ready for action."

So Joe led the way up to his room. He lay on the bed and Smokey sat on the floor, leaning against it, his head thrown back and his eyes closed. "Okay," he said, "take us away, mate."

But Joe couldn't fall asleep. He lay there, eyes closed, but they kept flickering open and he kept thinking about mundane stuff like all the homework he had stacked up, what Mum was going to cook for supper, whether Ben would help him with his coursework and why Liesel was so aggravating. There was no space for Learjets and curvaceous girls. Smokey would probably want them wearing something tacky like bikinis or hot pants. The thing that freaked Joe out was that whenever he thought about girls, he would get a flash of one of Nell's disapproving glares. She had this way of looking at him — withering, like weed killer or a really hot sun.

And there, suddenly, looking half astounded and half enraged, was a vague outline of Nell, standing at the end of the bed. Joe sprang upward, shook his head and bounded off the bed, his knee knocking Smokey's head. By the time they'd both calmed down, Nell's shade had vanished and Joe sank back onto the bed, out of breath.

"What the fuck was all that about?" Smokey was standing over Joe, his arms on his hips like a mother haranguing a child.

"I don't know. Look, there was something there, then it went. You missed it. I'm sorry, Smokey. I just can't do this Learjet business."

It was a relief to see Smokey swing away, clearly irritated but unwilling to alienate him any further. Joe listened to him running down the steps two at a time, not bothering to say goodbye to Ben, simply clattering out of the house. Joe stood up and went over to the chest of drawers. He took out the golden carpet from the previous night and shook it out. It was soft to the touch, cool and delicately scented. He smoothed out the silk, lay face down and closed his eyes. At first, the fringe at the edges of the carpet started shivering, as though a breeze had ruffled it. Then Joe could no longer feel the floorboards under the silk. The carpet had risen a little from the floorboards, undulating slightly, its graceful borders reminding Joe of manta rays he'd seen at the aquarium. He rested there, flat out, suspended inches above the ground. The carpet swayed. He rose and rose, higher and higher off the ground until he was several feet above the floor. He closed his eyes and finally drifted away from his day.

The carpet thumped to the floor so that his nose, knees

and forehead cracked on the wood. The pain from that was followed by a sharp series of kicks to his ribs, only partially muffled by the carpet.

"Explain to me, if you can. Explain exactly what I'm doing here." It was Nell, utterly infuriated.

Joe raised his head and looked at her. She was wearing jeans and a black sweater that clung to her curves. She had curves that he hadn't known about, since they were normally swathed in her school uniform. Her eyes were small and mean, her mouth was a tight, narrow line and her fists were clenched. He rolled over, pulled himself up and edged away from her.

"I don't know. It just happened. I can try to get you back, or maybe I could call you a taxi." He tried to sit up, but she'd really gotten him in the ribs. He nursed his rib cage and waited. Nell stood there, arms folded.

"How are you going to try to get me back? How can I be sitting in my room at my desk one minute then here looking at you snogging a carpet the next?"

Joe had had enough of evasions and half-truths. He was tired, he hurt and he didn't care if Nell thought he was deranged, because she'd thought that for the past three years anyway.

"If you must know, I fell asleep. I had a dream. You were in it. Somehow, when I have dreams, they come true."

Nell did not laugh. She did not make a sarcastic comment. She did not kick him again. She unfolded her arms and knelt down beside him. "Really?"

"Really."

"That's a bit odd."

"You think so?"

"Yes. See if you can get me back home. If it doesn't work, you'll have to get me a taxi. I can get the spare keys off the neighbors. My mum won't be back home for another couple of hours."

Joe stood up. He shook out the carpet to straighten it. Nell stooped to help. Once it was flat, he lay down again and began thinking of how he'd gotten Dill back home, even though he'd never been to Maycomb. It ought to be easier to get Nell back home, since he'd been to her house hundreds of times, just not recently. Her room must have changed. When she was ten, she'd idolized a couple of girl bands, and she'd had hung pictures of unicorns and wild horses. Her room had had lavender walls. She'd had a cabin bed with a slide and a mosquito net above it, a string of fairy lights in the shape of crooked red hearts over the bed, and beneath the bed low bookcases absolutely packed with stories. There had been a neat little desk where she used to paint, and there'd been patches of paint on the walls, one magnetic, the other which let you draw on it in chalks. They'd been plastered with drawings and photos of her mum and her little brother, held in place with blobs of purple and pink fur. She'd loved drawing as much as Joe but where he'd been into superhero-style drawings, she'd been obsessed with animals — tigers, panthers, flying horses and huge grizzly bears. On the floor there had been a rug shaped like a polar bear. There had been a shelf unit stacked with all these kits she'd been given at her birthday — sewing kits, knitting machines, bead kits and friendship bracelet kits, none of which she'd ever opened. And under the window had been the things she really loved, her microscope and telescope.

"Joe, we aren't in the right room."

He opened his eyes and saw the picture of a unicorn galloping along a moonlit beach, the wild horses thundering across the prairie, the mosquito net and the photos of Mrs. Brennan and Kieran.

"We are, but my room doesn't look like this anymore." Nell looked more amused and less irked than he would have predicted. He shook his head.

"Shit, I don't know how to do this."

Nell came and sat beside him on the carpet. "How weird is this? I can't put my finger on it, but I don't remember it being exactly like this."

"What does it look like now?"

"Lie back and I'll tell you."

Joe followed her instructions. She began talking in a low voice, softer than usual.

"The walls are different colors. One is a turquoise. The other three are cobalt blue. I don't have the bed with the slide anymore. I've got a double bed and it has a sea-green cover and pillows. I've got photographs of the sea on the walls. Well, posters of waves, but properly framed. I've got a dressing table. There's a mirror above it and to the right there are hooks for my jewelry and stuff. I've got two big bookcases and a couple of smaller ones under the window. I don't have that table anymore. Kieran has the microscope and the telescope now. Instead, I have a computer desk with my laptop. I think that's it."

"What about Mr. Speckles?"

"I've still got Mr. Speckles. He sits on one of the shelves in the bookcase. Turn around. You'll see him there."

Joe opened his eyes and found that Nell was right. There was Mr. Speckles, her old stuffed Dalmatian, his head drooping and slightly awry. Everything else was as Nell had described it.

"Where do you keep your clothes?"

"There's a cupboard on the landing."

"It's like being in a fish tank. It's like being on the bottom of the seabed. When did that happen?"

"About a year ago. Maybe more," Nell explained.

"Why did I dream about you?"

Nell stood up and went to sit at the chair by her computer. "You have to answer that one for yourself. Now how are you going to get home?"

"I'll be out of your way in a second or two." He lay down again and thought about his own room.

He seemed to explode back into it, as though he'd been cartwheeled or spun like a top, coming to an uneven stop tangled around the trestles holding his drawing board.

Somehow, he'd left the carpet behind in Nell's room,

where it had clashed with everything. He wished he could go back there. He remained curled on his floor, thinking about her, thinking about the calm of her blue space and aching.

A knock on the door... Joe slowly unwound himself and stood. "Yeah?"

"It's me. I heard a whole load of thumps. Are you okay?"

Joe went to the door and opened it. Ben was standing there, his hair on end. He looked Joe up and down. "You look gutted. Is everything all right?"

"Yeah. Yeah. I... It was stupid. I was spinning on my chair and I just fell off. Really dumbass." He forced his mouth into a wavery grin.

"You're sure you're okay, then?" Ben couldn't conceal his doubts.

"Yes. I'm fine."

They both heard their mother's key in the lock. Ben turned away. "Right."

Joe nodded and shut the door again. He picked up his book bag from the floor and began to unpack it. Homework was like taxes, inevitable and all the more painful if you tried to avoid it.

Chapter Nine

Miles High

The engine noise and the constant vibration roused Joe.

He was sitting in a beige leather seat surrounded by a symphony of cream, tan, buff, ecru and fawn. He gazed out at the clouds below then he peered down the aisle. He was only two seats from the cockpit. He could see the shoulders of a pilot and a copilot and limitless sky beyond. He twisted round to check out the back of the plane. Across the aisle and two seats behind was Smokey, his face as smug as a politician's after a landslide.

There was a feminine hand on his knee. He raised his glass to Joe. It was a champagne flute. It looked a little incongruous, a gangly teenager in hoodie and jeans, his puppy-huge feet in trainers, lounging in this luxurious steel cocoon.

A woman came forward and leaned over Joe. She was not tall, but conformed in every other respect to a standard blueprint for beauty—blue eyes, whose vividness was, Joe suspected, enhanced by contact lenses, long eyelashes, a trim nose, a full mouth, symmetrical face and shoulder-length black hair, slim as the stem of a wineglass and apparently as fragile.

"Can I get you anything from the galley, sir?" Her voice was huskily mid-Atlantic. Her breath was minty.

"Just some water, please. Sparkling, if you have it."

Her look of astonishment mixed with a little contempt vanished almost before Joe had time to register it. Perhaps she'd been expecting him to order more champagne or some extravagant treat like caviar and blinis. It was true that he felt peckish.

She came back in seconds so he asked what there was to eat, then listened to a list of gourmet delicacies that would have graced the delicatessen back home. A smoked salmon sandwich seemed a safe and swift option. When she brought it, he gestured to the banquette opposite. She sat down.

"Can you tell me where we're going?"

"Your friends said we should head for somewhere warm. Mediterranean. They suggested Sardinia, so we're taking you to Sardinia."

"Sardinia?"

"Yes. It won't be hot, but it will certainly be a lot more pleasant than the UK at this time of year. We should be landing in another ninety minutes."

"How long have I been asleep? How did I get onboard?"

"Don't worry about any of that, sir. Your friend took care of everything. Smokey, yes? Such a charming young man."

She turned and gave Smokey a hundred-and-ten-watt smile. He raised his glass to her. Joe noticed that the female hand he had seen before had reached the top of Smokey's thigh. Smokey nodded at her, and she leaned around to say hello to Joe. It was Nell.

Her hair was pulled away from her face in a chignon, highlighting features that she usually concealed under a curtain of light-brown locks. Kohl made her eyes huge and exotic. The rouge dusted along her cheekbones emphasized the stunning structure of her face, and her lips were full and gleaming with raspberry gloss. Her face had become a mask and it was impossible to read any thought into her normally expressive eyes. Joe felt a hollowness in his stomach that was a prelude to nausea. He closed his eyes and opened them again in the hope that it would be some other girl sitting there. But it was still Nell, still impassive.

"Join us, Joe." Smokey aped the manner of a sophisticate, swigging champagne and nodding casually toward the pair of seats across the aisle, behind Joe's seat. "Bit of a surprise finding Nell here."

Joe unsnapped his seatbelt and changed seats. He wanted both Smokey and Nell where he could see them. Nell was sitting back in her seat, toying with her glass. She was wearing a black dress—simple, sleeveless and short. Her legs were long and slim. Her sleek shoes had kitten heels. She was polished, groomed, buffed and gleaming, as unattainable as a Vogue model.

"Just like old times."

Joe and Nell exchanged glances.

Smokey talking drivel again.

The flight attendant came up and unfolded tables for them. Their walnut veneer matched the trim running down the cabin. She brought them food, but only Smokey helped himself, shoveling in sandwiches and chicken and lemongrass wraps as though he wouldn't eat again for years.

"Was it you who decided on Sardinia?" asked Joe. Nell nodded. He might have known. He'd have been astonished if Smokey had even heard of Sardinia.

"Are we staying in a villa or a hotel? I'd prefer a hotel. Room service and that, unless the villa has servants. Does the villa have servants, Joe?" Smokey's mouth was full.

"I've got no idea where we're staying unless Nell has fixed something up for us."

"I didn't have time. I just found myself on the plane as it was taxiing for takeoff. Don't you remember, Joe?" Irritation and anxiety infected her voice in equal measure.

"Not a lot."

"Maybe the pilot can radio ahead and find something and check if there's a car waiting for us. It's weird how you don't seem to know what's going on, Joe."

Since this is your dream… She'd left the words hanging unspoken. Smokey was blithely unaware of the tension between his companions.

"You've been a bit standoffish, Nell. It's nice to see you back in circulation."

"I'm not in circulation, Smokey, I'm here because Joe must have wanted me here. And what he thought he was doing, I have no idea."

Joe looked out of the window, which began to expand, allowing more and more daylight into the cabin, warping the window, spreading to the next porthole. He wanted to vanish into the sky and leave the jet to go its own way, just so long as he could be back in his bed and far away from Smokey's ramblings and Nell's suspicions. But Nell stood up and grabbed him by the shoulders, giving him a ferocious shake.

"Stop it, Joe! Stop that right now. We are in an exceptionally small plane. If you start any of your little tricks, we'll all buy the farm. Do you get me?" She stood over him until he made the window gradually shrink back to the same size as the others in the fuselage. Then she sat down opposite him. She was clearly not going to leave him in peace now. "Why don't you just wake up? If you don't want to be here, just wake up."

Smokey looked from one to the other in perplexity. "Not want to be here? In a Learjet on his way to the Med with bucketloads of champagne? What's he on?"

"You're the one who's on stuff, Smokey. And you're the one who set this up, aren't you? God knows how or why Joe decided he needed me along for this ride, but probably it was to stop him from getting both of you killed."

"Here we go, Little Miss Righteous." Smokey folded his arms in a huff.

"What's going to happen to us once we get to Sardinia, Joe? Can you make arrangements just like that? Do you think anything will be set up?"

"I don't know." He didn't want to be pushed any more. Nell chewed her lips, holding back a torrent of questions and abuse. But she did not badger him further, and each time Smokey tried to speak, she cut him off.

"If you could just fasten your seatbelts, we'll be coming in to land in about twelve minutes," said the flight girl. She took her own seat and belted herself in.

They landed, and there was a car waiting for them at the foot of the air stairs. There were no formalities, no passport control. Once their bags had been unloaded, they were simply driven away from the airstrip without ever setting foot in the airport.

"Do you think this is how rock stars really live?" asked Smokey in wonder.

"You are sooo trivial." Nell sat curled in her corner of the car, vulnerable, despite her slick getup. Joe sat silently, wondering how the driver knew where to go — or even how he himself had known where to go. Since he'd never visited Sardinia, it was a bit weird how this whole excursion seemed so organized. He'd have to go to the real Sardinia one day to see if it was the same as his dream version. It must be, he supposed. It was dusk, and the hills were bathed in a rich apricot and crushed berry glow as the sun dipped into the sea to their right, which meant that they were driving south along the western coast of the island. After what seemed like an hour, they turned onto a rough drive and rolled down toward a house that was in darkness until a door opened and light spilled from it.

Instead of entering the villa, Joe found himself walking alone toward a pool teetering on a cliff edge above a rock-strewn beach about a hundred feet below. Sunlight bounced and wavered off the chemically lurid water. In the distance a turquoise sea shimmered and hissed at the sand and rocks on the shore.

He realized that he was in trunks. He was alone. Beneath his bare feet, the wooden decking around the pool was warm but not burning. In each corner of the deck were huge potted plants, their fronds waving in a slight breeze. Three wooden sun loungers lay under a canvas canopy at the far side of the pool. Joe turned to look back at the villa. A light curtain billowed out of an open French window, perhaps one leading from his room. He stood, soaking in the warmth of the sun and savoring the silence. He walked to the edge of the pool and launched himself into the water. He swam along the bottom, surfacing at the far end with a great surge, releasing the breath he had held then taking in a great gulp of air. He floated, his eyes closed, conscious only of the heat of the sun and the warmth of the water. When he opened them, he saw a man standing at the shallow end of the pool, his back to the villa. The man wore a cream linen suit with a dark-red shirt, open-necked. Sunglasses concealed his eyes, but there was something about him that seemed familiar. The man stood, legs apart, hands behind his back, dark hair gelled back, face inclined toward the sun's rays. Joe pulled himself out of the pool and sat at the edge, the precipitous drop down to the beach only a few feet away.

The man took off his sunglasses. Joe recognized him now — the thief from the nightclub. The guy folded up his shades, eased them into the breast pocket of his jacket and stood watching him. Joe did not move. He simply met the stranger's gaze. The man shrugged, smiled and turned his back on Joe. He took two steps away then dissolved. The last thing Joe saw of him was a sort of X-ray image of his bones, fading in the bright sunlight. When he opened his eyes again, he hastily hoisted himself out of the pool, for it had become clouded and he could distinguish the silhouettes of frogs — what looked like hundreds of frogs — propelling themselves through the water. His skin quivered in reaction, as though he were still in the water, but sharing it with the jewel-like creatures, all neon reds and yellows and lime greens.

Next he saw Nell, standing in the same position as the nightclub guy, wearing the most unlikely clothes — a leopard-print skirt and crocodile-print halter top, her midriff bare and tanned. She looked as though she'd just been filming a pop video, bling dripping from her neck and wrists, her fingernails long, gilded talons. Smokey's fantasy babe. Joe stood up. She came around the side of the pool, apparently oblivious to its inhabitants.

"You've got to do something about Smokey. He's getting totally out of hand. He's wasted all the time. Where does he get the money for the gear, Joe? Where does the money for any of this come from?"

"I've got no idea."

"Joe, you've got to wake up. There's going to be serious trouble. Smokey's bringing weird people here. Please, try to wake up and get us back home."

"Wake up?"

"We're in your dream, Joe. We're living your dream. Get us out of here before something goes seriously wrong."

Joe struggled to understand Nell. A frog sprang from the pool and plopped onto the wooden deck. As the sun hit its back, it shriveled and blackened until there was only a faint scorch mark on the wooden decking. Joe ran for the French window, ran for the shower, leaving Nell behind.

In the shower, Joe curled himself into a ball, letting the water bounce off his back and skull. He kept his eyes tightly closed and tried to remember his room at home, the light over the desk, the bed, the walls, the trousers lying in a heap in the corner, the book bag he had just upended underneath the drawing table. He dragged himself back into the room, reaching high above his head and trying to haul himself up first by the fingertips, then by the hands, until he managed to get one elbow back into his own room. Then he felt the hand on his foot. He tried to shake it off, but the grip was firm, and he heard Smokey's voice protesting strenuously.

"No way, man. There's no way I'm going back, which means you can't go back either. Come on, Joe, just a couple more days. This has been the best holiday I've ever had. I've found some really great stuff. You've got to try it."

Joe kicked, but Smokey was stronger and now had him by the waist, pulling him back from his room and back into the shower stall, back into the villa and the sunlight — and the frogs. Joe fought back in earnest, prying away Smokey's hands and lashing out at him with fists, legs, feet.

He scrambled up and with a final lunge, tumbled onto the

floor and lay there panting. It was dark.

The light came on and Ben was there.

"Joe, what the hell is going on? You've been yelling your head off about frogs."

Joe looked around his room. His duvet was crumpled and he was wearing swimming trunks. His hair was wet, but the rest of him was dry. Ben knelt beside him and put a hand on his forehead. Joe tried to knock it away, but Ben was stronger.

"You're burning up, kiddo. I'm going to get Mum."

Joe sat on the floor, still dazed. He didn't ever want to see Smokey again, but he had to know if Nell was safe at home. He stood, but wobbled and sat abruptly back down on the floor. Sue Knightley came in. Like Ben, she held her hand to his forehead.

"Baby, you're sick. You've got to get back into bed." She hadn't called him baby in years. She tried to coax him off the floor and under his duvet, but Joe broke away from her and headed for the door.

"I can't, I've got to find Nell. You've got to let me find her."

Ben blocked his path and his mother clutched at his arm and held him back. He wanted to shake them both off, get rid of them.

Sue Knightley whispered urgently, "Joe, it's nearly two o'clock in the morning. Nell will be safely tucked up in bed, where you should be." Joe saw her glance over at Ben. "Check my bathroom cabinet. There's some ibuprofen in there. Hopefully it will sort out this fever, at least until the morning."

Ben watched as his mother propelled Joe back to bed, shook out his duvet, covered him up and sat beside him, stroking his forehead just as she had done when he'd had chickenpox. He began shivering. She tucked the duvet in close around his body and rubbed his arms. Ben went to get the pills and a glass of water.

They managed to get two Nurofen down him. He kept

muttering about Nell and the frogs, but his murmurs were increasingly slurred and subdued. He still shivered periodically.

Mrs. Knightley looked up at Ben, leaning on the wall near the head of Joe's bed. He pushed himself away from the wall and helped her to her feet.

"I'll stay with him, Mum. You try to get some sleep. If he's still like this tomorrow, I'll stay at home with him. I've only got one double lesson, and I can easily catch up. Zahid will get the notes for me."

His mother brought up Ben's bedding. Together, without speaking, they unrolled the single futon so it lay alongside Joe's bed. Then they shook out the sheet and duvet. Joe was still restless and shuddering.

"He'll need to go to the doctor, if he's not back to normal." She seemed to shrink before Ben's eyes. He reached out and drew her into his great bear hug. Her head barely reached his shoulder now. He dropped a kiss on the top of her head and eased her out of the door.

"Try to get some sleep. We'll work out what to do in the morning." He waited, listening, as she took each step down to her own room. Then he switched off the light before stumbling onto the mattress on the floor where he lay, listening to Joe and watching the minutes glowing past on the clock radio.

Chapter Ten

Gear

The sun woke Joe, not the alarm. He lay there watching it stream through the Velux window and thinking it must be really late. He sat upright and saw the bundled form of Ben on the floor, curled up on the futon. They were both meant to be in school. Friday was double biology followed by triple art. He leaned down and shook Ben's shoulder.

"Wake up! Wake up. We're late again, Elphick's going to kill me."

Ben pushed an ineffectual hand at Joe then tried burrowing deeper under the duvet, but when Joe wouldn't stop jiggling his shoulder, he emerged, his normally immaculate hair wildly askew, his eyes bleary and his face puffy.

"Mum rang us in sick. You're not going anywhere today, and I'm keeping an eye on you."

Joe leaped out of bed then stopped as he looked down and saw he was wearing his swimming trunks. "Why?" He pointed.

Ben shook his head. "You tell me."

"I've got to see if Nell's okay."

"Nell?"

"Yes. Nell Brennan. Something happened last night, and she might have been affected."

"What happened? You haven't been anywhere, Joe. You went to bed really early. The next thing we knew, you were yelling your head off about frogs, and you were so hot we could have fried eggs on you. What happened?" Ben was standing with his hands on his hips in a spooky echo of their mother.

Joe ignored Ben and headed for the shower. By the time he'd come out, he could hear the shower going in the downstairs bathroom, which meant that Ben was getting ready too. He threw on his clothes and rummaged around his bag for his notebook. At the back was a list of phone numbers. He did have one for Nell. She'd had a mobile since she started secondary school. He went downstairs to the kitchen and phoned the number, but he only reached the answerphone.

"Nell, call me to let me know you're okay."

He glanced around the room. It was nearly ten, which meant he'd have to wait an hour until break time, then, maybe, she'd turn her phone on. Unlike other girls, Nell would absolutely never keep her phone on during lessons, perhaps because she knew that scarcely anyone would call her. She wasn't exactly Miss Popular.

Ben came into the kitchen and insisted on checking Joe's temperature. It was still high, although Joe could feel nothing but a surge of energy that demanded an outlet. He felt as if he could run the two and three-quarter miles to school then do sixty press-ups. Ben somehow persuaded him to sit down and have some juice, but Joe could not keep still. His legs jiggled, his fingers drummed and his toes tapped. Ben brought more ibuprofen and stood over his brother until he'd swallowed the pills.

The medicine did slow Joe down. The brothers sat at opposite ends of the sofa, Ben holding the remote, the television blaring daytime nonsense that neither really registered. After the juice and pills, the energy drained out of Joe. His head sank lower and lower until it was resting on the arm of the sofa and his eyes closed again.

Ben watched until he was sure his brother was asleep then fetched a blanket.

Before draping it over Joe, he stretched out his brother's limbs and checked his forehead again. It was damp with sweat and his pulse was thrumming, but Joe was in a deep sleep. Ben remembered some platitude about sleep being the best cure for a sickness, and he hoped it was true. He covered Joe up, then fetched some books and settled in an armchair, trying to make notes for his next history essay.

The phone rang at ten-forty. It did not rouse Joe. Ben caught it on the second ring, hoping it would be their mother. A hesitant voice spoke.

"Hello?"

"Knightley residence. How can I help you?"

"Is that Ben?"

"Yes. Who's this?"

"Nell Brennan. You probably don't remember me, but I used to be a friend of Joe's."

Ben sighed. "Don't be daft, Nell, of course I know who you are. What's up?"

"How's Joe?"

"He's running a high temperature, but I reckon he'll survive."

"Would it be possible to see him? Could I call around this afternoon? I've got something of his. I think he may need it."

Although it sounded a bit weird, Ben remembered how insistent Joe had been about wanting to speak to Nell, needing to know that she was okay. He watched Joe steadily for the next two hours, but when the phone rang again, Joe woke up, his face flushed and ridged where he'd been lying against the sofa fabric.

Ben spoke quietly. "Joe has been asleep since around ten. The temperature seems to be coming down, and it's a really deep sleep, so I think he may be on the mend." Joe stirred, causing Ben to turn around. "He's just woken up. I'll get him some lunch, then he can ring you himself." After a little more nodding and hemming and "yeah, right," Ben put the phone down and asked Joe how he felt.

Ben watched carefully as Joe woozily put his feet to the floor, rocking a little as he sat up.

Then Joe asked him, "Who was that on the phone?"

"Mum. You gave us quite a fright last night. Are you feeling better?"

"I don't know." Joe sat with his head in his hands for a few moments, then he stood up. He moved slowly toward the door.

"Can I help you?" Ben offered.

"I'm just going to the loo. I feel really odd still. My head's all furry on the inside."

It took Joe a little time to come back, and he shuffled as if he needed a hip replacement. He clambered onto the sofa without Ben's help, but he lay down immediately and reached for the blanket. Ben went over and shook it out, then felt Joe's forehead again.

"It's definitely coming down, but you're still pretty hot."

"Did anyone else call?"

"Yup. Nell Brennan. She's coming around after school." Ben waited, but Joe scarcely reacted, just whispering something about 'Nell' and 'a relief' before falling back asleep. Ben rang his mother to tell her the latest then settled down again for another bout of reading. Now that Joe seemed to be calmer and cooler, it was actually quite pleasant to sit there quietly doing some work and chilling out. It was the first time in ages that Joe hadn't fled at the sight of him. Of course, it would have been better if he were choosing to be with Ben while fully conscious, but it was perhaps a start to rebuilding their relationship.

It hadn't occurred to Ben that anyone in the family would freak when he brought his first boyfriend home. He had felt confident that neither of his parents would be judgmental or horrified that their son might be gay. He had simply assumed that his brother and sister would feel the same, and Liesel had been fine about it. Of course, Joe had heard about it in less than ideal circumstances. It had been unfortunate that Charlie Meek had seen Ben kiss Zahid goodbye on the High Street as he caught the night bus home after an evening at the Honey Club.

Ben glanced at Joe and returned to his books. When the

doorbell chimed a while later, he jumped. The tumbling books roused Joe, but he was too dopey to do more than raise his head.

Nell Brennan was standing on the doorstep, her uniform neat, her backpack immaculate and a large carrier bag in her left hand.

"This is for Joe."

"Come in for a cup of tea. I know that Joe wants to see you, Nell."

"I should be getting home."

"Are you looking after Kieran?"

"No, he's with his childminder. I'm still too young. I can't be left in charge until next year."

"So what's the hurry?"

Nell looked over Ben's shoulder. Ben turned to see what had caught her eye. There was Joe, rumpled and looking a little confused, wearing his customary black long-sleeved T-shirt and jeans. He seemed to have grown during the day. Ben clocked that they were nearly the same height now. He stood aside, and Joe stepped forward.

"Are you okay, Nell?" asked Joe. "Please come in."

She shrugged off her backpack and squeezed into the hallway past Ben and Joe.

There was an awkward pause as they all went into the kitchen and Ben made tea, but then he muttered about getting back to his books and went off to the living room. Joe waited until he heard the door closing.

"I'm really sorry."

"Not half as sorry as you're going to be." Nell's grimace was wry. "Smokey's selling something he brought back with him. And he's told a couple of people how he got it. They thought he was bonkers, so he gave up talking about it, but I thought you should know."

"What did he bring back?"

"I think it's coke. He offered some to a girl in my tutor group. He's being a complete div. He's virtually doing it under the teachers' noses. He'll get caught in a day or two.

But if he starts talking and brings you and me into it, I don't know how either of us are going to explain it." Nell sipped at her tea.

"You're really calm about all this."

"You've gotten me home safely twice now." She reached down for her carrier bag and handed it over. "Here's your rug. But in return, I want a full explanation. Time got all warped in Sardinia. It was like we'd been there forever, then like no time at all. I didn't see you. But I woke up in the same room at least three times. You were never there. Smokey was never there, I was all alone in this villa with a load of books and some music. It was like a slice of heaven. Then I'm standing in front of you wearing Beyoncé Knowles' wardrobe and giving you some sort of warning."

"You said that Smokey was bringing weird people to the villa. If you were in your room the whole time, how did you know that?"

"I don't know. It was like I had a script in my head, and I just repeated what was there. But you know something?"

"What?"

"It must be real." Nell loosened her tie and unbuttoned her shirt a little. Joe pushed his chair away from the table. Then she reached into her shirt and pulled out a chain. Attached was a pendant in the shape of her name, covered in shining stones. She fingered it then slipped it over her neck. She placed it on the table then slid it across to Joe. "I took this to a jeweler. These are real diamonds."

Joe shoved the pendant back toward Nell as if it were molten. He didn't know what to say.

"How long has this been going on?" asked Nell.

"Just since Monday. When I dream, it comes true, just like I told you when I got you back to your room. Sometimes I can control it."

"Like how?" Nell was both skeptical and curious. Joe stood up and led her to the garage. He opened the door and switched on the light then let her go ahead of him. She stepped down and stopped. Then she walked up to the

Lamborghini and walked around it. She reached out and touched it. She looked across the roof of the car at Joe.

"Real car. Real diamonds. Real cocaine. Real shit. You are in really deep shit."

Joe ran a hand through his hair. "I guess so."

Nell came around the car, stroking its gleaming surface. She stood at the bottom of the two steps leading back into the house. "Do you want help?"

"How can you help?"

"I don't know unless you tell me you need help. Do you need help, Joe?"

He swallowed. "Yes. I need help." Nell came up and he stepped back to let her through the door. Joe followed her into the kitchen. She sat to finish her tea. When she plunked the empty mug down on the table, she took another look at him.

"Okay. Time to tell me the whole story. How many dreams have you had, what have they been about and why do you think this is happening?"

It occurred to Joe that Nell was even more frightening than his mother, but he started talking, hesitantly, nervously then with greater assurance and a sense of relief that he had someone to talk to.

He told Nell about the fish, the car, the nightclub, about struggling to escape from Smokey and waking up this morning with only the dimmest notion of what had been going on in Sardinia, then fell silent. She had been watching him, but once he stopped talking, her glance veered away as she thought through all she had been told. She chewed a little at her lips, scrunching her mouth, her eyebrows wiggling and knitting as she concentrated on what she had heard. It made Joe feel comfortable watching her mobile features, a sight that he had seen in the classroom daily since they were four and five.

Ben came through to tell Joe that he was off to collect Liesel from her dance class. He seemed relieved that Nell showed no sign of disappearing and said before Joe could stop him that he hoped she wouldn't mind keeping an eye on Joe until he was back. She grinned and said, "Of course not," somewhat to Joe's irritation.

The front door slammed, and Nell focused once more on Joe's situation.

"There are some things you've got to sort out. Smokey's the number one problem. That coke came from somewhere, and someone is going to want it back. Then there's this carpet. I don't think you should hang on to it. And finally, there's this bloke, the thief guy. If he's turned up twice, my guess is he'll turn up again."

Joe wanted to ask Nell how she could think so clearly. She had always been like that. She had the brain of a chief executive trapped in the head of a child — a ruthless, manipulative, driven chief executive. She stood up and put the kettle on, then collected the mugs, dug out tea bags and milk. She thought aloud as she moved around the kitchen.

"So, you could take out Smokey's stash by dreaming about it and getting it off him. But the chances are you'll lose control of the dream and get into even more trouble. I don't think there's anything you can do about the pickpocket until you dream about him again. Once you do dream about him, you need to find out his name and where he comes from. It may be that he's connected with Smokey, since he's appeared in both the dreams you had for Smokey. That's such a stupid name." She brought two mugs of tea back to the table.

"What were you doing with your hand on his thigh?"

Nell rolled her eyes. "Trying to calm him down and stop him from asking that flight attendant for a blow job. He is such a plonker. Aren't you embarrassed having such a complete tosser for a friend?"

"Yes," admitted Joe and smiled. Nell smiled back. Then she chuckled. Joe chuckled too, and Nell began laughing uncontrollably and Joe couldn't help laughing too. Then they couldn't stop, and it began to hurt, but each time they caught each other's eye, they fell into another river of laughter that brought tears to their eyes and an ache to their ribs. Joe knocked over his tea, and they laughed even more. Gradually, they calmed down as they mopped up the tea and cleaned the floor where it had dripped. Nell sat back on her knees by the table, her hands full of soggy paper towels.

"I haven't laughed like that for ages."

"Me neither." Joe paused. "I've missed you, Nell."

"Yeah. Likewise." She dumped the paper towel in the bin, then sat down again. "You need to give that carpet back. Try to dream up this Karabashi man. It's the simplest dream."

"Why give the carpet back?"

"It doesn't belong here. It's like Dill. He had to go back in the book, and you found a way to do it. You have to do the right thing."

The front door clattered as Ben came back with Liesel.

Nell collected up her stuff. She made swift, polite conversation with Ben and Liesel, who went into the kitchen. Joe followed her to the door. "I'll try not to get you involved in any more of this. The thing is, I couldn't help it. You just came."

She tilted her head and examined his face. Then she blinked and nodded, confirming something for herself. "Don't beat yourself up about it." He watched her leave, walking down the street toward the bus stop with a bounce to her step, head held high.

Joe closed the door and went to the kitchen. He felt uneasy, but he had to thank Ben for looking after him all day.

Liesel was at the table, and Ben was standing there with the carrier bag Nell had left behind. "Nell's left this behind. If you run, you can probably catch her up."

"That's okay. It's mine. She wanted to give it back to me." Joe reached out, and Ben handed the bag over. "Thanks, Ben. Thanks for everything today."

Ben smiled. "Any time. You know that, Joe."

Joe nodded and headed upstairs. Nell's words came back to him. 'You have to do the right thing.' Telling Smokey about the dreams had been so wrong. Maybe giving the carpet back would make things a little bit more right.

Chapter Eleven

Karabashi

When Joe next opened his eyes, he was in an orchard. It was walled and enormous. He was close to a gate, and spreading out before him were rows upon rows of trees, carefully tended. Their branches were thick with blossoms, and the air was rich with scent. The place was silent, apart from the slight rustle as a breeze meandered through the trees and there was a subdued drone of bees. Underfoot there was grass and, in every direction Joe looked, there were simply more and more trees stretching into the distance in ranks as regular as an army. At first, he could only see apple, and possibly cherry, but otherwise, they just seemed one great mass of tight-packed flowers in shades of pink and white, as though the trees were preparing to be married off. He stepped forward into the mass of flowers, winding his way through the branches until he had lost track of where he had come from and where he was going. He looked down. He was wearing a light, open-necked cotton tunic and trousers in the same material. He was carrying the golden carpet he intended to return to Karabashi. His feet were bare, but the grass was so soft and rich underfoot that he might have been walking on silk.

There was no need to panic. The trees were planted in such orderly rows that sooner or later the corridors between them must lead back to the orchard walls then to the gate. So Joe wandered farther and farther into the trees, randomly swinging from left to right, caressed by the soft petals and soothed by the delicate susurration of leaves against leaves. He recognized the blossoms. Now, he could identify cherry and apple, peach and plum. He'd helped his parents collect the fruit from their garden often enough, but he didn't think he'd be able to distinguish the different types of nut trees. The almond he did know. There was a tree in the garden, though it had never produced any nuts. But as he walked, he was able to tell the difference between pistachio and walnut, as if he'd known this place all his life. A bird began calling, a honeysweet trill into the blue sky, perhaps warning its fellows that their territory had been invaded, perhaps simply singing for the joy of the fresh day.

Gardeners would have to tend this orchard from time to time, but it would be weeks and weeks until the next harvest. Joe knew exactly what would happen, as though he'd watched the harvest himself every year that he could remember. Hundreds of slaves would be driven into the orchard and there they would spend backbreaking days collecting fruit for the sultan — peaches and cherries, pistachios, walnuts, almonds and plums. The orchard would resound with men calling to one another, hefting up great baskets and carrying them away for cleaning and serving to their monarch. In the meantime, the orchard was left to itself, its blossoms forgotten by all but one man.

Through the screen of leaves and petals, Joe made out a white parasol thickly embroidered with thread the shade of lapis lazuli. Only the stark incongruity of the blue thread gave away the existence of this artificial canopy. Joe walked quietly toward it, then some small sound gave him away and a deep voice asked who was there. Joe said nothing, simply drew closer to the parasol.

Beneath it was sitting the scholar Karabashi, cross-legged on a rug that seemed to weave together every shade of red. His turban was smaller and less snowy than when Joe had previously seen him. He wore a simple gown of blue damask with a pink sash embroidered in gold. He held a book but was no longer reading it, watching out instead for

Joe's approach.

"Our host and our wise counsellor." He did not seem surprised to see Joe again. He put his book down and indicated that Joe should sit down. "We followed your advice."

Joe wasn't quite sure what to do. It didn't seem right to walk up and plonk himself down beside the scholar. He bowed before Karabashi. After all, he had to apologize for hanging on to the carpet, even if it hadn't been intentional. He handed over the neatly folded package which Nell had tied with string, probably so she could control it as she'd wrestled it into a carrier bag. Joe had pulled the carpet out of the bag and had held it as he'd gone to sleep, hoping that would ensure it came with him if he managed to get to Karabashi. It had worked.

Karabashi took it, unfolded it on the rug and stroked it.

He looked up at Joe.

"Come. Sit. You have made a great journey to return this to me. Take some refreshment."

"I don't mean to interrupt." It seemed strange that they could understand each other. Surely Karabashi must be talking Turkish, yet Joe understood everything, and even though it felt as though he was speaking English, he couldn't be, because Karabashi understood everything he was saying. Karabashi brushed aside Joe's hesitant comment.

"Come." He indicated once again that Joe should join him on the rug. "You relieve me of the need to read a wearisome text."

Joe sat down under the shadow of the parasol.

Karabashi reached behind him into a wicker basket and drew out an earthenware bottle, cup and a little box. He poured a glass of some liquid into the cup and handed it to Joe. Never the most adventurous eater, Joe was slow to put the cup to his lips, but when he did, he found it was simply mint tea. He drank a little then set the cup down. Karabashi proffered the box. Inside were delicate pastries made of nuts and honey. Joe took one and swallowed it in a gulp. Karabashi had kept the box at the ready and offered him a second. Joe took it, but this time he nibbled at it with a little more refinement. He vaguely remembered his father saying that in the Middle East, it would cause offense to refuse food or drink and that the best thing to do was to eat very slowly so that you didn't keep having your plate refilled.

"What happened when you told the emperor where the bowl came from?" Joe asked.

"He was astonished. At first he was angry, but then he was delighted that his own craftsmen had acquired the gifts that the infidels from the east sought to conceal from us. So your advice was just, and we are in your debt."

"I didn't mean to keep the carpet. It just stayed behind." Joe looked around the orchard. "This place is very beautiful. What year are we in?"

"We are in the year 1004, in the month of Sha'ban. Does this mean anything to you? I believe that in the calendar of the popes, it is the year 1596 after Christ."

It felt safe, being over four hundred years away from school and Smokey and all the other niggling irritations of his daily life. Karabashi was a restful person to be with. He did not bombard Joe with questions or even talk at all. They simply sat and contemplated the trees and the blossoms, taking occasional sips of mint tea as bees hummed and birds sang.

Joe fiddled with the grass. It felt lush and thick and real, like the carpet on which he sat and the tree trunk against which he leaned. Time evaporated. Other worlds evanesced. For the first time in a week, there was space. Joe lay back and gazed up at the sky, as blue as the embroidery of the parasol under which Karabashi sat, once again immersed in his book. Eventually, Joe levered himself up on one elbow and asked, "Excuse me, but what are you a scholar of?"

"History. My friend Lokman, whom you met the other night, and I are engaged in a history of our sultans."

They fell silent once again, but after another half hour, Karabashi closed his book and wrapped it up in a silk cloth before placing it in a basket. Then he started asking questions of Joe. Where had he come from? By what means had he traveled? Why had he come?

The answers were not as straightforward as Joe had hoped. He had come from England, by dream, to return the carpet that had inadvertently remained in his room, but explaining how he had traveled was a challenge. He decided on the truth.

"I traveled through my dreams. My dreams come true."

"True?" Karabashi could not disguise his skepticism. "Perhaps it would be fairer to say that your dreams have become real."

"Perhaps it would, but isn't it the same thing?"

"There is a difference between truth and reality," Karabashi explained.

Joe pondered this notion. If Karabashi was right, something could be true without being real, and it could be real without being true. This could explain the Lamborghini, which was real but not a true Lamborghini.

Karabashi continued. "For example, we are here in this orchard. This is real to you and me. We can both feel the grass beneath us and the bark of the trees and the scent of the blossom. But no one would believe me if I said that a child from the future had come to visit me and returned this carpet — for which, I thank you. Once again, I find myself in your debt."

"Just because no one believes you doesn't mean it's not true." Joe's head was beginning to ache slightly. He sat up and rubbed his temples. "I am truly here. You know that because if you look at your flask of mint tea, it has gone down, and you wouldn't have eaten so many cakes if you had been on your own."

"The mint tea and baklava are manifestations of reality, not truth."

Karabashi was beginning to display one of Joe's father's

more irritating characteristics — a willingness to occupy his brain with a question that had no answer, spiraling through skeins of arguments just for kicks. Joe didn't care about semantic definitions of truth and reality. He simply wanted advice over this dream thing.

Then Karabashi asked if Joe needed help. Joe was forced to listen to the scholar more closely.

"Not really." Then he took it back. "That's not true. If you knew anything about how these dreams work... If you could help me get them under control, that would help."

The scholar stroked his beard and his dark eyes were distant as he considered this conundrum. His brow creased then cleared. He stroked his beard again, then seemed to come to a decision. "I have never heard of a man whose dreams took on the form of reality, but I will investigate. But this is complicated. Should you remain here while I complete my research or should we arrange to meet? There is no point in your coming unless my research has produced results, but how am I to indicate to you that such an advance has been made? How can we communicate?"

Joe's heart leaped and fell as Karabashi offered his assistance then predicted obstacles. But then, he had managed to insert himself into Karabashi's world when the need had arisen. If it could be done once, it could be done again. He pointed this out to the historian, but it only gave rise to another issue.

"I believe that you must chronicle your dreams. You must note the time, the place and the purpose of the dream. You must list the people you meet and why you are dreaming this dream. There will be a pattern, and once you have the pattern, you have the key to understanding."

This was a sensible suggestion, but it would take a good deal of time. It was the sort of long-winded way of proceeding that all teachers loved, a way that required a student to do a lot more work than the teacher, who simply had to read the record and tick it, except that Karabashi would not be able to mark his work, since he would be unable to read English. Joe sighed. It certainly wasn't an exciting thing to do, but it did make a sort of dreary sense.

Karabashi continued to muse on Joe's situation. He wondered how time functioned in Joe's dreams and whether they would be able to arrange a suitable time to meet. "There are times when it would be inconvenient for both of us if you were to appear out of nowhere, as you have done this afternoon. It would arouse comment and might lead to accusations of sorcery and treachery. Yet you must come again, and I suppose I must simply ready myself."

He looked at Joe, then blenched. "Young man, I can see inside your body!" He reached over and took Joe's hands. He looked wonderingly at them. "I can see your bones and your veins. I can see the blood flowing around in you and your lungs drawing breath. What is happening?"

Joe had no idea, for he felt no different, but he looked down and understood what Karabashi meant. Light was streaming out of his body, rendering his skin translucent, muscles and tendons clearly visible, organs operating and all individuality erased, for he had become like a drawing in an anatomy book, a three dimensional model of a human corpse. He stood up, disconcerted and fascinated, then began patting at himself, even though he knew that would not make his skin opaque again. Karabashi also stood, his calm imperturbability shattered, panic and revulsion rising within him. He bent down and grabbed the carpet, which he threw to Joe.

"You will need this to return, I am sure. Come back when you can. Come back whole. Has this ever happened before?"

"No," replied Joe, clutching the carpet and staring as Karabashi, his parasol, his rug, his orchard and its enclosing walls were now engulfed by a white fog which rolled in thick swirls as dense as candy floss.

Mrs. Knightley was standing over him, calling out his name over and over. He caught hold of her hand and said,

"Mum, I'm here."

She sat down on his bed and picked up the carpet cradled in his arms. She reached up and felt his forehead then under his chin, checking his glands.

"You were so deeply asleep that it terrified me. I thought you were unconscious. I had to wake you up, Joe, just to check you were okay."

"I'm fine. Much better."

Her expression was dubious, but she relaxed as she stood up. She wandered over to the Velux window, which was closed, and looked out. It was dark, and all Joe could see was the orange glow from the streetlamps. She pulled down the blind then walked back over to him.

"Do you feel up to supper?"

"I'm not hungry."

She bent and tousled his hair. "That must be a first. You've had hollow legs for the last few months. I could bring you up a sandwich or something."

Joe loathed having crumbs in bed, but he could see that his mother wanted to do something for him, so he nodded, even though he would hide the sandwich under the bed and wait until she wasn't looking before sticking it in the bin.

As soon as she had left, he threw back his bedcovers and looked for a place to keep the carpet until enough time had gone by for Karabashi to have made some sort of progress.

Now three people knew about his powers — Nell, Smokey and the scholar. It was reassuring to think that two of them wouldn't be interested in badgering him into having dreams on their behalf.

He opened his cupboard and put the rug on a high shelf over the hanging space, tucked away where no one was likely to disturb it. He looked around his room and thought about reading a book. Then a wave of dizziness hit him, and he lurched back to bed. He lay there, gazing at the slope of the ceiling, covered with cartoons mostly too small for him to decipher. So much more had happened to him this week than any other week of his life. This time last week he had been cocooned, protected from the unknown and sheltered from harm. Now, he had been flensed and was faced with tasks to complete. For Karabashi, he must prepare an account of his dreams so far. For Nell, he must work out what to do about Smokey and for himself, he must discover the identity of the stranger who had twice invaded his world.

The possibility of dreaming himself back a week, before all this had started, also occurred to him. It would be much easier to stick at being Joe, the quiet, doodling kid two rows back. But somehow, Joe knew that even if he tried it, the dreams would not let him rest now.

Chapter Twelve

Smokey and Mirrors

When his mother returned with the sandwich, she insisted on sitting at Joe's desk while he ate it. No hiding it under the bed, then. After that, she insisted on changing his sheets and putting him back to bed as if he were four. She considered aloud whether Ben should spend another night at his brother's bedside, but Joe's demeanor showed that he would not welcome that invasion. He could see that if he obliged her in everything else, she would give way on that idea. So he was very pliable and almost chatty, although he found that quite difficult. When she came across an old book full of steam trains that he had kept for the drawings, he even let her read to him and found himself nodding off as she murmured the tale of an arrogant engine trapped in a tunnel for his snootiness.

He did not dream that night. He might have, but when he woke on Saturday morning, he remembered nothing of his dreams and had only a wonderfully light sensation in his bones, his skin and his muscles.

Joe went downstairs and ate two bowls of cereal, three pieces of toast and a banana. His mother watched him with a contented smile as she flicked through the paper, snorting at the occasional news item, brow furrowed over others. Afterward, Joe took his dishes, rinsed them and put them in the dishwasher. Then he came over to his mother and gave her a hug.

She hugged him back and said, "You're still sick. You must be. You never clear up after yourself."

"I do now." Joe gave her another squeeze and asked if he could go on the computer. It was so calm in the house without Ben and Liesel about, just the time to send an email to his father. No one would be trying to look over his shoulder, insisting on doing their practice or looking up the price of dance clothes on the Internet.

It was the start of a quiet weekend for Joe. That afternoon, Mrs. Knightley took the three children for a squashed ride in the Lamborghini, judiciously timed to avoid the rush of cars around the shopping center on the edge of town. In the evening, they ate Chinese takeaway and played Scrabble, as they had done when Dad had been home, and once again, Joe had a dreamless night. On Sunday morning he even agreed to go for a walk with the others before lunch. He did not acknowledge but he did notice Ben's efforts to shield him from Liesel's sniping. He went up to his room after lunch to do some coursework. He pulled out a piece of paper and began sketching. He thought of Karabashi's advice about keeping a record of his dreams and understood this was the way to go about it. So he began sketching out and dating the drawings — first the fish business, then the Lamborghini, then the nonsense with Dill and the key, and getting him back to Maycomb, the night out with Smokey, the encounter with Karabashi and his pals in the palace scriptorium, extracting Nell from her room, the Sardinian holiday and, finally, the orchard. On each cartoon, he noted the date, the time of the dream and the amount of time that had seemed to pass within the dream.

Try as he might, Joe could discern no pattern or consistency in the dreams. He could dream under coercion, when Smokey or Nell had made him. He could dream up what he wanted, but he was also subject to whim and accident. He did not know why his sleep had been uninterrupted over the last two nights, and he had no idea what limits or rules governed his dreams. It seemed amazing — wild, entrancing and chilling — so frightening that Joe felt as though a solid block of ice had taken up residence in his chest. If he surrendered to the fear, the ice would engulf him, but if he held it back, perhaps it might melt a little and the pressure would lessen.

It was just before supper that Joe checked his diary for the week ahead and listed the tasks to be completed. He had a fresh piece of paper on his drawing board and had doodled Smokey's name in a swirling, fat script, bulbous and jagged, a miniature graffiti signature. In a few swift strokes, he had outlined Smokey's greedy face and hands, with a speech bubble saying, "Come on, old mate, just a tenner for the best marching powder ever."

He had no idea how much coke Smokey had managed to get, where he would have hidden it or whom he would have sold it to. He would have had all day Friday to flog it at school, but Joe wondered if he was stupid enough to take it onto school premises or whether he would have simply set up meetings so he could sell off packets over the weekend. It might already be too late, because Smokey would probably have sold off as much as possible over the past three or four days, assuming that he could force Joe into getting more supplies. There would be pressure. Joe was sure of it. A running campaign of cajolery, flattery and threats to get Joe back to the island where he'd got his first batch.

That meant finding some way of stopping Smokey now.

At supper, Joe was distant and distracted again, to the dismay of his mother and brother. Liesel was subdued, tired by a day spent with her friends in the park, until she remembered her news.

"I saw your friend Smokey in the park today. He was pretending to be so cool. You know he's got an iPod, one of the brand-new ones that takes pictures and everything," Liesel related.

"How could he afford that?" asked Mrs. Knightley, astonished. His parents were coping financially but they didn't have the money to splash around on sophisticated electronic gadgets.

"He was selling stuff," said Liesel.

"What stuff?" demanded Mrs. Knightley.

"You know. Drugs, I suppose. Little packets. He was really posing—fist bumps and handing over little bags or folded up pieces of paper, counting up his money. Loads of people were coming up to him—Charlie Meek and that lot, and some of the girls, all flirty."

Mrs. Knightley whipped round to Joe. "Do you know anything about this?"

"No." He shrugged. "Not really. Nell told me he'd got something to sell, but I don't know anything more than that."

She reached for the phone and tapped out a number. "I've got to tell Maria about this. What exactly was he selling, Liesel? Was it weed or was it something stronger."

"Stronger. I think it was coke. It was white powder anyway."

No one answered the phone at Smokey's house. Mrs. Knightley left a message asking his mother to call urgently, then she put the phone down. She turned back to Joe.

"Promise me you have nothing to do with this."

"I promise. I don't know where he got it from. I don't know who he's selling it to and I don't want to know. We hardly talk anymore."

Liesel was irrepressible. "So what was he doing hanging around you the other day? He came home to look at the Lamborghini, then Joe took him up to his room. It was Thursday night, wasn't it?"

"He came to look at the Lamborghini. That's all. He didn't say anything about drugs. He just talked about wanting to fly in a Learjet. That's all."

None of the children had ever seen their mother look so forbidding. Her eyes were chill, her mouth a harsh line in a hard face, so different from the warmth they were used to. Joe glanced at Ben. Even he was frightened by her expression.

"If I find you have lied to me, Joe, there will be

consequences. You understand."

"I understand."

In a way, it was a relief when Liesel blabbed. It was an even greater relief when Sue Knightley absolutely forbade Joe from inviting Smokey around to the house. She tried calling his house again after supper, but there was no answer. Joe went upstairs and rang Nell on his mobile. Either she would already know what was going on, or he would be preparing her for a storm the following day. That was how he justified it to himself, but he knew that he was really phoning so that she could tell him what to do.

She was in, and he gave a succinct explanation of what Liesel had seen. Nell swore. She hadn't heard anything about this, having spent the day visiting relatives.

Joe didn't think much of her advice. She wanted him to dream Smokey into a safe zone where he could neither sell drugs nor get caught. When pressed, she thought a safe zone would be like a bubble or a space capsule, something totally cut off from all other human contact. She warned Joe against going anywhere near Smokey.

"Let him sweat it out on his own. Don't talk to him, just isolate him. Try to control his environment."

Joe didn't know whether this was possible. He thought back with fond regret of his first dream when he'd had no constraints. His mind had been totally free, inspired by Crosbie's pictures — which gave him his next idea. He said goodbye to Nell and went down to his mother. He put the phone back in its cradle and asked if he could take a look at her art books.

"Why do you want to look at those?" she asked, bemused. She'd studied history of art at university. She'd built up quite a collection of catalogues and reference books, but she'd hardly ever looked at them, not since she'd taken her solicitor's exams just after Ben had been born. "God, it's over fifteen years since I looked at any of those seriously."

"It's a project. Art, you know. Books are easier than the Internet sometimes. You can look at each picture for longer somehow."

She led him to the master bedroom where all the big books were tucked away in a bookcase on her side of the bed. He took three and asked if it was okay for him to take them to his room.

"Sure. You can hang on to them if you really want them. Ben's not interested, and we can always dig them out from your pit if Liesel needs them."

Joe searched. He was looking for a picture in which Smokey would be unobtrusive but alone. He might need food. He would need shelter. Then Joe smiled and settled down to his drawing board. He started sketching, creating a set of triangles across the page. Then he drew in some curves and there was an arcade on the top half of the paper with four arches. Shelter.

In the bottom half of the drawing, he outlined bananas, around twenty in bunches, sitting so that they would not bruise. To the left, he drew a cascade, a man-made fountain. Finally, in the center, he drew a plinth. On the plinth he lay Smokey down in a deep sleep, wearing his baseball cap as normal and a jacket over a T-shirt. But he made Smokey's legs those of a goat, hairy and tipped with dainty cloven hooves. Curled in his hand was a long tail, thin as a whip and tipped with a small dark flap of flesh shaped like a spade from a deck of cards.

Joe got out his watercolors and gave the painting a series of washes. The sky was a murky pond green, the land was drab olive, the arcade a musty yellow color, the bananas vibrant and Smokey black from head to toe, more like a shadow than a breathing boy. He sat back and looked at the painting. Something was missing. So on the horizon, he painted in a steam-train, a great smoke trail billowing into the sky.

Now it felt finished.

When Joe woke up, he half expected to be in that strange courtyard, but he was in his own bed. When he checked the picture, it looked exactly as it had when he finished it. Then he looked harder at the statue of Smokey. It was almost imperceptible, but Joe was convinced he could see the chest of the statue rising and falling with the regular breathing of a person in a deep sleep. And he thought — but he wasn't absolutely sure — that he could make out the distinctive white wires running from earpieces to a pocket inside the sleeper's jacket which indicated the presence of an iPod. Weirdly, lying beside the plinth where Smokey was sleeping, there was a head that Joe knew he had not drawn. It was the sightless head of a woman with what appeared to be a stone fruit bowl instead of hair. She looked like some sort of Greek goddess.

He flipped his sketchbook shut. The picture was dry now, and Joe wanted it with him, just to check that things were okay in Smokeyville. And he could also show it to Nell and see if she thought it was a safe enough place for the moment.

* * * *

Joe did not have another chance to check up on the picture until break time. The figure on the plinth had turned its back on the table full of bananas. Joe counted up the number of bananas. There were now fewer in each bunch, and he could see the traces of at least two banana skins tossed aside in the arcade. Smokey was absent from English. No one had seen him that day, but this concerned no one particularly, least of all Thomas, who was clearly delighted to be minus a pupil who made the presence of a wasp in the classroom seem like a minor diversion, even when all the girls stood on their chairs shrieking and batting their arms about.

At lunch, Nell found Joe. Although she was in school uniform, he could not quite dispel the image of her in that little black dress. Her hair was down and fell across her face as she flicked through the sketchbook to Joe's picture. What they saw gave both of them a shock.

Smokey's torso was pressed up against the front of the

painting, his arms outstretched above his head, banging furiously against the surface, as though he were behind glass. They watched then as Smokey ran around the edges of the painting, disappearing between the arches of the arcade, bouncing back into the center, then up to the edge of the sky, pushing as if he could lift a lid off the top of the picture to escape from it. They could see that all the bananas had now been eaten, and most of the skins were lying around the ground or on the tabletop, smushed and browning, with the clear imprint of dainty little hooves squelched into them.

Nell kept her mouth clamped tightly shut, but her shoulders shook as she watched Smokey racing around the picture, teetering on his hooves. She started snorting and holding her stomach when he turned his back on the front of the picture, did a handstand and tried kicking at the surface. Joe half expected the picture to smash like a pane of glass hit by a stone, but it held, shuddering a little as the solid little goat's feet struck over and over again at the enclosing air. But they both sobered up when Smokey's arms gave way and he fell. He landed in a heap on the ground, and his baseball cap rolled away. Then he cradled his head in his arms and started to sob. Joe was glad he could not hear him.

"You have to keep him there until we've found the drugs." Nell closed up the sketchbook and handed it back to Joe. He slipped it into his bag.

"There's no chance of getting them. Liesel saw him dealing in the park yesterday and my mum will have phoned his mum by now."

"Do you think they know he's missing?" Nell folded her arms and gnawed at her lips. Joe felt bad about causing her anxiety — again. He shrugged and ran his fingers through his already-ragged hair.

Neither Nell nor Joe could concentrate for the rest of the afternoon. Ms. McKechnie made it abundantly clear how little she thought of their distraction during her lesson, a distraction which caused Nell to slip up on delivering an answer to a fairly simple equation in class. Her false step inspired McKechnie to announce an extra algebra test, raising a groan of mingled disbelief and fury from the other students in the class.

Then it was Crosbie's lesson. Joe made his way there, half hoping that Smokey would be there, but he wasn't. Nor was Crosbie, and Elphick was doing cover, so there was no chance of doing anything other than filling in worksheets on citizenship. It was dark by the time the class finished. Joe caught the bus home and let himself into the empty house. He had the place to himself for another couple of hours.

First he checked on the picture of Smokey. He was back on his plinth, asleep. Joe wanted to give him some fresh food. He thought about rubbing out the banana skins and drawing in some more food, but it would probably wreck the page. But Joe remembered a lesson in symmetry. He dug around in his portfolio chest and found a simple mirrored pane of glass. He positioned it so that it reflected his sketch then drew the reflection on the opposite page so that now the arcades were on the left of the picture, the statue remained in the center but now faced backward and the cascade tumbled down the right hand side of the page. He sketched in pizza, some chocolate fudge cake and a big bottle of mineral water. He'd thought about Coke, but the red was going to be too virulent. He colored it and left the picture to dry. When Smokey woke up, everything would be different, reversed, but at least he'd have a decent meal. Joe felt bad about messing with Smokey, but then he remembered Liesel's account of what had been happening in the park. He ripped the old picture out of the book, scrunched it into a ball and chucked it through the mini-hoop over his bin.

Joe then turned his attention to his homework, working his way through McKechnie's batch of sums first. She'd be the least forgiving of his teachers if he failed to do his homework. It took nearly an hour, and he hadn't quite finished when he heard the front door opening. He looked at the Smokey picture and put it away, just as he heard his mother summoning him downstairs.

Mrs. Knightley was in the front room, looking unusually disheveled. She was wearing her office clothes, a grey tweed suit and black silk shirt. She had her usual silver chain on with the pendant Dad had given her when Ben had been born, but her dark hair was wild and her eyeliner was a little smudged. Joe's uncles were always saying that Joe looked like her, but he couldn't see it. This evening, suddenly, he could.

"What's up, Mum?"

"You haven't heard, then?" She stopped pacing and leaned back on the arm of the sofa, her arms folded.

"About what?"

"Silas. Smokey. He's in the hospital. He went wild this morning. Maria had to get him sedated and into the psychiatric ward of the Royal this afternoon, so that's where he is."

Nausea swept over Joe. He doubled over, his hand over his mouth, but the wave passed and he sat down in the armchair, curled up like a hedgehog.

"There's more," said his mother, less harshly. "The police have been called in. Maria found over half a kilo of cocaine in his room."

Joe looked up at his mother, his face suddenly haggard with evident shock. "You know I don't know anything about all this."

"I hope you don't, Joe, and I hope that's what you'll be able to tell the police. They're coming over to question you about all this sometime this evening. The sergeant who rang me up said about eight p.m. Maria had to provide a list of all of Smokey's friends, and you're on it. So I really hope you were telling me the truth, and I also hope you'll have the wit to tell them the whole truth."

Then she hauled Joe through to the kitchen to help her get supper ready, and he spent the next hour and a half watching the clock inexorably tick toward eight, too distracted to pay any heed to the rest of the family's speculations about where Smokey had got the drugs and what was going to happen to him.

Chapter Thirteen

Dr. Dolon

Two police officers came to interview Joe, and they behaved nothing like his expectations. They were plainclothes detectives from the drug squad, in their early thirties, dressed as if they were about to go clubbing — the man wearing a T-shirt and Levi's with Camper shoes and the woman in red tights and a swirly, patterned mini-dress. They didn't try any right-on talk. They just got on with the interview in a rather clinical fashion. They seemed to accept Joe's tale of a disintegrating friendship and his rather lame explanation of bringing Smokey back to the house on Thursday evening to catch up on GCSE coursework. He didn't exactly *plan* to conceal the Lamborghini's existence, but he saw that it would arouse all sorts of suspicion, and if his mother had said nothing about it to them, there was no reason why he should.

Mrs. Knightley came up to his room that night. He was ready for her. The police interrogation had sharpened him, and he was still feeling refreshed from his weekend's uneventful sleep. She quizzed him about the Lamborghini, about Silas, about drugs, about his cartoons, about every aspect of his life, gnawing at inconsistencies, tugging at the loose threads in the responses he gave.

When she had gone, Joe shook out the carpet and lay down, still dressed. He closed his eyes and the first thing that came to mind was Nell's face. He did not know how she would feel about seeing him now, but he was beyond merely *wanting* to see her. He ached for her.

When he opened his eyes, he was still on the carpet. Nell was sitting there too, legs crossed, arms propped on her knees, deep in a book, her hair hooked behind her ears and swinging forward against her cheek. She was wearing a maroon fleece top, striped green and maroon pajama bottoms and sheepskin moccasins. He raised his head and she gave him a thoroughly unimpressed look.

"What am I doing here now, Joe?"

He explained about Smokey, about the police, about his mother. Nell did not begin to look any more sympathetic, but she did appear less affronted. She sighed as Joe trailed off.

"You have no idea how this dreaming thing works, do you?"

"No."

"Can you control whether you dream or not?"

"I'm not sure. I didn't dream this past weekend."

"Did you draw anything?"

Joe thought about it. He'd fiddled about with his Life at the Knightleys strip for Dad, but other than that and the painting of Smokey on Sunday evening, he had not drawn anything.

"Hasn't it occurred to you that you dream when you draw?"

"But I didn't draw the Sardinia dream—or the nightclub dream when Smokey and I went out in the limo. And I've never drawn you." Although even as Joe said that, he knew that what he wanted most at this very minute was to draw Nell and keep her with him forever. Having her near was the only good thing that had come out of this whole business.

"Did you find the Turkish scholar guy?"

"I did. He said he hadn't heard anything like it before, but he would see what he could do to help."

They stopped talking. The carpet was hovering above a manicured lawn which undulated away on all sides as far as Joe could see. Above was a cerulean sky. That was all.

There was no other relief to the scenery, just mown grass as though the carpet had become a raft on an emerald-green sea.

"This is actually quite restful," said Nell after a long while. Then she returned to her book. Joe agreed with her, although he didn't say so out loud. He reached out to see what she was reading. She held it away from him and said, "You just have to ask, you know."

"What is it, then?"

"It's by Freud. It's about wish fulfillment. Do you know what your wishes are, Joe?"

"I have no wishes." Which was a lie.

Nell didn't say, 'Oh, yeah,' out loud but her expression was perfectly readable. It occurred to Joe that he really didn't know what he would do with a wish. He'd wished for a car without thinking twice about the consequences, and now he was lumbered with a huge yellow monster he wouldn't be able to drive for the next eleven years.

He looked again at Nell, watching as her eyes ran over the print before her, noting the fine bones of her hand and wrist as she turned the pages, the elegant length of her limbs and the delicate elongated fingers with neat, trimmed fingernails. Her hands were those of a woman, not a child. She wore no rings, no earrings, no jewelry at all. He still did not know what he wished for. She put down the book.

"Where are we?"

"Here." Joe looked round again at the emptiness. "Wherever this is."

"What about our physical bodies? Smokey's physically in the hospital, but he's also in the picture, isn't he? So where are our bodies?"

"In our rooms at home, I guess."

"Does that mean we're in a sort of coma? This is weird."

Joe lay back and closed his eyes. To Nell's alarm, the carpet began to move.

"Hey, what are you doing now, Joe?"

"Wait and see."

The carpet rose about a meter above the ground and as it moved, the sky darkened to indigo, the stars like pinpricks in its fabric. Nell put out a hand, as though she could scoop up the color and hold it. It grew colder and colder as they rushed through the dusky air, and the stars were soon quenched by the streetlights of the town below. The carpet began its descent and Nell started to recognize landmarks from the town, from their zone, from her street, from her house. Then they were hovering outside her window.

"Look inside. Is your body there?" Joe did not open his eyes at first, but then he squinted to see what was going on.

The carpet hovered at the window. Nell put her hands on the ledge and peered in through a chink in the curtains. "I think I can see my legs. Now let's go to your house. We can see through the Velux into your room, unless you've drawn the blind."

They skimmed over the rooftops, avoiding aerials and chimneys, disconcerting one cat out on the prowl and rousing several dogs into a frenzy of unnerved barks. Somebody threw open a window and called out into the unheeding night, "Shut that bloody dog up, or I'll do it for you." The dog was summoned inside, which only slightly muffled its bemused baying.

Then they were fluttering over the Knightleys' house, the carpet shimmying a little as Joe kept it steady, allowing Nell to look in.

"You're there. You're lying on your rug. Your ordinary rug, not this one."

Joe steered the carpet away from the window and back toward the light of the great meadowlands where they had first found themselves. The carpet was silent as a glider. They could hear only a faint whisper of air as they traveled faster and faster toward the sunlight.

Joe opened his eyes and sat up. The carpet landed on the grass, which was lush and soft.

"So we're there, but we're here. What happens if someone comes in and wakes us up? I suppose the whole thing disperses if it's you and if it's me, they think I'm unconscious and freak out."

The idea clearly did not appeal to Nell. "I think we should go and visit Smokey in hospital tomorrow, check up on him. And if he looks really out of it, I think you're going to have to get him out of that picture."

"What if I got all the teachers into a picture? Then they'd all be sick and they'd have to close the school for a while. You can't have kids in school if half the teachers are absent."

"What picture could you get them into? But you'd have to draw them all. It would take you forever. You'd have to do, what, fifty portraits?"

"Probably more, just to be on the safe side, and I don't know half of the staff. There are all those people in the sixth form section who never come near us." Joe started thinking about pictures into which he could dump the teachers — crowd scenes, maybe from some of the French Revolution paintings that he'd looked up for his history project or perhaps one of those crazy medieval paintings that Crosbie loved so much with roses growing out of people's bottoms. It was a great distraction from facing up to what Nell had said. Joe didn't want to see Smokey. He remembered his other problem.

"What was Meeky doing today?"

"Don't know. I never see him around. He was horrible at primary school, and I don't suppose he's improved any. We're not in any of the same classes."

"Bet he's tried to muscle in on Smokey's operation. I just hope Smokey hasn't blabbed about where he got the stuff."

"What's he going to say? 'I got this really great gear from a lightning trip I took to Sardinia courtesy of my good friend Joe, who will dream you to your ideal holiday destination, with or without narcotic substances.' Get a grip, Joe. Your secret is safe."

"I'll have to bring Liesel tomorrow. It's my turn to pick her up, and no one will be at home to look after her. Ben's off at work on Tuesdays and Thursdays."

"That's fine. I can keep an eye on her while you go to see Smokey."

* * * *

So the next afternoon, much against Liesel's will, Joe and Nell levered her into the thirty-nine bus that went past the Royal Hospital, and they bribed her with a teen comic and a bag of Maltesers to sit still in the waiting room. Nell took out her books and Joe reluctantly edged down the corridor, surprised at how empty and quiet the place was. Given all the bulletins on the news about overcrowding and bed shortages, the place was spookily silent. He could see one nurse at a reception desk. He went up and asked where he could find Silas Murphy. She had warm brown eyes and a Ghanaian accent. She pointed him across the passageway to another door, and he went in.

Joe hadn't known what to expect. He'd had a vague idea that it would be like an ER and that there'd be machines bleeping and buzzing everywhere. But it was just Smokey, lying there, his mum holding his hand, her eyes sunken and her shoulders rounded. Smokey looked smaller than in everyday life. His crinkly hair had been shaved off and there was one electronic sensor on the side of his head just above his ear and another on his neck, both stark and white against his café au lait skin. His eyes were closed tightly, the dark eyelashes furled like scimitars, his usually mobile mouth quiet and closed, his chest rising and falling steadily. When Mrs. Murphy turned around to see who had come in, Joe noticed the silvery tracks of tears on her cheeks, as fragile as a snail's trail. He swallowed.

"How is he, Mrs. Murphy?"

"No change. It's good of you to come, Joe, especially when he's in such trouble."

"I'm sorry, Mrs. Murphy."

"So am I, Joe, so am I." Her shoulders convulsed and she raised her hands to cover her face. He could only just make out her words. "Where did we go wrong? Where?"

"You didn't. It wasn't you."

But Mrs. Murphy didn't hear him. Joe stood there, feeling so out of place it ached, and knowing he had to return home to get Smokey out of the picture immediately. But he couldn't leave just yet. He had to spend a bit of time with Smokey, otherwise it would look really odd.

Just then, a man's voice came through the door.

"Mrs. Murphy? We've got the latest test results here. Do you want to step outside and we can discuss them?"

Joe looked up at the doctor. He was wearing a pale-blue open-necked shirt and navy chinos under his white coat. His eyes were puffy and ringed with dark circles, but Joe still recognized the man from his dreams. The thief from the nightclub. The man standing on the decking by the swimming pool in Sardinia. The doctor blanked him, but Joe knew he'd registered his presence.

"Would you mind sitting with Silas while I talk to Dr. Dolon, Joe?"

"Of course not. However long it takes."

The two adults left the four-bed ward for the main corridor, just within Joe's sightline. Dr. Dolon lifted a clipboard thick with paper. He showed the first page to Mrs. Murphy then flicked through the rest of the pages.

Joe leaned forward. He felt uncomfortable about taking Smokey by the hand, but he felt equally lemon-like just sitting there gazing at the body of his friend. He couldn't imagine talking to him. The idea made Joe squirm. There was a noise at the door. Nell was there.

"The day nurse is keeping an eye on Liesel. She said if I wanted to visit, this would be a good time." She looked over at Smokey. Her jaw clenched, her lips thinned and she crossed her arms. "Poor guy."

"You don't like him."

"I don't. And I laughed when I saw him racing around that painting. But this is awful. How are you going to get him out?"

"Repaint the picture without the statue in it. That's the way it worked last time. I drew him in and he was trapped there."

Nell waited until Mrs. Murphy came back. She and Joe stood up, and she caught a glimpse of Dr. Dolon. It looked to Joe like she didn't recognize him at all. As she exchanged platitudes with Mrs. Murphy, Dr. Dolon turned and met Joe's eyes full on. He smiled. It wasn't a proper smile, more like a threat. His eyes did not crease up and he seemed to be keeping himself leashed, a lean feline simply waiting for its moment. He slipped one hand into a pocket.

Dolon sounded professional and kind. Silas should show some signs of improvement in a day or two, but in the meantime, he had to be kept under observation. If they came back later in the week — say Friday — they ought to be able to see him up and about. But no one would be discharging him for quite a few weeks. He'd have to go into the psychiatric wing once he'd come out of this coma, then there'd be months of therapy. After that, the police were talking about prosecution and a term in some sort of juvenile detention center. Mrs. Murphy drew a tissue out of her bag and wiped her eyes before they could brim over. Then she blew her nose, straightened and dismissed the two kids.

"There's no need for you to hang about here, dears. It was very good of you to come, but Silas is out of it for the moment. If you like, I can call as soon as he surfaces."

"Yes, please, if you would," said Nell. Joe shook hands with Mrs. Murphy. Then he had to walk past Dolon and the doctor's steady, suspicious gaze. Joe could feel the doctor's eyes following him down the corridor. Once they turned the corner into the waiting area, he turned to Nell and whispered where he'd met the man before.

"Just wait until we've got to your house. Then you can talk about it."

Liesel was sitting flicking through the dog-eared pages of a celebrity magazine, muttering "split up, together, split up, split up, split up, together, rumored to be splitting, split up, split up, split up."

She looked up. "They've got like forty couples in this magazine and only about five of them are still together. Do you think there's a curse if you appear in it?"

"That's not a new idea, Liesel."

Liesel dumped the magazine and put on her coat and bag without a murmur. Joe shook his head in disbelief. He'd have been given a nonstop earache if he'd tried the same move with his sister, but Nell made it seem totally natural to shepherd her out of the hospital.

"How's Smokey?"

"Out cold," replied Joe, "but they say he should be okay in a couple of days."

"His sisters are really worried. They keep acting as if he's going to die or something. Is he going to die?"

"No. He is not going to die. He is going to be fine. He'll be back plaguing Carmel and Louise in a week, if not sooner." Joe didn't say so, but he did think that Smokey's sisters were little madams who'd be milking this episode for all the sympathy they could get, since they scarcely got the time of day from most people under normal circumstances.

Their bus came and Liesel decided to embarrass the other two by interrogating Nell at full volume about whether she was dating Joe and if she fancied him, and how Nell ought to know that he was a real minger, even if girls did fancy him. The rest of the bus failed to stifle their chuckles and stared mercilessly at the two teenagers. As they walked from the bus stop to the Knightleys' house, Nell said to Joe, "Perhaps I should go on the bus with Liesel more often. It's one way of convincing little old ladies that I'm not going to happy-slap them." Then she looked down at Liesel. "So which girls fancy him then, Liesel?"

"Why'd you want to know? Are you going to have a bitch-fight?" Liesel asked excitedly.

Nell crossed her eyes at Liesel and said, "Nooooo! I just want to tease them about it at school tomorrow."

Having established that Nell simply wanted to embarrass Joe further, Liesel happily catalogued a list of about six girls who she claimed thought Joe was hot. Joe did his best to ignore the implausible tally of names Liesel had gathered.

* * * *

Back home, Liesel headed for the TV. Upstairs, Nell watched as Joe repainted the piazza with arcade, food-laden table and train for the third time. This time there was no statue in the center of the picture, although he did include the female head that had appeared there. Then Joe took the other two pictures he'd drawn and carefully tore them up into tiny pieces.

"What time is it?" asked Nell when he'd finished.

He looked at his watch. It was half-past six. Nell noted it in her diary. "Let's see what time Smokey comes out of his coma."

A wave of disbelief suddenly swept over Joe. The last week began to seem to him so much nonsense, a bizarre fantasy game that he had somehow conned Nell into playing.

Nell continued her thought. "We have to find out how he got the drugs."

Joe sat back in his chair, twizzling round slowly on its stem, his long legs dangling, his arms folded tight against his body. "Do we? Why?"

"So that we can work out how to put them back."

"It's too late for that."

"I don't see why."

"Because he's already sold a shed-load, and we can't replace what has gone."

"You could draw the stuff that's missing."

"I just don't see the point." Joe knew he was being obstructive, but he couldn't admit just how scared he was.

"We could sit back and wait, or we could go back and see if we can work out where he got the drugs," Nell offered.

"Enough with the Nell Brennan, Girl Detective act. We're

not looking for the drugs. They came from someone giving them to Smokey for some reason and probably expecting payment. And do you know who I think gave them to him?"

"Who?"

"That doctor. Dolon. The guy who's treating Smokey. He's the guy I was talking about, Nell, but this time he's outside the dream world and in real life. How does that work?"

Of course Nell asked whether Joe was totally, absolutely, utterly sure. He didn't say anything, just rolled his eyes and huffed as he might do when his mother was on his case.

"At least you've got a name to work on, then." Nell glanced again at her watch, then said that she needed to get home. Joe followed her downstairs, where he shrugged on his coat.

"What are you doing?"

"Coming with you. There's no way you're going home alone in the dark."

"What are you? My mother?"

"No, but my mum would go mental if I let you go on your own." He went into the kitchen where Ben and Liesel were sitting together drinking tea.

"I'm walking Nell home. I'll be about half an hour."

The walk was awkward. Nell wanted to start in on investigating Dolon, but something about the doctor made Joe's skin crawl and he wanted nothing more to do with Smokey or Dolon.

"There's Karabashi. I need to find out more about how this dream thing works before I get tangled up in any more stuff."

Nell snorted when they reached the end of her street. "I can make it on my own from here."

Joe nodded. Nell paused, looked hard at Joe, then turned and walked away. In a movie, thought Joe, I'd have grabbed her and kissed her. And if he had kissed her, she'd have kicked him or slapped him. Because this wasn't a movie and Nell was intrigued by his situation, but not so much by him, he watched as she went through the little gate and into her front garden. He waited until he heard the door close behind her, then he ran back home.

Chapter Fourteen

Feast for Beasts

Back home, Joe had no time to himself. Mrs. Knightley was there, chopping vegetables, asking about Smokey and his mother, getting Liesel to lay the table, Joe to get drinks and Ben to stir the sauce, inquiring about Joe's homework and eventually, casually mentioning the phone call she'd received from Mrs. Elphick that afternoon. Having poured out juice and water for the rest of the family, Joe slumped in his chair and did his best to evade his mother's gaze.

"She's genuinely worried about you, Joe. She said you'd been getting into fights."

Ben's eyes switched from his mother to Joe.

"There's been a bit of hassle. Nothing I can't handle."

Liesel had stopped chucking the cutlery onto the table and was now positioning each piece with delicate precision.

"She said you'd been falling asleep in class."

"I've just been a bit tired."

"She thinks I should take you for a blood test, see if you've picked up mono."

"You only get mono from kissing, and no one would ever kiss Joe," said Liesel. Ben barked at her to go upstairs until she'd learned when to keep her trap shut. Both Mrs. Knightley and Joe snorted as Liesel wailed that he was really mean then shot out of the room. He muttered about good riddance then turned back to the stove and the sauce.

"So, Joe, fights, flaking out in class, friends falling into drug-induced comas..." The garlic under his mother's cleaver was being pulverized almost to pulp under the forceful rhythm of her chopping. "I think I'd be negligent if I wasn't concerned. Don't you?"

"The fight thing was just Charlie Meek being stupid. Then a couple of his sheep thought it would be a good idea to play the same game." Joe wanted to go no further. Neither his mother nor Ben would be happy to hear the reason for the scraps. Ben was hardly going to give up Zahid because having an openly gay brother made life uncomfortable for his little brother. Besides, however uncomfortable it made Joe feel, Ben's sex life wasn't really his business, even if it did get him into fights.

"And the sleeping thing?"

Joe had no ready answer for that one. Ben spoke. "It's probably hormones, I should think. Joe's growing like he's swallowed magic beans. His voice has broken. He's all over the place. I was a bit like that. Remember?"

"I certainly don't remember calls from your anxious teachers about catching forty winks during lesson times."

"I just never got caught. It's a wonder more kids don't fall asleep. Terminal moraines and the periodic table aren't exactly gripping Most of the teachers in that place make ditchwater look like a zappy little cocktail."

"Which brings us back to Smokey."

"I told you everything I know last night, Mum. We haven't been talking much to each other recently. He's been getting into some stuff he shouldn't have. Anyway, he doesn't think I'm cool enough anymore, and he ignores me."

Ben spoke up. "Joe's on the money. Silas Murphy is a user and a loser. He tries to use people and he's definitely into drugs. If he thinks Joe has something he wants, he'll hassle him, but otherwise, Joe's just too straight for Smokey's kind of shit."

Mrs. Knightley scooped up the garlic and put it into a jar with several tablespoons of olive oil and a splash of vinegar. She screwed the top on tight and shook it hard.

"I don't know what to say to Maria. She's terrified of telling Denny what the real problem is. He just thinks

Smokey collapsed. She's managed not to let on about the habit just yet — or the dealing. He was away on some golfing thing the whole weekend and had a work crisis as soon as he got back, on top of all this."

Joe stood up and went over to the counter where his mum had left the lettuce in a dryer. He found the salad bowl and started tearing the lettuce and dropping it in. His mother handed him the salad dressing jar and turned her attention to the oven to check the chicken she'd been roasting.

"How did you leave things with Elphick?" asked Ben.

"I said I'd get Joe tested for mono. We agreed that we didn't think he was on drugs and she said that Charlie Meek was facing yet another exclusion for some other misdemeanor, so hopefully the fighting will be curbed. She said that Joe was a target, not an initiator, and she wasn't having that. She's tough as old boots and not putting up with any further disruption with her school, thank you very much. You'd think she owned it. What does that head figure do? Sit in his office all day twiddling his thumbs?"

"He's never there," said Ben and poured the sauce into a jug with a flourish before dumping the pan in the sink and carrying the jug to the table. Then he drained the vegetables while their mother carved the chicken.

"You'd better go up and make you peace with Liesel, Ben. Get her down here as quickly as you can."

Once they were all at the table, Liesel still pink about the eyes, Joe was grateful when the conversation veered away from school and him and onto Christmas and the hope that David Knightley might make it back in time for Christmas Eve. It was about five weeks away. Liesel began compiling a wonderful list for Santa, composed chiefly of plastic junk she had seen on TV, and Ben kept coming up with additional items of such sparkling pink girliness that Joe and his mother pretended to retch violently.

As soon as supper was over and cleared up, Joe went up to his room with his mother's approval. "And turn that light out promptly, Joe. It's the only way to crack this sleep issue. I don't want any more phone calls from Ms. Elphick."

He only had a couple of pages reading to do for the next day. He was in bed with the light out by nine-thirty, his eyes closed by nine-thirty-one.

When he opened them again, he was standing in a doorway leading to an enormous banqueting hall. The walls were hung in red damask, with gilded pillars on one side framing great swathes of red taffeta curtain that concealed huge windows. On the opposite wall, between each set of pillars, hung four immense tapestries in rich greens and blues. Beneath the tapestries were sideboards laden with four punch bowls of beaten silver, each shaped into the likeness of a cornucopia of fruits, matched in abundance by the platters of real fruit that punctuated the table with a tumble of apricots, peaches, grapes, strawberries, cherries and lemons, their peels razored off into crazy spirals. Joe was mesmerized by the length of the table and the variety of its contents. He saw peacock and swan, each dressed in its own feathers, suckling pig, hams, pies, pasties, jellies and marzipan favors shaped like chess pieces. He saw puce lobsters, crabs furled tight, melons cut and whole, capon, woodcock and, glinting between the food, crystal glasses blown in fabulous colors — cough medicine pink, lime green and turquoise, ewers of silver and crystal, chased gold goblets and salvers, knives with elaborately carved ivory handles. As the flames from hundreds of candles in sconces and in the two great chandeliers over the table flickered and spat, their reflections danced in the gleaming silverware and great mirrors.

He took a tentative step into the great room, terrified that someone would hear him or see him and tell him off. He looked up at the ceiling and saw it was vaulted into three sections, each one painted in scenes from Greek mythology. He could make out the strict stance of Artemis, her head sporting a bandeau with a crescent moon above her forehead, linen held up to conceal her shapely torso as she pointed at an abject Actaeon, discovered spying on the squealing maidens who attended their mistress at her bathing. In the center, the Olympians gazed calmly on as Persephone was restored to Demeter. Joe twisted around to look again at the tapestries, which displayed scenes of country life—a milkmaid at her post in an abundant copse just outside a wealthy village, a hunter preparing to fire his arrows at a skipping hare, a rural dance and a shepherd tending his flock.

Joe had been dragged occasionally to National Trust country houses by his mother, but he'd never taken much notice of the rooms. He could not remember seeing anything like this extraordinary abundance of food and art and artifacts. It was like stepping onto a movie set, but there were no actors, no cameras, no sound at all, just the disconcerting thump of his own heart. He took another step forward, then another, until he was standing at the table. He reached out to see if the food was real. He was not planning to eat anything, simply to squeeze a fruit. Then he heard a distant hubbub and he was paralyzed by the prospect of discovery. The doors at the far end of the room opened inward, and a crew of men burst in. They were not guests. They were serving men and boys bearing still more food, cakes and sweetmeats, cheeses, bread, great platters of vegetables, all laughing and joking and apparently oblivious of Joe standing in their midst. He listened to their chat, and as with Karabashi, he had no difficulty in understanding their speech, even though they were not speaking anything resembling modern English.

"What time is his lordship expected to sit down?" asked a crooked man, hunched and twisted.

His neighbor, stout and short with warts on his nose, replied, "At once, I hear. He's starving. His guests are starving. He's furious with Master Perkin, and the only thing that will soothe that savage breast is the finest feast our kitchen has ever seen, or we'll pay for it with our hands and our heads."

"He'll cut them off?"

"Yes, and cook them up for a broth or a stew afterward, I've no doubt."

The tide of men flowed around Joe, tweaking here, rearranging there, adjusting the contents of the table and the bottles and the urns around the room with purpose. They did not wish to lose their limbs in the service of their lord. If he was such a tyrant, Joe wondered why they continued working for him, but before he could pursue the thought, another man entered the room, and they all snapped into position. This man was blubbery and voluble, with a drooping moustache and drooping eyes and drooping nose, all hauling his face southward like guy ropes on a marquee. He walked down one length of the table then up the other, his inspection minute and accompanied by a commentary grumbled through his dark whiskers.

"Dolts, incompetents, fools, idiots, puny sheep-biting indigents, slobbering malmsey-swillers... How can I be expected to serve my art and my master when I am surrounded by malingering malcontents and butter-fingered wastrels?" He twisted around and grabbed a boy by the ear, twisting it until the child, several years younger than Joe, was howling and hopping. "You, you bloated, beetle-brained bladder! You've been sitting on your arse all day, snaffling titbits from all the trays, and yet you can't be trusted with a simple arrangement of apples and pears." He dropped the boy and lashed out at another servant then another, clipping one about the head, backhanding another, shouting in one's face, covering his victim with frothing spittle. The spectacle made Joe feel nauseous and repelled, but he still seemed invisible.

Then the half-mad cook—for this, Joe gathered, was his position—clapped his hands, said "Well, it will have to do, but if he decides that it's not good enough, my cleaver is ready to remove fingers from hands and hands from wrists. Be prepared, you lumpen miscreants!" The servants filed out, and the loathsome walrus turned one last time to examine the table, giving a sigh of satisfaction and raising to his mouth a marzipan mouse that he'd palmed in his inspection.

In a sudden wave of panic, Joe realized that he had become the marzipan mouse. He felt himself being swung upward by a tail then he was dangling, swaying above a huge red cavity, hot as a furnace but reeking of garlic and rancid meat. The hand pinching at his tail lowered, and Joe tried to scrabble away from the gaping maw, but he was trapped in an almond-paste body and he could now feel the cook's hot breath rising up like sulfurous fumes from a volcano.

He jerked himself awake. If he had been eaten, would he now be dead? Joe had no wish to put it to the test. Dying had always seemed a remote prospect, but just then, it had been imminent. He would have been mashed, crunched and macerated, before descending into a foul crucible of gastric juices. Joe's stomach writhed and twisted. He felt as though knitting needles were using his guts for yarn. He leaped out of bed and raced for the sink, reaching it only just in time.

Afterward, he brushed his teeth. As he returned to bed, he drew his arm across his forehead, and it was slick with sweat. He glanced at his clock — ten-thirty.

When he opened his eyes again, his stomach heaved and plummeted because he was back at the doorway to the great dining hall. He checked it out more closely. It seemed identical. The same rich reds, the same abundance of food and furnishings, glass, gilt and silverware, identical tapestries, except they weren't quite identical. This time the bucolic rural scenes had been skewed and leering beasts now slavered at the sight of the milkmaid and her goat. Hounds were now ripping the hare to shreds. The shepherd was aged and withered. The dancers were now skeletons. He glanced up to check the Olympians above. Now Actaeon was being flayed by his hounds, and Demeter had her hands up to her face, her mouth a dark cavern as she watched Hades carrying Persephone down to his underworld as their siblings and cousins watched, impassive onlookers.

This time, he reached forward and plucked an apricot from the closest fruit-stand. The faint racket of approaching feet sounded the same as before, but this time, when the door opened, the men behind it stopped short and stared at Joe. He stood, immobile, juice trickling down his chin. Before he could run, two men came forward. One plucked the apricot from his petrified fingers, the other pinioned his arms. Then they man-handled him back through the doors. Joe remembered the poor boy whose ear had nearly been twisted off, and his own ear began to tingle in sympathy.

The men stopped before the quivering belly of the huge chef. This time, his features were inverted in mirth, his rheumy eyes framed by heavy blond eyelashes, his moustache waxed into a curved bow, his mouth a scimitar of delight below, framed by dimples and laughter lines.

"You mischievous manikin, what imp has set you on to sample our wares? Are the apricots ripe?"

Joe glanced around the circle of men watching their exchange, expectant and amused at the sport to be had. He nodded. The apricots were ripe.

"Excellent! Are you one of his lordship's guests come early to the table? Are you faint with hunger? Come to the kitchen. There's plenty to sate you there."

Joe was hustled down to the kitchen where he was forcibly seated in the middle of a bench at a long table, and, surrounded by the serving men and sous-chefs, was obliged to taste sauces and savories, sweetmeats and specialties, his every nod or grimace recorded and noted by the company. Although all were welcoming and friendly, he felt uncomfortable, reminding Joe of a visit to his mother's aunt after lunch and when they were obliged to eat a complete high tea with Mum looking daggers whenever anyone tried to avoid another bite.

Then he was rushed back upstairs, once again prevented from speaking by the hurry and bustle of the men themselves.

There seemed to be no women in the place at all, which struck him as odd. Then he was propelled so fast along the corridors and up the stairways of the house that he lost all sense of direction. Someone opened a door and popped him into a room. A panicked manservant nervously paced the parquet floor. Joe's gray pajama bottoms and T-shirt were swept off him, and he was prodded and prinked into hose, a cambric shirt, a padded jerkin heavily embroidered with gold thread and seed pearls, matching sleeves and three-quarter length drawers and delicate leather shoes that reminded Joe of the Clark's sandals his mother used to make him wear as a small boy, with a strap across his foot and a clanking buckle. The valet took a comb and wrenched it through Joe's thicket of dark hair, yanking and hauling at the knots.

At last, he was chivvied back down the stairs, down corridors, round corners until he found himself at the head of a massive staircase of white marble, gray-veined and chill as the whisper of angels.

There was no time to listen to whispered warnings that bombarded him as he stood there, numerous and dry as leaves falling from autumn trees. He shook his head to dispel the noise and ran lightly down the shallow, commanding steps that curved around into a vaulted hallway. Flambeaux sat in angled sconces, leading the eye down a parquet gallery and to the dining hall at its end. There was only one direction to follow, and Joe took it.

This time when he stopped at the doorway of the great room, it was because the place was heaving with guests. Every one of the hundred or so seats was full, and the guests were deep in their cups and at their platters. And what guests, for everyone was only half human. He saw hydra-headed women and centaurs, sphinxes, lupine figures with tawny eyes and paws, snake-haired gorgons, men with pigs' snouts and trotters, a minotaur whose weighty neck and head threatened to send him toppling backward when he poured the contents of a goblet down his throat, a fellow as shaggy as a bear with eyes quite as small and mean, and, intermittently, sheep-like creatures, their fleeces whiter than winter ice, their little hooves nervously tittuping against their plates and glasses as they registered the hungry stares of their fellow diners, who seemed ready enough to bare their fangs and rend their ovine neighbors. All of them were grabbing at the array of foods before them, cramming it into their mouths, slobbering and belching and rising up to haul before them another loaded trencher of the glorious delicacies.

A soft voice insinuated itself into Joe's horrified consciousness.

"Quite grotesque, don't you think? But so very entertaining."

Joe twisted around to see who was speaking to him. He looked up, only a short distance, and into the eyes of the man he knew as Dr. Dolon.

Chapter Fifteen

Eidolon

Instead of the doctor's coat, chinos and a pale-blue shirt, Dolon now wore clothes even more dazzling than Joe's. His starched ruff was four or five inches deep. His white satin doublet was trellised with black velvet and silver silk. He wore white silk hose and his puffed drawers were in the same material as his doublet, but in a slightly different pattern. On his fingers gleamed rings rich with gems and in his left ear dangled a huge and creamy pearl. His dark hair was swept back into artfully unruly curls, and this time, he sported a tailored moustache and beard tapering to a fine point.

"Now that we finally meet, perhaps we should introduce ourselves properly," suggested the doctor. "I am Eidolon."

"Pleased to meet you," said Joe, holding out a hand for Eidolon to shake. It was ignored. "Is this your home?"

"I suppose so. For the moment, until I tire of it."

Around them, the sounds of the feast continued — the buzz of conversation, the gulping and chewing and delighted murmurings, the clink and chink of glass, knives and silver. Never had Joe seen quite such single-minded and sustained consumption. It entirely dispelled any appetite he might have had, but Eidolon led him to the far end of the table where two seats awaited them. At once, menservants were at their elbows, pouring wine, selecting succulent morsels from five or six of the dishes closest to them. Joe half expected someone to come and pop the food into his mouth.

"So, young man, what is your name?"

"I'm just a friend of Silas's. Your patient."

"Yes, that unfortunate boy. You haven't touched your glass. Surely you'd like to sample the wine? It's an excellent Burgundy."

"Surely you should be at the hospital?"

"But I am, just as you are in your bed. At least, I assume you are in your bed." Eidolon sat back in his chair, fingering a grape in one hand and the stem of his glass in the other. Joe remembered everything his mother had told him about stranger danger, everything his father had said about never giving anyone too much information — parental hang-ups he'd taken for granted and at times considered a touch paranoid, but not now.

"Probably." He tried another question. "Why were you nicking things at that club?"

"To see if I could get away with it. Why were you there?"

"Because Silas wanted to go. What were you doing at the villa?"

"I'm not sure. It was just the place I was taken. You and your friends…"

The hubbub of the feast around them made it hard to concentrate, but Joe knew he had to remain on guard. There was something about that soft, penetrating voice, the sweep of the eyebrows and the gleam of the hazel eyes that generated fear rather than confidence. What Joe could not work out was why he had been invisible the first time he had entered this scene, but now he was only too visible and vulnerable. He looked away from Eidolon and around the room again. The edges of the floor and the ceiling seemed to be fraying and warping, as if he were seeing the place through a distorting lens. Perhaps, if he chose, he could wrench himself out of here, much as he had escaped from the chef's ravenous appetite for sugared mice.

"You're a very interesting individual." Eidolon continued his close observation of Joe, then took a sip of wine. "You're the first person to cross into my world. Normally, people are quite oblivious to me. But we've met each other three times now, and I don't suppose that is an accident. How do we keep getting tangled up?" He replaced his goblet on the tablecloth daintily.

"Chance."

"I don't think so." He finally popped the grape he had been fiddling with into his mouth. "Some force is arranging for this to happen."

"Is this your dream or mine?" asked Joe.

"Don't you know?"

This just irritated Joe. Eidolon reminded him of the more sarcastic teachers at school, the ones who loved to condescend to their students and used any opportunity to massage their own egos with smart remarks. He tried to remember how he'd escaped from Perkin. He wasn't quite sure how he'd done it, but he'd had to somehow burst out of the boundaries of the mouse body and back into his own. It had hurt. Now he wasn't present in any other body, and it would probably hurt even more, but that seemed preferable to exchanging inanities with this Eidolon person, who interrupted his thoughts as if Joe had spoken aloud.

"It's no good. You'll have to meet a challenge to escape this place now."

That sounded ominous — ominous and unpleasant. "What sort of a challenge?"

Eidolon smiled then steepled his fingers, tapping his pursed lips. He tilted his head first to one side then to the other as he pondered how best to trap Joe.

"I don't see that I have to present you with any challenge for the time being. I don't believe you can leave here until you've met the challenge, so if I delay setting it, you can't go anywhere, which suits me very well."

"Why?"

"I want the stuff Silas took. I want it all back. He ruined a little project of mine I'd been nursing along. A touch inconvenient. I'm sure you understand."

"Why don't you ask me to get the drugs back? That could

be my challenge. If I fail, I have to return here whenever you want."

Eidolon considered Joe's proposal then shook his head. "No, that won't do. It's a neat enough idea, but I can retrieve my goods without your participation, which means I can dispose of you whenever I please. Because" — and here Eidolon bared his teeth, which were neat and square and startlingly white for some sixteenth century courtier — "I am going to dispose of you. What with my misplaced goods and my tiresome arrest the other night, you've wasted quite a bit of my time. I can't allow that to continue."

The valet appeared at Joe's elbow, and Eidolon nodded.

The servant led Joe back to the room where he had been dressed, helped him unlace himself out of the elaborate clothing he wore then bowed and locked him in.

Questions plagued Joe. He had never before slept in a dream. If he had a dream within a dream, would it come true? If he dreamed about being home, could he get himself home? Could he call in on Karabashi and see if the Turk had discovered any useful information? Could he get a message to Nell? Had Smokey woken up? Was Eidolon really a doctor at the hospital?

He reflected on the conversation with his manicured host — or jailer. He hoped that he'd concealed his name. It seemed atavistic, but vital, to withhold his identity from the stranger. Anyway, what sort of a name was Eidolon?

At least he'd managed not to eat or drink anything, which surprised Joe, because he was in a semi-perpetual state of starvation. But this evening, neither thirst nor hunger assailed him. Perhaps that was just another aspect of being in a dream, except that he recalled that in Sardinia he had eaten quite happily. The inconsistencies were beginning to trouble him, especially since both Nell and Karabashi thought that identifying consistencies was so important.

He paced. When the valet had left, Joe had found his own pajamas, whipped off the huge white nightshirt the valet had placed over his head and put his own things on. He gazed out of the window but could make out very little of his surroundings. He had been left with a candle fizzling in its stand. He didn't like the look of the heavy wooden bed with its richly embroidered hangings. It looked dusty and uncomfortable. Although it was tall and imposing, he wasn't convinced that he'd actually fit in it, but there was no alternative. He had to lie diagonally because, although it was as wide as a standard double bed, it was nowhere near as long. The sheets were clean but clammy. He remembered reading somewhere that in the sixteenth century, most people shared their beds and their fleas and lice, so supposedly, he was privileged, but he would almost have welcomed being bitten if it meant he had company.

The only course open to him was to dream his way out of this. But Eidolon had made him nervous. If he dreamed, the man might follow and find out who he was, who his family was, where he came from. Then Joe remembered that Eidolon was theoretically Smokey's medic, and since Smokey was hardly the soul of discretion, it was only a matter of time before Eidolon tracked him down.

First he would try going back home. He wasn't sure what he would do if that didn't work, but he would think of something.

So Joe sank back into sleep. He found himself on the stairs at home, halfway between his own attic floor and the second floor where his parents, Ben and Liesel all had their rooms. He went upstairs first. He opened his door and heard his own breathing. He looked up. Light was shining in through the Velux window, the reflected glow of streetlamps. As his eyes adjusted, he saw himself, the breath rising and falling as he dreamed on, his eyelids restless and twitching. He was lying on his back. Normally, he never lay on his back. It disquieted him to be watching himself this way, so he went downstairs two steps at a time. He paused outside his mother's door, standing for perhaps five or six seconds before reaching out to turn the handle. But his hand flowed through the doorknob. He reached for the painted panel and found that his hand disappeared into it. He drew it back, then tested it again. He tried knocking on the door, but his knuckles passed silently through the wood. He bit his lip, because if he didn't, he would start whimpering.

Then he stepped forward and walked through the door.

The solidity of the wood gave way. It was like getting into a swimming pool, shifting from one element to another. Then he was on the other side, in Mum and Dad's room. He turned and looked at the door. He stepped back so that he was in it. He remembered going through the wall during the fish dream. Tucker had seen him, which meant that perhaps Mum would be able to see him, even if he could pass through walls. He went to her bed. He glanced at the digital clock on her bedside table. Two-fifty-one a.m. She was not going to be happy...if he managed to wake her.

She was curled up on her side, her head on one pillow, her arms wrapped tightly around another. He prodded her shoulder. No response. She swayed a little but did not stir.

Then he grasped her shoulder and gave it a shake. Nothing. Then he bent down and whispered in her ear.

"Mum, it's me, Joe. Please go upstairs and wake me up. Please go upstairs right now and wake me up. Please, Mum, it's really urgent."

But she did not move. He sat beside her. He wasn't sure what to do next. He supposed he could try Ben and Liesel, but he was certain that if he couldn't wake Mum, they'd be impervious too. Still, he should try.

He went into Ben's room first. He'd fallen asleep with the light on. The room was really tidy, with work laid out for the next day and a lever arch lying open on his desk, his steady, even handwriting crisscrossing the page, complete with bullet points, numbered items and highlighting for key dates, names and events in three different fluorescent colors. He lay in bed, one foot escaping from the duvet, his book open on his chest.

Joe went over and eased the book from under his hand. At last, he had some effect on a real object. He picked up the bookmark lying on the floor, marked Ben's page and positioned the book on top of the lever arch. It gave him an idea. He found Ben's notepad and a pen and scrawled a message. Go and wake up Joe right away. Please. Then he tried waking Ben, but like their mother, he was immune to Joe's proddings and pokings.

And when Joe walked past the desk, he noticed that his message had faded into invisibility.

There seemed little point in trying to rouse Liesel, but Joe went to her room anyway. She was spread-eagled on her stomach, her loose plait of hair snaking down her back, one arm hanging over her bear. For the first time that Joe could remember, he felt a wave of tenderness for her. He leaned over to stroke her head. She muttered and turned her head away before settling down into a deeper, calmer sleep. There was nothing Joe could do here. He walked back onto the landing.

It seemed all too likely that Eidolon was spying on him and laughing, perhaps maniacally like a hammy villain in a horror movie, but Joe decided it was time for Plan B. He hadn't yet established what Plan B was, but that would come, he thought, as soon as he began another dream.

He sat back on the stairs where he had entered the house, rested his head against the wall and closed his eyes. When he woke, he was curled up in the hideous four-poster, the bedclothes tangled about his body. He lay there for some minutes, then shook out the sheets and blankets and wriggled about until he was comfortable again. As he closed his eyes, he decided it was time to try Karabashi.

He found himself in a marble hall, spotted by rosettes of sunlight shafting down from the great vaulted dome overhead. All around he could see curved Moorish arches receding into the distance, their pillars striped in gray and red marble.

Beneath the dome spouted a small fountain, sending delicate ripples into a marbled pool. A wiry man with an abundant moustache — a tellak, or bath attendant — signaled to Joe to follow him.

They walked down one of the arched corridors into another domed area. Here, the man gestured to Joe to remove his clothes. Then the tellak wound him in a towel and placed before him some wooden clogs. Joe put them on, and they rattled down another row of arches until they came to a chamber wreathed in steam. In the center was a huge octagonal slab where several men in their towels lay, their clogs in neat pairs at the foot of the steps leading up to the slab. The attendant indicated that Joe too should remove his clogs and lie face down on the slab. Joe complied and lay prone, waited for whatever was meant to happen next. Every pore was absorbing heat, and he felt his limbs loosening and relaxing, his pores opening, his mind emptying. He lost track of time and his bones all seemed to be dissolving, leaving nothing but a puddle of jellied skin on the slab, but the attendant came and led him to another room where men were being pummeled and kneaded like so many loaves of bread being prepared for the oven. The tellak showed Joe to a bench then clicked his fingers. Another small but formidably muscled man appeared. He poured oil on his hands and began gouging his thumbs along Joe's spine, in and around shoulder joints, lifting his arms and twisting them around, slapping and pounding at Joe's flesh, molding and squeezing his muscles. He was bent and stretched into different positions. At first he tried to resist, but then he realized that this caused more pain and diminished the pleasure of being released into a normal position once the hold was complete.

Next he stood while an attendant doused him with water and, with long sweeps of the arm, scraped at his skin with a coarse glove. Joe felt as though he was a horse being groomed. Afterward, his skin tingled, and he felt cleaner than he'd ever been in his life. He was allowed one final dousing before being taken to a great pool into which he climbed and sat, his body weightless and limber. He leaned back, propping his head on the edge of the bath, gazing upward at the shafts of sunlight shooting down toward the water. Then the attendant ordered him out, toweled him dry and handed him his clothes. Instead of his own pajamas and singlet, he was given a starched kaftan in heavy white cotton with dozens of white silk embroidered buttons. When he had slipped this on and some baggy white under trousers, he followed the servant to a cool room where there were cushions and small boys operating huge fans. Joe curled up cross-legged, his back against a wall opposite the door. He waited, loose-limbed and relieved to be visible and tangible again.

Karabashi came and stretched out beside Joe. His long fingers were meshed and resting on his stomach. He had the air of a cat that has hunted successfully, slept soundly and stretched thoroughly.

"So, you have found me again."

Joe nodded. Karabashi smiled and continued. "I have read now of one man who was able to travel through the land of his dreams. This he documented, but whether it is true is impossible to say, for the book claims to be history, but it has several inaccuracies that cast doubt on its reliability."

"Can you tell me more?"

"I will tell you as much as I am able, but before I do, I must warn you that this individual did not come to a happy end. He was ambitious, he was foolish and he was eventually arrested, tried and executed for treason."

"Where did he travel to?"

"He claimed he traveled into the past. He claimed he traveled to distant and savage lands, far to the north, far to the west. He noticed certain things — that in some dreams he was visible and in other dreams he was not. In some dreams, he was accompanied by his friends, in other dreams he was alone. He could repeat his dreams and alter them. At times, he could dream what he wished. At other times, he was at the mercy of the dream. He wrote this book in prison, as he was awaiting execution. In it, he said that his physical death would not matter for he would have departed his body by the time they came to kill him. And this was true, for he was found dead the morning of his execution, but still they took his body, beheaded it and threw the remains in separate sacks into separate rivers, for the sultan wished to extinguish the evil that was breeding in this man."

"What was his name?" asked Joe, but he thought he knew already.

"He had a Greek name." Karabashi paused. "Eidolon."

Chapter Sixteen

Know Your Enemy

There had been a certain grim inevitability to Karabashi's response, Joe thought. Now he needed more information.

"What evil was breeding in him?"

"Eidolon had acquired great power. He had become Grand Vizier to the sultan, and he used this position of command purely for personal gain. He took revenge on those he felt had obstructed him. He orchestrated the downfall of anyone he believed was his enemy. He sated his own unpleasant appetites in a hundred different ways, and he had many unpleasant appetites. He enjoyed watching the suffering of others in both body and mind. He wrote of all this, of all the means he had at his disposal in his own world and in that of his dreams to torture anyone he considered a threat and many that he did not consider any threat at all, but were too insignificant for notice. He wrote of all this with pride. You may read it, if you wish to accompany me to the library in the palace."

Joe agreed, and they went into the streets of Stamboul, climbing until they arrived at an unobtrusive door in a great white wall. Karabashi unlocked it and held it open for Joe.

They went through walled courtyards and along corridors, up some stairs and around corners. Snatches of conversations and songs and wrangles accompanied their passage through the back ways of the great palace. Joe heard the cries of children and the calling of nursemaids, the slap of wet cloth as they passed the steaming laundry, hammering, the sizzle of cooking, gusts of laughter and the gurgle of fountains mingled with women's giggles. As they neared the library, the sounds died away, apart from the ever-present murmur of water.

The library was a huge, shelved cavern, protected from external light, cool and dim. On the shelves were ancient books bound in tooled leather, some tiny enough to fit into the palm of the hand, others huge tomes that would need more than one man to carry them. There were also scrolls and maps and paintings and all the tools for book-binding — the knives and scissors, needles, thread and stamps, paints, ink, brushes, pens and all the paraphernalia associated with making books. The place smelled of glue and spirit, leather and fresh paper, a heady mix as though all the knowledge contained on the pages of the books created there could be inhaled simply by standing in the center of the room.

A skeletal man who towered over Karabashi approached them. He bowed and indicated that Karabashi should follow him. Joe and the scholar were seated at a table. Then a lamp on a stand was brought over. Only after it had been lit was the book they had come to examine brought to them.

It was very ordinary compared with the rest of the library's tomes, scrolls and manuscripts. No exquisite miniatures colored with lapis lazuli and gold graced its pages. It was a simply bound volume about the size of a paperback.

Joe picked it up and went immediately to the back of the book and started reading the text. It was several minutes before he looked up at Karabashi and said, "How is it that I can read this? I can't read Arabic script. But in my dreams, I can speak Turkish and read this script."

"Do these words have meaning for you?"

"They do."

Karabashi went to find another book, sat back down again and left Joe to his perusal of Eidolon's memoirs. The man's dreams had started as Joe's had, when he was fourteen, at first random and unmanageable. Eidolon simply stated that he had gained mastery of his dreams, frustratingly failing to describe this process for his readers. His dreams had been full of pneumatic dancing girls and wine drinking before he had turned his attention to the acquisition of money and power. Eidolon was chillingly self-seeking, happily causing the deaths of first his parents and siblings, then his cousins and uncles, allowing him to inherit their possessions, before moving on to the seizure of goods and whole estates belonging to friends and acquaintances. He wrote of betrayals and double-dealing with delight, displaying an insouciant relish in the downfall of his victims.

By and by his tastes darkened and his interests kinked.

He described in loving detail how the people at his mercy writhed and moaned in torment. He devised ever more elaborate and cruel tortures for them, seeming to forget that he was a man inflicting suffering on his fellow men. For Joe, the book was almost impossible to read, and Karabashi turned in concern when he winced and pushed the text away. The fear that he too might be afflicted with the desire to bring pain to other people sickened Joe.

"We read so that we learn. What is it you need to learn from this memoir?"

"How to defeat him. How to avoid becoming like him."

Karabashi looked at Joe warily. "But he is dead. It is documented."

"He is not dead. I have met him. He is keeping me prisoner."

"How can you be here?" The scholar fidgeted uneasily with the clasp of the manuscript he had been reading.

"In much the same way as I have been here before. In my dreams. But I believe I am also a prisoner in his dream." Joe's gaze did not waver. "I need your help. I have to defeat this man. He is alive. I don't know how, perhaps by inhabiting someone else's body, but however it comes about, he is still alive."

"You are not the same as he is?" Karabashi half stated, half asked of Joe.

"I am not. I don't want to do any of these things that he does. He's vile and revolting. He's wicked. He deliberately dreamed that his family was killed, so that they really died. I'd never do that. Never."

"Does that mean you could not dream that he is killed?"

"I don't think I could. I think I'd have to try to kill him myself, without dreaming it, otherwise what proof would I have that it was true?"

"But if it takes place in a dream, then it will still be a dream. You must discover how his spirit survived his execution." Karabashi stroked his beard and thought. Then he took Eidolon's book out of his hands and examined it carefully. He returned it to Joe and said, "Continue reading, if you can bear to. I know when the book was written, and there will be traces of this creature in other histories of the time. Let me find these out and perhaps we will discover enough to help you."

Karabashi rose. With a swirl of his robes, he went to the bony librarian and was directed to a corner of the library. Joe returned to Eidolon's boastful, repellent account of his loathsome life. The accounts of dreams dwindled but not the accounts of horrific acts. Then Joe stopped and reread a section. He flicked back through several pages, read them again and began to think.

Any challenge issued by Eidolon would undoubtedly feature the subject's humiliation. The challenge would be organized in one of three ways — Eidolon would demand the fulfillment of an impossible task, perhaps clearing the Augean stables or sending a camel through a needle's eye. Except that Joe knew that a needle was another name given to one of the horseshoe-shaped gates which marked the entry into a walled city in the Middle East. Eidolon set riddles, and riddles could be solved.

Alternatively, Eidolon might require Joe to go into unequal combat, to fight a lion equipped only with a net and a short sword or perhaps duel with a fully-trained swordsman. But it occurred to Joe that if he could read Arabic script in this dream, he might be able to fight, even if he were in Eidolon's dream.

Finally, he might have to seek out some unattainable item—a phoenix or its egg, a dragon's eye or its hoard, the feathers of a winged horse or the horn of a minotaur. But Joe thought that kind of challenge unlikely as Eidolon would have to send him out of captivity to find whatever item he wanted.

From Eidolon's memoirs, his favored option seemed to be grossly unequal combat. After all, most of his victims were not warrior material, Joe included. But perhaps, if Eidolon nominated a champion, he too might name someone else to fight on his behalf. Whatever challenge Eidolon picked, however, he was likely to cheat to win it.

Karabashi approached Joe. "I have discovered more about this man. On the night before his execution, he had a visitor. The guards saw the visitor depart. They saw the prisoner before his final night's sleep. He protested that he was not what he seemed. His hysteria was dismissed as the ravings of a condemned man. When the guard changed, they did not check the prisoner. But by the morning, he was dead."

"So Eidolon used the visitor. He switched bodies. Is there any record of the visitor's identity?"

"There is. The jailer noted the arrival of the executioner. He always visited his victims the night before their death. This particular executioner was extremely effective. His career was long and his pension substantial. He was succeeded by his son, who was equally competent."

"Eidolon would have enjoyed being an executioner. But it can't have held his interest for long, not if he'd been the second most important person in the kingdom." Joe looked at Karabashi. "I wonder if I could switch identities?"

The scholar's gaze and tone were dry. "I do not propose offering my identity."

Joe grinned. "Of course not."

But it gave him enough of an idea to be going on with. He wasn't sure that he wished to be exiled from his own body, but if that was what it took to fool Eidolon, he was prepared to do it. The next thing he wanted to discover was exactly whose body Eidolon was currently using.

Although Joe thought about taking Eidolon's memoirs with him, he doubted he would be able to read the text outside his dream, rendering the book useless. Instead, he spent as long as he could be reading and memorizing Eidolon's traits and twisted plans. But as evening approached, even Karabashi could not keep the librarians from pointedly suggesting that his young friend had spent enough time with his book and that it might be time to leave.

Karabashi led Joe away from the library. They found a deserted courtyard and sat in the shadows as the faltering sun gleamed on the rippling water of a rectangular pool.

Joe bade farewell to the scholar. "I hope we meet again, but if we don't, thank you very much for all your help."

"I don't know that I have done so very much. I almost wish we might change places so that I might meet this enemy of yours and examine your world as you have had the opportunity to examine mine."

Joe shook his head. "I don't think you'd enjoy meeting him. But if I can find a way to show you my world, I will. Be ready, just in case."

"I will."

They shook hands, then Karabashi left with a sweep of his robes and a final wave of farewell. As Joe watched his silhouette recede into the cool of the palace corridors, fear gnawed at him, but he suppressed the urge to call the man back. It would only mean delay. Joe wanted action.

* * * *

When he woke, still in Eidolon's dream, it was still dark, but there was a change in the quality of the light, and Joe rose from his bed. Shivering, he went to the window. It opened into the room, but then he had to unbolt the shutter and push it out. There had been snow overnight, and the gray half-light of those winter minutes before sunrise allowed Joe to see where he was.

His window was three stories up in a red-brick house with gables and wings. He was in the southernmost of three wings, each with great mullioned windows. To the east lay rolling acres of field, to the south, woodland, black and jagged against the pristine sheet of snow that covered the land and trees. To the north were hills, and there Joe could see still more snow clouds gathering. He could see no hamlets or villages before him. Even if he could get out of his room and the house undetected, there would be little chance of a full escape. There must be horses somewhere in the establishment, presumably in stables somewhere near the house, although not visible from Joe's window. But since Joe had never sat on a horse, he imagined that finding the stables would be a futile exercise.

Although given that he had been able to read Arabic, there was no reason to suppose he couldn't ride a horse or engage in swordplay.

Joe went to the table by his bed and saw the candle with a tinder box beside it. He spent anxious moments trying to raise a spark sufficient to light a spill, but eventually he managed it.

With the spill, he lit the candle and thoroughly explored his room. There was a massive dresser. He opened it. It had drawers and each held clothes. There were smallclothes, shirts, doublets, sleeves, ruffs, buskins, cloaks and caps in velvet and damask and taffeta, silk and woolen stockings, muslin cloths and heavily embroidered garters, handkerchiefs and kidskin gloves. There were ostrich feathers and swans down trimmings, ermines, ocelot, sable and ribbons and laces of mulberry and raspberry and crimson and navy. Everything was so carefully folded that Joe did not dare disturb the exquisite array.

He closed the drawers and the great doors before investigating the huge chest at the foot of the bed. There, he found some things he thought might be useful. Leather belts with loops for scabbards and two slender velvet cases, each over a meter long. He took out the dark green velvet case first and flicked up the catches. Inside was a simple rapier with a sweeping hilt designed to protect the sword hand. Joe held it up in the classic fencer's pose he remembered from films. He flexed his wrist, pointing the sword up, down, then drawing circles in the air with it. He moved forward a few paces then back. He lunged forward, and it was as if the sword led him, for he began to parry, feint and strike out as if he were confronting a real opponent. He stopped. He glanced around the room then once more imagined he had a real opponent before him and fought, pressing his enemy hard with a flurry of passes that should have left his arm aching, but it did not hurt at all, just as if he practiced daily.

He replaced the first sword in its case and removed the second one. It was far fancier than the first, with jewels in the hilt and in the *ricasso*, below the hilt and above the sharpened section of the steel. It also had a matching dagger. He examined both, gazing at the jewels there, the rubies and diamonds winking in the dawn light. He was surprised by the lightness of the weapons until he thought about using them in a sustained fight. It would be no good having heavy weapons that would wear out your arm muscles more quickly.

It seemed best to replace everything where he had found it. He hoped that it would not cross Eidolon's mind to arrange a duel. However competent he seemed to be with a weapon here in the privacy of his room, he was not at all sure that he would keep his nerve when faced with a challenger of true ability. The fact that he could fence at all was also a useful secret against Eidolon.

Joe measured the length and breadth of his room as he turned over and over in his mind any possible means of escaping Eidolon, overcoming and finishing him off. There had to be some simple way of eluding the man, but the solutions to his problems evaded him. Stray sounds from the house distracted Joe — the call of servants, a cockerel, a distant crash and raised voices as someone broke something and received a scolding.

The key turned in the lock and the silent valet entered, carrying a tray with a bowl of some steaming mess and a tankard. He plonked it on the bed and said, "Eat this quickly. The master wishes to see you as soon as you are dressed."

Joe sat on the bed and picked up the bowl, smelling its contents. It reminded him of one of Mum's soups.

"It's just pottage," said the valet. As Joe continued to gaze dubiously into the bowl, the man sighed. "It's what we servants have for breakfast. Vegetables, mainly from last night's table all cooked up in a broth and mashed a bit so it has a bit of substance. You'll need the strength."

He dipped his spoon into the indeterminate hot sludge. He lifted it to his lips, aware that he had not eaten the banquet the night before, nor while visiting Karabashi. He had not wanted to eat Eidolon's food the night before, but he was too hungry to stop himself now. Hoping that it wasn't drugged, Joe ate. It tasted bland, with a hint of seasoning as if someone might once have passed a stick of cinnamon over the cooking pot then thought better of it. After a few mouthfuls, he took a swig from the tankard and nearly spat it out again. "What is this?"

"Small beer. Why?"

"I don't suppose— No, you've probably never heard of tea."

"Tea? What is tea?"

"A drink that will catch on in another fifty years' time, I should think. It comes from the orient. It comes from a plant, and you brew it with boiling water then you add sugar and milk. It's delicious." Joe took another swig of his small beer. It tasted much sweeter than normal beer, but serving it at room temperature did the flavor no favors. He was about to ask for water, then thought it would probably be germy beyond belief.

The valet ignored Joe, focusing instead on the delicate

issue of what clothes this guest should wear. He opened the great clothes press and fiddled and hummed as he chose this, rejected that, hemmed and hawed over the other and finally assembled a complete ensemble.

Joe was to be dolled up in a sleek blue velvet outfit, liberally embroidered with silver thread. There was no ruff, but his shirt collar was stiff with seed pearls and his silk stockings were white. The fellow had chosen a pair of blue leather shoes with white rosettes. Joe was relieved that there was no mirror in the room. It was embarrassing enough having to wear this get-up without having to see his reflection. Nell would be smiling in derision. That was for sure.

There was no clock in the room, so Joe asked the time. The valet thought it was between seven and eight, but time here was not so precise as Joe was used to. He hoped that the dream was speeding on much faster than real life and that back home, it was still deep night.

Once he had been laced into his clothes, the valet stood back and examined Joe carefully. "You'd look better with a decent head of hair, but I suppose you'll do well enough. At least a hat can hide the worst." He had a sort of beret with a fringe at the ready that he tweaked into place.

He went to the chest at the foot of the bed, pulled out one of the sword belts and strapped it around Joe. "I don't suppose you know how to handle a sword, being more familiar with tea and so forth. But you must wear a sword now, for you're nearly a man, and gentlemen do wear swords here."

Joe shrugged. The valet took the plain sword out of its case and handed it to him. Joe made a great show of struggling to get it into position, appearing to find the thing unwieldy and almost impossible to manage. The valet raised an eyebrow.

"You'll have to manage better than that, or we'll have no fun at all this afternoon."

"What do you mean?"

"The master has set up a challenge for you against another guest, an expert swordsman from Padua, I hear. Out for blood, he is. Well, there's a line of gentlemen waiting to fight him, so I daresay we'll get some sport out of it, even if you aren't up to providing it."

Joe finally managed to get the sword to cooperate, and he was ready. The valet held the door open for him and led him back through the labyrinth of staircases, passageways and turnings until they were on the ground floor once again. They stopped before a set of double doors, which the valet threw open. The room was packed with a glittering array of gentlemen, at the center of whom—like the pupil of an eye in dense black and dazzling diamonds—stood Eidolon.

Chapter Seventeen

Escape

The pack of men turned to stare at Joe as he stood on the threshold of the room. It was paneled in oak wainscoting, with an oak floor on which the heels of the men clicked as they shifted. When they saw that he was a mere boy, they turned their backs on him and continued their conversations, Eidolon included. Joe edged through the doors just before the valet shut them.

Once he was confident that no one was watching him, Joe made his way to the windows. He oriented himself. The chamber was a mirror image of the great dining hall, with the same number of huge windows. Both looked out onto a terrace, which gave onto a parterre of low box hedges and turf. He must be on the other side of the house from the bedroom where he had spent the night, facing west or southwest. A brick wall surrounded the formal garden and beyond that was parkland with several great oaks and horse chestnuts, their silhouettes bare and black against the pewter sky.

He continued around the hall, listening to scraps of chatter about people he did not know and about foreign affairs he did not understand. The men were mostly talking about Spanish gains in northern France and how the French king would go about recovering Calais. They made ribald comments about the king's romantic entanglements, laid wagers on the sex of the child his mistress was carrying and whether the old queen would agree to send any further troops to France to help him in his wars against the

Spaniards. The men were clearly waiting for something, although Joe was not sure what. He looked for somewhere to sit. There were no chairs, but there was a great table, covered by a carpet which Joe recognized as a Turkish carpet, like those he had seen in Stamboul with Karabashi. On it stood a blue-and-white bowl, over half a meter in diameter. The sight of it made the back of his neck tingle and his breath quicken. He was sure that it was the bowl that Karabashi and his colleagues had been discussing the night he'd first met the scholar.

"Do you like it? A particularly fine piece by the great Chinese master Wu Xianyang." Eidolon had appeared at Joe's side. "A gift from a dear friend."

"It's very impressive." Joe decided against making any rude comments about Iznik potters or the fact that there was no way of knowing who had made it since the marks on Ming pottery did not normally specify the name of any craftsmen. It had taken Joe a quick search on the Internet to discover that, but perhaps Eidolon was a bit of a technophobe. But the name was the same that the Ottoman scholars had mentioned, and Joe hoped that Karabashi was safe.

"Feast your eyes while you can. We're about to go hunting."

It amazed Joe that these gentlemen in their silks and velvets were contemplating a hunt, but they began filtering out of the room. As they entered the hall, their menservants awaited them, ready to help them remove their fine doublets and put on longer, heavier coats or tunics trimmed and lined with fur. Then they helped them tug on boots and buckle on enormous swords, daggers and spurs.

Joe lingered. His valet was ready too. He slipped off Joe's fancy shoes, eased on the soft leather boots, fiddled with the spurs, removed Joe's sword then strapped on a heavier, longer scabbard and garniture. Finally, he added a hunting horn made with silver mouthpiece and rim. He followed the crowd of gentlemen who had filed down the great stairs to the carriageway. To the left of the stairs, a little way off, men were struggling to control a writhing mass of dogs, yelping and moaning in anticipation of their morning's sport. Their pelts gleamed under the winter sun, some smooth and polished as pebbles on a beach, others shaggy and brindled. There were several different breeds as far as Joe could tell — a few slack-jowled, flop-eared beasts similar to bloodhounds, several pairs of more ferocious-looking creatures with big square jaws, neat little ears like devil's horns and the build of Great Danes and perhaps eighteen or twenty greyhounds.

There were also three pairs of mastiffs with huge chests and heads, wearing spiked collars laden with jewels and iron chains for leashes.

Then there were the horses — restless, bearing gold-embossed saddles with barding and reins in scarlet or green with gold studs, their breath steaming in the cold morning air. Each horse was controlled by a groom, with another servant standing by holding spears and gauntlets. Joe lagged behind, waiting to see which horse would be his. It was a bay, looking enormous, but with less elaborate harnessing than some of the other horses around him. He went to the left side of the animal then placed his foot in the stirrup. It was a straightforward matter to hoist himself into position. He took the reins in his left hand and the horse whickered but did not move. It seemed quite natural. Then someone blew his horn, and the huntsmen mounted and most of the lighter dogs were lifted onto horses so that they would not be worn out when it came to loosing them at the prey. At last the cavalcade set off at a tidy trot toward the forest east of the house.

They rode for about half an hour, deep into the forest made up of oak, birch, beech and sycamore, mostly mature, their branches bare, some twined with ivy, others distinguishable by their bark and shape. Quite soon the scent of log-fires rising from the brick chimneys of the great house had faded and the only sound was the jingle and clink of the horses' saddlery, the soft thump of their hooves on the mulchy paths into the wood and occasional murmurs from the dogs. They were following huntsmen to the last known bed of the beast they were hunting. Joe had still not been able to discover exactly what animal that might be, but from the scraps of conversation that he managed to overhear, he had discovered that the animal was mature and cunning.

So far, the horse was behaving itself too, and Joe had worked out that a simple twitch of the reins would indicate to the animal where it should go. At first, it had seemed content to lag behind the main body of riders, but as Joe's confidence grew, he began to outpace some of the other riders and gradually he drew nearer to Eidolon, who was surrounded by five other gentlemen. One was elderly, with a white beard tidily squared off about three inches below his chin. Two others were middle-aged, their eyes creased and their faces beginning to blur about the jaw line, their beards streaked with gray.

Another man was in his prime, with dancing blue eyes, a dark beard and a mischievous, curling mouth. He was doing much of the talking, making the others laugh and smirk. The youngest member of the party was a fellow in his late teens or early twenties, with light, unamused eyes and blond hair waving from beneath his dark hat, adorned with a single white feather. His hunting coat was trimmed with white fur and his saddle was the most elaborate and luxurious of all. He rode a chestnut horse, a little larger than the other men's mounts, and he looked weary and somewhat irritated by his companions.

Eidolon largely ignored the older men, accompanying this young man most closely and pointing out to him various sights that he apparently thought might be of interest, but the fellow scarcely acknowledged his host at all. Joe found him haughty and hoped he would not attract the interest of the only other person in the group of a similar age.

By now the huntsmen had tracked down their quarry and the horn sounded, accompanied with great cries of, "Ho moy, ho moy." A relay of the bigger dogs was released and the men spurred their horses forward. Joe's horse raised its head and harrumphed before picking up speed, its gait shifting from a steady trot to a canter then into a full-fledged gallop. Joe's body took over once again from his mind, steadying itself with the stirrups and sitting lower in the saddle, swaying as the horse's legs began steadily pumping as the animal swerved and veered across the uneven forest floor.

It was so hard to keep his seat that Joe did not notice that his horse had outpaced the other riders. It came to a sudden halt almost on top of six of the fiercest dogs, all poised in a clearing around a black, hairy creature making a frenzied, squealing noise, its small eyes red, its mouth wide and saliva dripping from its livid mouth. The boar feinted first to its right then to its left, but was kept at bay by the snarling dogs.

Joe adjusted his hold on his spear. It had been positioned into a slot at his stirrup, but now he knew he would need it. The dogs would not be able to hold the creature for long, and he sensed that as the largest target, he was the most likely object of its imminent attack. He leveled the spear, working out the best angle. His horse seemed blessedly calm, and he wondered if it would stay that way while he struggled with the boar. He hoped that other hunters were not far behind. He had no idea which section of the boar's anatomy he should aim at, but he knew it needed to be low and dense, otherwise the boar would twist away from the spear and if he were to succeed in merely wounding it, it would become even more dangerous. It was making noisy panting sounds now, its feet churning up the earth beneath it as it readied itself to charge. Joe held his horse steady, then it came at them. As the boar hurtled forward, the hounds leaped and twisted out of its way and onto its back, one burying its teeth into the nape of the beast's neck, one savaging its spine, a third grasping a thick hindquarter while a fourth slid beneath its feet and whined as the fearsome tusks tore at its flesh. Joe closed his eyes as he plunged the spear into the side of the animal, and the force jarred up his whole arm, but he held steady and urged his horse forward. He did not know which was stronger, the boar or the horse, but he knew that if the horse gave way, it would lose its balance, leaving both of them vulnerable to a goring. He would not let that happen, and he grappled with the boar on the end of the spear as it wrenched and writhed under the onslaught of dogs and iron. Blood pounded in his ears, but over the harsh breath of beasts, he could hear the halloos and cries and horns of the other hunters.

The hooves of both boar and horse were scrabbling at the earth then more dogs burst out of the undergrowth. With another blast of the horn, the dogs fell back from the boar, its pelt now running with blood. With a rush of feather and two dull thuds, a pair of crossbow bolts embedded themselves in the boar. Joe held on, though he could feel his horse's strength waning. As more blood pulsed from the boar onto the leaves and earth below, its force began to ebb, and the dogs came back, worrying at it. It jerked, almost hauling Joe's arm out of its socket as it writhed and twisted to escape the hounds.

With his last remaining strength, he yanked his spear clear and watched as the boar circled, its life receding, its small eyes confused as it blundered. Its rear legs gave way and finally, it fell with a crackle of leaves and twigs, twitching for seconds that seemed to stretch into minutes before finally going limp.

The grove where he'd killed the boar filled with horsemen and huntsmen in an instant. Joe threw down his spear and caught his breath. He was shivering. He kept his left hand, which held the horse's reins, steady on the pommel of his saddle while he tried to control his shaking. He wanted to throw up. His nausea increased as he watched some of the men take their knives and begin flensing the corpse. Others started a fire, and he heard the hooves of the main body of hunters drawing near. Swallowing back the bile, he looked around and saw an opportunity to escape. There was no way he was going to cope with some sort of swordfight later today, and he certainly didn't want to spend any more time at Eidolon's mansion. Now was the time to escape. Once he was clear of Eidolon's land and people, he could sit and think about how to get out of this dream.

He guided the horse away from the clearing. The animal was tired, he could tell, and it was also so richly dressed in its bright leather that he knew it would be conspicuous. He dismounted and led it to where some of the hunt servants had tethered their animals. He lifted the reins over its head and tied it next to one of the other animals. He looked up and down the line of animals and found what he was looking for—a small, sturdy horse with a plain saddle that had eaten its fill of the hay that had been spread for its fellow creatures. He untied it and led it, the bulk of the resting horses shielding him from the gaze of the hunters, and he unsteadily climbed into the saddle, his right arm sore and aching.

He encouraged the horse into a walk then a trot. He could see the sun through the trees beginning to sink to the west. Following it would lead him back toward the mansion. It felt counterintuitive, heading into the darkness, but since the terrain was entirely unknown to him anyway, he didn't see that it made much difference.

At first, he was concentrating so hard on making his way through unfamiliar terrain that he had no time to think. It was only after he had reached a path that cut through the forest that he could relax, and it was only when he relaxed that he began to think. It was only when he began to think that various problems occurred to Joe.

His worries crept up on him stealthily. First, he wondered how long he had until Eidolon noticed his absence. Then he wondered what Eidolon would do. A mislaid guest would not look good in front of men he was trying to impress, however insignificant that guest might be. With thirty or more hunting hounds at his disposal and expert trackers who had been able to read the size and weight of their quarry from the spread of its hoof-prints in the woodland earth, Joe did not hold out much hope for his chances of permanent evasion. He had become legitimate prey.

Added to which, he had still not worked out how to break out of Eidolon's dream.

He did not want to get caught. If he could remain free, even in Eidolon's dream, it was better than being locked up in that house with no idea of what would come next. But he could almost see the men in charge of the lymers receiving their orders, and he knew that once they were on his scent, his flight would be over.

He slowed the horse and looked around him more carefully. The path was cut into a slope. To his left, to the north, was the hill down which he'd come, to his right the ground fell away, the steep slope broken by tree trunks and heavy undergrowth. This was when common sense came to his aid. There must be a valley nearby, and if there was a valley, it meant there was a stream or even a river, either of which he could use to confuse anyone if they were tracking him. The path was leading Joe down to the water.

He spurred the horse forward into a lolloping canter. It was a much rougher ride than his previous mount, but he knew that this one was fresh and that was what would count.

It did not take long for the path to level out beside a brook. Joe urged his horse into it. The animal skittered as the cold penetrated its forelocks, but he used his spurs again, and it stepped into the water and began daintily splashing as its hooves hit the gravel bed of the stream. He encouraged it to carry on walking downstream, but it was not happy. Ahead the trees thinned out, and he saw a ford with a road leading eastward up the opposite side of the valley. He could either carry on downstream or he could see where the road led. Not feeling confident of his ability to keep the horse to the water, he took the road. He let the horse have its head, and it thudded up the hill.

The trees dwindled as the road continued uphill. The horse, for all its enthusiasm, slowed as they reached the hilltop, allowing Joe to get his bearings. He had emerged from the forest, and far in the distance he thought he could see the chimneys of the house where he had been imprisoned. The forest seemed still and silent, but Joe was sure that by now, Eidolon was tracking him.

He could see fields, but the land before him was mostly grassland and forest. He could see no sign of habitation, although he looked for plumes of smoke or clearings. It didn't matter. It was time to get moving. He wasn't sure quite what he was going to do about shelter on a cold November night, but there were still several hours of daylight to be had, and he'd better make the most of them.

It was a shame that horses didn't come with a fuel gauge. Joe had no idea how far his beast had come or how far it was going to be able to take him. He decided to keep to a steady trot with an occasional canter rather than trying to ride the animal flat out, even if it did mean he'd be giving any pursuers a chance to catch up with him.

The emptiness was eerie. No birds sang, the hedgerows were still and there was scarcely a breeze beyond that caused by his passage through the air. Back home, there was always noise — traffic, voices, snatches of music, shouts, cries, airplanes, rattling, banging, motors, lawnmowers, footsteps on pavement. Here, the only sound was the pounding of the horse's hooves. Back home, sooner or later, he'd have come to a signpost or a postbox, a streetlamp — some sign of human occupation. Perhaps this world was so empty because it was part of Eidolon's dream, but all the men visiting Eidolon must have come from somewhere. They must need to go somewhere. There had to be people in this place. Of course, there might be bandits who would see an isolated traveler and do away with him, especially a richly dressed man with an expensive sword and fur trimmings.

Behind him, the sun was sinking fast, and the horse

was becoming restless, turning its head homeward as if considering making a break for freedom. It was a relief to come upon a deserted stone hut, large enough to lie down in, even if it was on the bare earth. What he was going to do now, with no food, no tinder box, nothing to give the animal, he wasn't sure, but he was sure that it was time for him and the horse to stop.

He dismounted. He had no idea how to take the saddle off, nor was he sure that he'd be able to put it back on again, but it seemed mean to leave the saddle on the animal. He looked beneath it and found a set of buckles and straps. He undid them and the horse shook itself with relief as he lifted the saddle off its back. He lifted the reins over its head and wondered how to stop the animal from wandering off in the night. Then he saw a rusted iron ring screwed into the wooden frame that served as an entrance to the hut. He fastened the reins there and was relieved to see the animal began immediately cropping the tufty grass around the hut.

It was only when he sat that he realized how stiff he was. His arm still ached, and the cold was beginning to bite at his extremities. If Eidolon found him now, Joe would hardly be able to stand up, let alone defend himself. Running away was one of the crazier choices he could have made, but perhaps it had bought him a little time to work out what to do next.

Chapter Eighteen

Titan

At first, Joe dozed. There was nothing else to do—no meal to prepare, no means of making himself a fire, no teeth to brush. He thought of Mum always in the kitchen fiddling about with food, and Ben and Liesel bickering, all the usual routines and chores and comforts, and Nell. He cleared his mind. He had plenty to tell Nell. He needed to remember the route he had taken this afternoon. He had to forget about his own thirst and hunger and work out what to do next.

The shivering soon began. He rose and paced round the hut and the horse in widening circles, even though every bone and muscle creaked. It was better to be walking and aching than sitting, aching and freezing. As he walked, images of Eidolon flashed at him—in T-shirt and jacket at the nightclub, standing on the deck by the pool, in that doctor's coat, in ruff and velvet for the banquet, in fur and velvet for the hunt. Joe tried to imagine him in the robes first of a vizier then of an executioner. It was easy to picture him with a sword raised high over some unfortunate victim's bowed head, ready to sweep down. He'd smile just as he had done in the nightclub as he lifted possessions from handbags and pockets.

Whether Eidolon had followed Joe into his dreams or Joe was intruding on Eidolon's made no difference. If Joe tried to break out of this dream, he was almost certainly exposing people to Eidolon in some way. Joe couldn't work out how the guy had tracked down Smokey and insinuated himself as a doctor in the hospital, but he had. Then there was the great porcelain basin. The guy got everywhere.

But when he was in Joe's world, he couldn't be in his own. So the thing to do was to find out Dr. Dolon's duty roster and work out when the registrar would be at work and when he would be kipping at the hospital. It was time to visit Smokey again.

Joe made his way back to the hut. The horse had lowered itself down to the ground. Joe stroked its neck and nose. Liesel had such a thing about horses, always clamoring for a pony and saying that he'd been prejudiced against the animals, but now that he'd had to depend on one, he felt a surreptitious fondness for this one as well as the bay that had resisted the boar so stoutly. The horse whickered. Joe positioned himself against its sturdy body. Curled together, the two creatures fell asleep.

* * * *

The hospital smelled simultaneously clinical and grimy. Joe waited, leaning on a wall in the empty hallway outside where Smokey was, until he was sure that no one was around. He walked onto the ward. It was dark and there was very little noise. He could only hear the hum of a heating system—what a relief to be warm again—the persistent but forlorn shriek of a telephone ringing and remaining unanswered and someone snoring and snorting in their sleep.

Smokey was in a four-bed ward, each bed curtained off. Joe eased through the curtain and stood by Smokey's bed. He was still attached to a machine monitoring his heart rate and breathing, but he was not unconscious. In fact, his eyes were open—terrified, dark pools of panic. Joe approached his bed.

"Joe, is that you?" His whisper was hoarse. "Jesus, you scared me. I thought it was that creepy doctor again."

"Can you see me?"

Smokey gave him a 'what are you on' look. "Yeah. 'Bout bloody time too. What the hell are you wearing, anyway? If you've got time to play fancy dress, you've got time to help me."

"I'm not having anything to do with your stash. Whatever you've done with it, you're going to have to sort it out on your own."

"It's too late. I've sold most of it, and the pigs have got what was left. They searched my room and they've found it, but that Dolon guy, he wants it too. And Charlie Meek is going to try to take a chunk out of me. I'm in deep shit." Smokey was more indignant than repentant. The man in the bed opposite stirred, his snore cutting short then resuming.

"Where did you get hold of it in the first place?"

"In the villa. Didn't you see it? Someone had wrapped it up and dumped it in the freezer — a kilo, wrapped up like it was coffee."

"Why did you take it?" whispered Joe.

"Because when I saw what it was, I knew I could make a killing."

"But didn't you think that someone would notice if it disappeared? And get just a little bit shirty?"

"It was put there by a crook who deserved to have it nicked. What were they going to do? Run to the cops and say their coke had vanished? It was perfect."

Smokey was so exasperating. It wasn't as if they hadn't seen enough mafia movies to know that stealing someone else's gun or drugs or women or territory would lead to major trouble. But no, Smokey figured he was invulnerable.

Joe unhooked the chart at the foot of Smokey's bed and began reading the patient's notes. The man in the bed opposite stopped snoring. It was a relief, until he started making a much more worrying noise, a sort of gurgling, choking sound.

Joe left Smokey and checked out the really sick guy. He had been propped up in his bed and was struggling for breath, clutching his throat and making desperate retching sounds. Joe began pulling at cords and pushing buttons by his bed, switching on the light and a TV before finally locating an emergency buzzer.

He returned to Smokey. "I've got to go. There'll be nurses all over this place in a minute or two."

Joe shrank into a doorway as two nurses made for the ward, muttering about poor old Mr. Garside, that chest infection still playing up. Joe found the reception desk where they'd been sitting and checked the files. There was one for Smokey, fuller than the notes at the end of his bed. And even better, typed up with Dolon's signature at the bottom. Then Joe noticed a white coat hanging on a peg. He slipped it on and snapped the poppers shut over his doublet and hose getup. Then he walked away, taking the folder with him, reading all the while. He walked down the stairs two floors and found a floor plan of the hospital. It was clear enough, but he couldn't begin to work out where he'd find Dolon. He sat down on a bank of chairs in another hallway, dumping the file beside him. He stuffed his hands into the pockets of the white coat. And there was the answer. A pager.

He picked up Smokey's folder again and checked the details more thoroughly. He found Dolon's pager number and even better, a list of his duty nights when he'd definitely be in the hospital. Joe smiled. Dolon was at work. He walked briskly down a corridor and found another vacant reception desk.

There were three phones. First, he tried simply punching in the pager number. It didn't work. But then he found an outside line and the pager responded. He put down the phone and walked away. No one stopped him. He left the hospital and headed home. He didn't know what else he could do. He didn't know what to expect.

He was walking down a quiet street when he dissolved. At first, he tingled, then he felt that he was disappearing, as though he was walking into invisibility—his nose, his fingers, his feet, then his chest and chin and arms—until he'd been absorbed into his body back home. He was in bed, lying face down under the covers, but instead of his usual singlet and pajama bottoms, he was naked. It was just after four in the morning.

Joe didn't wake up until Ben was standing over him, shaking and tugging at him. "Didn't you hear your alarm? It's been going for the past half hour. Mum's going mental."

Joe groaned and shoved his head under the pillow. His head felt heavy and his body still ached all over. In fact, it ached more than ever. He winced as he shifted around and levered himself out of his pit. His right shoulder and upper arm felt as though they'd been wrenched out of position, and he was surprised to see that his right arm was still the same length as his left. His inner thighs felt as though hot skewers had been used to fasten his legs to his body. Standing up was a slow and hideous process of unfurling himself from the bed. He stumbled to the shower. Gradually, the heat and steam of the water worked on him, unknotting the tangled tendons and muscles that had never previously been so mauled. Today would definitely be a slow-motion day, but at least there was now a possibility that he would survive it.

Getting dressed, getting to the bus stop, getting to the school gates were all agonizing. Ben noticed and badgered Joe with questions that he shrugged off, his whole being concentrating only on maintaining some movement. Irritating Ben wasn't intentional, but it did have its satisfactions.

School did not start well. He'd made it to his form room safely enough, but on the way to his first lesson, Charlie Meek, now accompanied by two different acolytes, accosted Joe in the corridor. The three boys shoved him against a wall, and Meek hissed at him, "Your mate is dead meat. I told him in the hospital and I'm telling you now. I'm the only one who deals here. You got that?" He opened up his jacket and showed Joe a knife handle. "You get in my way, you try selling on my patch, and I'll cut you."

Joe refused to lower his gaze, peering into Charlie's pink-rimmed eyes with resignation, waiting for the oaf to finish mouthing off.

"You disrespecting me? You got that, dickface?"

"I have that, dickface. Are you finished?"

Charlie gave a Rottweilery snarl but his sidekicks restrained him. They waited until he was calm, then released him. Charlie twitched so that his jacket realigned itself with his sloping shoulders. He took off his baseball cap and smoothed his hair, then popped his hat back on. Joe wished he had a rapier again so he could take a quick stab at the track-suited bottom that swaggered away from him, not that anything he did today was going to be quick.

Nell swung into view. "I have that, dickface? That's your best line for Charlie?"

"I'm not at my best today. Do you know when Smokey came out of his coma?"

"Six-thirty. We can't talk, McKechnie's coming."

* * * *

Nell did hang around for break. She'd noticed how stiff Joe was and when he explained about horse riding and boar fighting, she laughed.

"Yeah, right, you killed a boar. I would say 'in your dreams' but of course, that's exactly where it happened."

"Do you remember Smokey's doctor?"

"Vaguely. Tallish guy, dark, a bit hot but with small eyes."

"Hot? You think he's hot? He's a psychopath and he's a trained executioner!" Joe couldn't believe girls. Every male they met was instantly assessed for hotness. It was disappointing to discover that Nell was no different.

"I said a bit hot, which means not really hot at all, just the kind of guy other girls would think was hot." She clocked the rest of his comment. "You've learned quite a bit in the last few hours."

Joe nodded and winced as somebody jostled him, jolting

his right arm. Nell pulled on his left hand and led him out of the canteen and into the big hall where students could mill around, provided they weren't eating or drinking. She went to the stage and leaned against it. "So talk."

Explaining about dreams within dreams made the whole night seem even more confusing and implausible. Annoyingly, Nell niggled at details, like what might have happened to Joe's clothes and how he had not been able to wake his own family. But she fixed on the key issue like a heat-seeking missile.

"This Eidolon guy wants to get rid of you. He's tracked you down because you're the only other person in the world who can do this dream stuff. He wants to find out the source of your power. Then you'll be expendable."

Although Joe had thought this through without Nell's assistance, it was somehow worse hearing her say it out loud. The only upside he could see was that it was better to know that he was the target of some crazed sociopath than just carrying on as normal only to be ambushed and cut off without a chance to fight back. Well, better in the same way that it was better to have a greenstick fracture than a compound fracture—or to have kidneys for supper rather than liver. Better in a not good way at all.

The bell went and so did Nell, picking up her book bag and giving him a careless wave. It was fine for her to be casual. She wasn't the one with Charlie Meek and a vindictive thousand-year-old man on his trail. The germ of an idea crossed his mind. He couldn't yet see how to get it to work, but it was swilling around there, along with the rest of the sludge that passed for his brain.

Joe coasted through the rest of the day. He felt inert but this didn't seem to register with anyone apart from Crosbie, who came up to him in art and asked why he wasn't as enthusiastic as usual.

"What's this dead fish act? I've seen haddock at the supermarket looking livelier than you. Where's the grand sweep? Where's the vision? We're looking at Fauvism here, not Elizabethan miniatures. Go wild, Joe. Go wild in the country."

Perhaps he was trying to be funny, but it was just irritating, although better than being a boar's public enemy number one. Joe tried the sweep thing, but it hurt too much. He tried working with his left hand. Although it was messy, it was certainly big. It struck him as kindergarten stuff, two curving hillsides, a couple of trees and lying beneath them, a wobbly, indistinct figure. Crosbie came over again.

"That's the stuff. Much better. Once you get a bit of color in there, it'll be fantastic."

Unconvinced, Joe continued left-handed. On his way home, he decided to visit his favorite shop. It would still be open for another hour or more, plenty of time for a good browse. He got off the school bus a couple of stops early and waited for another bus to take him into town. As the bus rumbled through the streets, he looked into the windows where lights blazed and lives continued, catching glimpses of a girl at a desk, a man pumping iron, a woman feeding a toddler and countless souls curled up on sofas as the glare from their TVs flickered about their rooms, a miniature aurora borealis in every home.

Titan was tucked away a couple of streets behind the main shopping streets of the town. It was owned by a silent man who sat at the back of the shop, constantly on his computer or talking in a low voice over the phone. The place was actually run by two students who spent more time in the shop than at their lectures. Tom was chatty and enthusiastic while Zach was world-weary and always knew of something better than the comic that his customer was currently buying. "That's fine, but there's a really great Alan Moore coming our way in a couple of months that'll blow this out of the water."

Joe had first come to Titan with his dad as a kid of eight or nine, but now he dropped in every couple of weeks to check out what was new. The shop did most of its business online, but there were people who made their pilgrimage to the shop, driving four or five hours to spend a precious afternoon in the cramped, airless place, most of it in the basement where the used comics were on display.

Tom was on duty when Joe walked into the shop. They chatted briefly then Joe went to his favorite corner and sat down with a stack of fresh stuff. He didn't read for the story anymore, but spent most of his time working out the perspective, noting any tricky maneuvers between frames, checking out the range of colors and tones that were being used. He would sometimes make notes, but mostly, he'd just indulge his eye and absorb the images.

After a while, Tom came over with a slender book. "Just in from Brussels. Zach put it aside and told me to show you if you came in."

The book had a black cover with silver-white lettering and an almost invisible silhouette of a face only distinguishable because it was printed in matte format on the gloss board. It was called *Dream Master* and had no credited author or artist.

Inside, the drawings reminded Joe of a Belgian cartoonist whom his dad loved, Edgar Jacobs, whose heroes, Blake and Mortimer, were two bluff Britons of the old school. Joe had liked the pictures well enough, but he'd found the text too wordy and didn't know enough French to read them easily. But here there were scarcely any words at all, and the drawings freaked Joe out.

The first one looked familiar enough. It was a long shot of a school. Then there was a drawing of a classroom with a projector and desks of uninterested children, one of whom was asleep, his cheek pressed against the wall, great ZZZZs emerging in thought bubbles. And in the next frame, the other students had the heads of fish and were gaping and gasping for air as the teacher reached for a great stop-cock and a gush of water flowed into the room.

There were the Lamborghini, the Learjet and the carpet. There was Eidolon. Every dream that Joe had had in the past ten days was lovingly reproduced in line and color wash. The final frame showed Joe curled up against the horse beside the hut in the middle of nowhere. The rest of the book was blank.

He took it over to the cash desk. "Do you know where Zach got this?"

Tom shook his head and asked if Joe wanted to buy it.

His first impulse was to hand it back and forget about it. "How much is it?"

"Dunno. Isn't there a price on it?"

There was nothing, not even a barcode. Tom took it to Titan's owner. "Here, Al. This one's got no price tag." He passed the book to his boss.

The guy, in his thirties with a bald head and a stripe of a beard running in a slender line down the center of his chin, picked up the book and turned it over, flicked through it then came to the desk and examined Joe head to toe. It was the first time in seven years that Joe had ever heard him speak.

"It's yours, if you want it. No charge." He held out the book. "Be careful how you use it is all."

"Use it?"

"Yeah. I've heard of one other book like this. Bloke in America. He went a bit wild with it. Didn't make the grade. Had it taken away from him. Ended up a bit...well, dead, really. So be careful."

"Yeah, sure. Thanks."

"No need to thank me. I'm just the messenger." Al went back to his desk, and Joe stood there, lemon-like, the book in his hands until Tom said, "Is that all then?"

Joe nodded, packed the book away carefully into his bag and left the shop.

Chapter Nineteen

Zahid

Preoccupied with what he'd learned in Titan, Joe ambled along without really noticing where he was going or what he was doing. It wasn't until he came to a crossroads that he realized he'd taken the summer route away from Titan. The summer route took him through the backstreets of the town and down a couple of alleyways that it was better to avoid unless it was daylight. And sure enough, in the second alleyway, he heard first a grunt then a moan and the smack of a fist and a lot of heavy breathing. As he stood there, frozen, torn between running away or running toward the trouble, one of the assailants looked up. It was Kevin, one of Charlie Meek's brain-dead chums. Kevin hollered.

Afterward, Joe did not know why he'd done it, especially since he couldn't do it very fast, but when Kevin yelled, Joe yelled back, lifted his backpack up and started swinging it around his head like a mace and began running at the clump of boys standing around their victim. They all looked up with gormless, gaping mouths. Then as Joe bore down upon them, they fled.

They left behind them a huddled fetal thing that gradually unfurled and tested its limbs before standing up and checking the blood that was still bubbling from its nostrils and the side of its mouth. Joe looked up in shock.

"Zahid, what the hell are you doing here?"

Ben's boyfriend did not initially reply, still dazed from the attack. He started searching his pockets and mumbled, "Tissues?"

Joe fumbled in his backpack and found one of the mini-packets that Mrs. Knightley always tucked in their bags every morning. He handed it to Zahid, who took one out and held it against his lip and nose. When he'd staunched the blood flow, he removed the tissue and said, "Thanks."

They heard footsteps. They looked down the alley.

There was Charlie Meek, returning. Joe did not stop to think, just grabbed Zahid and yanked him back down in the direction he'd first come. Charlie followed them, and the sound of footsteps behind them multiplied.

"It's only Joe Knightley. We can handle them both. Two for the price of one. Come on." Charlie's gang was revved and followed him with yells of anticipation.

Joe and Zahid were both slow and in pain. The footsteps were getting closer. They turned down a side street and around a corner. Joe doubled over, caught his breath and looked up. "Shit! Shit, shit, shit!" It was the loading bay for the local furniture shop — a dead end.

He pulled Zahid into the darkest corner of the loading bay. They waited. The slap of footsteps faded then paused. Joe could almost see Charlie turning and looking about him, realizing that his prey was still within reach.

Joe had no alternative. He shut his eyes and slowed his breathing, and in the distance heard Zahid muttering about picking this moment for a quick kip.

They were lying in a tangle in an airless room with a tiny window set high in the wall. Beneath them was a kilim. There was a desk and a high stool. On the stool sat Karabashi.

"Is this a long stay or are you just passing through?"

"We're on our way," replied Joe. "You know Eidolon's been here? He had that big bowl you were all freaking about on a table at his home. He's in your time — or he was."

And he closed his eyes again and summoned up an image of his own room. Once he'd opened his eyes and found himself still clutching Zahid, but in his room, Joe relaxed. Zahid did not. He stood up, clearly in pain then hobbled into the shower room. Joe heard water running. Then Zahid was leaning against the frame of the door, his arms crossed, his eyes narrow with suspicion. "So what the fuck was that all about?"

"If you promise not to tell anyone, I'll explain."

"Not even Ben?" Joe grimaced as a response, so Zahid muttered a grudging, "I promise."

"I can make dreams actually happen. If I dream, it comes true. I can sort of control it, but to do it, I have to go to sleep."

"You're telling me that you dreamed us out of a beating."

Joe nodded. Zahid couldn't entirely control his eyebrows, which revealed his disbelief. "I suppose I have to believe it, since you took me with you." He paused. "Thanks for getting me the hell out of there. They were ready to mince me."

"No problem." Which was facile, but the easiest thing to say. Joe wasn't wild about having saved Ben's boyfriend from a walloping.

"Does Ben know anything about this sleep thing?"

"No. I don't think so. He knows something weird is going on, but I'd appreciate it if you keep your promise and don't mention it to him."

"Is he in? It's going to be a bit tricky explaining what I've been doing in your room if he's around."

"He shouldn't be. It's dance class for him and Liesel. Do you want to wait downstairs? You shouldn't go home on your own."

Zahid looked a little better now that he'd rinsed his face, but his lower lip was puffing up. Bruises were beginning to emerge around his left eye and cheekbone, and there was blood on his shirt.

"Would you mind calling me a taxi? My parents are expecting me. I'll just tell them that I was mugged then a good Samaritan came and put me in a cab. Don't mention anything to Ben. I'll call him later."

Once Zahid had left, Joe went through to his mother's bathroom. He ran the water and squirted in bath foam. As he lay in the tub, he remembered the book and the questions hurtled at him. Who was the Dream Master? How did the book work? Would the two swift dreams he'd engineered appear in it now? Was there a book full of Eidolon's dreams?

It did occur to Joe to wonder why Charlie Meek had gone for Zahid, but before he could wrestle with that, he heard the key in the door and the clatter of people coming in. He registered Ben's voice, calm and low, then Liesel's higher-pitched squeak. He could also hear his mother's voice. She must have picked them up. She did occasionally, especially if Liesel's teacher was ready to run a mini-display of some routine.

The phone rang. He heard his mother answer it. Then she called Ben. First Joe heard Ben's deep tones on the phone, then he heard his mother's footsteps racing lightly up the stairs to her bedroom.

She dumped stuff on her bed before noticing the open bathroom door.

"Why are you using my bathroom and not the family one?"

"Liesel always wants a shower straight after dance class. I needed a long soak, and I thought you wouldn't mind."

Mrs. Knightley muttered that he was a chancer and turned away. Then she turned back.

"Why do you need a long soak? Have you been thumped or something?"

"I'm just feeling a bit stiff. I don't know why. I must have wrenched something in PE." Joe groped for an explanation, but his mother wasn't letting go.

"Come on, Joe. They don't make you do anything that strenuous in PE. They're too scared of getting sued." She looked at him, but his body was safely concealed beneath the bubbles. "You haven't been in a fight, have you?"

"Not exactly." He decided to confide in his mother. "Don't tell Ben, but I helped out Zahid. He was getting clobbered in an alley, and I helped him get away. I was a bit excessive. I didn't hit anyone or anything. Okay? Please don't tell Ben.

He'll be really fed up if he hears about it."

"Zahid is going to tell him, even if you don't." His mother pondered. "Why would Ben be fed up? He'll be grateful."

"He'll just beat himself up about not being there and feel all guilty. Then he'll take it out on me. You know what he's like."

"I don't recognize the Ben you're describing, actually, Joe, but if you don't want me to say anything about it, I won't."

Joe heard her going back downstairs to the kitchen.

When he joined the rest of the family, they were all still talking about Zahid's news. Liesel was quick to tell Joe how he'd been set on by muggers, but then they were disturbed and some nice guy had put him in a cab and made sure he reached home safely. It was quite amusing to hear Ben, the normally woolly liberal, become the right-wing ranter, banging on about chavs with nothing better to do than wear hoodies and nick mobile phones.

"The problem is, Zahid is so skinny, and he does nothing to look after himself. He should really go to some sort of self-defense class." Ben couldn't let it go.

Mrs. Knightley had had enough of the subject. Joe could see that she was uncomfortable knowing the truth and lying by omission to her elder son.

* * * *

The subterfuge proved entirely useless the next day in any case, as Charlie Meek went around the school boasting about beating up Ben Knightley's boyfriend. He swaggered and crowed and threatened to mash any poof who came near him.

The showdown came in the main school canteen after the big rush for lunch, when seven of Ben's sixth form friends quietly formed a wall around Charlie Meek. Then Ben appeared. He was nearly a foot taller than Charlie. His sharp, symmetrical features, tidy nose, floppy dark hair and chocolate-brown eyes made most girlish, and some boyish, hearts flip.

Before him, undersized, pasty, pink-eyed Charlie looked like a malnourished ferret shorn of hair, shivering and undignified.

"I've been hearing things, Charlie," began Ben. Charlie did not answer. His eyes shifted away, focusing on the laces of Ben's tan work boots. "Things about the way you've been talking to my brother. Things about the way you've been talking about my boyfriend. The way you've been talking, Charlie, is going to get you into a lot of trouble, unless you apologize to me and to my brother and to Zahid. A nice formal apology right here. I haven't decided exactly when you're going to be apologizing, Charlie, but it will be in the next couple of days."

"You can't do anything to me here," said Charlie. His defiance was short-lived when Craig McDonald looked at him. Craig was a champion of the Schoolboy Boxing League. He was about to move into the Seniors as a light heavyweight.

Charlie tried to step back and found himself making contact with Connor Reilly, who had reached fifth dan in his judo classes. They were Ben's friends.

"I'm not saying anyone is going to do anything to you anywhere, Charlie. That would be a threat, and threats are against our Anti-Bullying Policy. You do remember the Anti- Bullying Policy, don't you Charlie? I seem to remember you have to sign a contract at the beginning of each school year." Ben held out a hand. Connor handed over a blue spiral-bound diary. Ben flicked through it.

"That's my prep diary," yelped Charlie. "I been looking for that."

"Not hard enough. It's been in the Lost Property office for over a month, so I thought I'd return it to you and remind you of the contract you signed." Ben held up the relevant page for Charlie. "See. You made your mark. Now, I'm assuming you have trouble reading, so I'll just refresh your memory."

Ben started reading the school behavior contract. "Respect others. You do that every day, I'm sure, Charlie. Behave well. You're conspicuous for your good behavior, aren't you, Charlie? Follow instructions given by a member of staff. You jump when they say to, don't you, Charlie? Come to all lessons fully equipped and prepared to learn. You equip yourself with other people's belongings, don't you, Charlie? Shall we go through the contract again, Charlie, just remind ourselves of the deal you signed?"

Then one by one, other sixth formers planted around the canteen stood and began to speak the words in chorus with Ben.

"Respect others. Behave well. Follow instructions given by a member of staff. Come to all lessons fully equipped and prepared to learn."

The call was repeated then reduced until it became a simple chant of "Respect others." All the hordes of year seven, eight and nine children who had been terrorized by Charlie for weeks and months and years rose up and took up the call, repeating over and over again, "Respect others. Respect others." They did not shout, simply spoke. Charlie looked around him and saw the faces, some spiteful, some rejoicing in his situation, others neutral and blank.

Ben and his friends stepped away from Charlie, melted back toward the doors. The space between Charlie and the other children in the canteen widened. They were all retreating from him, but they sustained their steady repetition until the bell went, and he found himself standing alone in an echoing cafeteria where a row of dinner ladies stood, their arms folded, nodding at the sentence passed on Charlie.

He was frozen in the canteen, rage surging through him, aware that his humiliation was being relayed around the school by every kid who'd been at lunch. His reign had been dissolved and his crown was rolling around in the gutter. There would be no more acolytes. His spell had been broken.

Then an adult walked through the canteen—a new one, a supply teacher, surprisingly dapper for a schoolmaster, wearing a freshly ironed shirt, pale blue, toning with his trousers and his tie, his hair a little on the long side, but swept back from his brow, his eyes pale and detached, his beard and moustache neatly trimmed.

"Where are you meant to be, Charlie?"

"How do you know my name?"

"I made it my business to find out."

"Who are you, then?"

"I'm Mr. Dolon. You must have seen me around. I've been here, teaching drama."

"Drama's for poofs."

"If you knew anything about it, I might take that remark seriously." Dolon crossed his arms and inspected Charlie with a faint air of disappointment. "You'd better get to your next class."

Charlie mooched off, but he turned and looked at the new teacher before leaving for sociology. Dolon was standing there, his arms still crossed.

"What are you waiting for, Charlie?"

Charlie shook his head and replied, "I don't know."

Dolon smiled. "You don't now, but I'm sure you'll find out soon enough. See you in detention, Charlie-boy."

* * * *

Joe heard about the canteen showdown from various people who'd seen it. He'd been in the library, wondering how to discover at lunchtime the source of his evolving dream-traveling, so he'd gathered only stray whispers and murmurings as the afternoon had worn on. He had to leave promptly to collect Liesel. As he walked out of school, he saw various villains mooching into the classroom where detentions were held. A teacher was there, walking from desk to desk. Joe didn't recognize the slim blue back, although his casual air, the thick sweep of dark hair and the stance with one hand in a pocket pinged some bell in his subconscious. It was only sitting on the bus, tuning out while Liesel prattled, that he realized who it had been.

Chapter Twenty

Ten Thousand Doors

Joe did not want to dream. He wanted to rest. He wanted his aching body to recover and he wanted to avoid Eidolon, whether in the guise of a doctor, a teacher or his own suave and polished self. In the still of the night, he woke over and over, sometimes drifting to consciousness then regressing, other times smashing into wakefulness as another place or time beckoned. Once, he found himself being sucked against his will toward another world that he knew was Eidolon's and he had to heave himself back into his own, scrabbling for purchase in a deep tunnel of some friable material. He woke just before the alarm went. There was no point in snatching any more time in bed. In fact, it was almost a relief to have made it through a night with no complications. He rose and set about the routine of the morning, although a residual stiffness from the riding hampered him from moving as smoothly and unselfconsciously as normal. Every action, from putting gel in his hair to slinging on his shirt was creaky and ungainly.

He grunted over breakfast. This time last week, he had been ill, thanks to Smokey's intervention in his dreams. Now it was Smokey who was sick. Even if he recovered, it was highly likely that he'd be permanently excluded from school, thanks to his fundraising activities over the weekend. He'd be lucky to escape a prison sentence. According to Mrs. Knightley, the police had already told Smokey's parents that he would probably be sentenced to something called an STC—a secure training center, basically, a kid's prison. Smokey hadn't been told yet. He was going to be in the hospital for another week, having tests. Then he'd be arrested and charged with possession and supply of a class-A drug. His parents were devastated. They'd known things weren't going well, but they hadn't imagined that their son would break the law — still less that he'd get caught, face trial and a custodial sentence.

Sooner or later, Joe thought, someone would demand to know where Smokey had gotten hold of the cocaine. There was more than enough of it to test. Joe guessed from what Liesel had said about his deals in the park that Smokey had been bagging it up in half-gram measures, hiding the bulk of it in his bedroom. If Eidolon wanted it back, he'd have to dream his way into the police station or wherever evidence for court cases was stored, since the gear had been seized from a shoebox in Smokey's room.

There was half a kilo left, but enough had gone to get him nailed for supplying.

On the way to the bus, Ben said, "I wonder if Charlie Meek got the message yesterday. I want to break that fucking maggot's face, but I'm not going to play his stupid games and get done for hurting him."

"What are you going to do if he carries on like yesterday morning?"

"He won't dare, because I'm going to get in there first. Wherever that little toerag is, I'll be there too, and when I'm done, it will have penetrated even his thick skull that he's not getting away with beating anyone up."

They'd reached the bus stop by this time. Joe leaned forward. "Listen, Ben. Be careful. He's got a knife, and if you get him riled, he's just the sort of cretin who'd actually use it."

Ben's face hardened. "How do you know this?"

Joe managed a save. "Just something I've heard. You know, his mates put it around. Maybe it's just to make him seem harder, but maybe it's true."

"He was threatening you the other day. He didn't pull a

knife on you, did he?"

Joe shook his head. The bus came and they were crammed in too tight amid the drizzle-dampened bodies to talk.

As they reached the school gates, Ben turned to his brother. "Don't forget that it's your turn to get Liesel. I've got a rehearsal this afternoon, and I can't do it, okay?"

"Okay. Mum only told me a hundred times over breakfast. I won't forget."

Joe ambled toward his form room. It was open. He took out a maths book to do more revision for McKechnie's latest test. People began piling in, all talking about Charlie Meek and how no one had seen him that morning. It would be quite an achievement if Ben and his friends had stopped Charlie from coming to school. He was all kinds of hoodlum, but sadly, the one thing he'd never done was to play truant, much to the distress of the kids in the forms beneath him.

There was almost a holiday air about the kids in the lower school, free for once from Charlie's malignant presence. At break, Joe was in the canteen. All sorts of little kids emerged like moles blinking in daylight, sniffing the air in case their nemesis appeared, but gradually relaxing, scoffing crisps and fruit gums without fear of a grim hand appropriating them. They chattered like starlings, swigging their Cokes and Sprites from the vending machine instead of taking surreptitious sips, laughing, recalling and replaying the moment when Charlie had been left alone as the last of his tormentors turned their backs on him.

Even if he did come back and try his old tricks, Ben had provided the lower school students with a chant against him. They would just start reciting the school code of conduct. It was easy to talk when there was no sign of Charlie.

It was only during break, after his maths test, that Joe remembered having seen the new supply teacher. The thought curdled his enjoyment of the day. It was time to track down Eidolon and find out how he was managing to juggle two stressful jobs simultaneously.

Subterfuge did not come naturally to Joe, but he had to try something. He went up to the reception desk at the main school entrance. Miss Wickens had steel-gray hair falling straight to her shoulders and a fringe, like a chain mail helmet. Her eyes were ice chips and her skin was leathery from her regular trips to Valencia. She was always showing off her latest snaps to the two secretaries who worked in the same office.

Her voice could laser through armored steel. Very few students ever went near her and those who did were always subdued in her presence.

He stood at the hatch behind which she sat like a vulture, hunched over the school switchboard. She ignored him for minutes. He gave a little cough. She continued to ignore him, but she was running three different conversations simultaneously with her colleagues and two different callers, her raucous voice bouncing around the small office without modulation in tone or volume.

She put the receiver down and looked at him. Her eyes were like knives. He could almost hear her flicking through a mental filing system that contained salient details about all one thousand, two hundred and thirty-nine students in the school.

"Joe Knightley. What you want?"

"I've got a message for a new teacher. Mr. Thomas told me to pass on a message to him, but I don't know who he means. He just said the new temporary teacher who did detention cover last night."

"What's the message then?"

"Just to go and see Mr. Thomas at lunchtime for a meeting in the English department. Is he going to teach English then?"

"None of your business." Joe could have sworn she muttered the word *scrote* at the end of her sentence, but he knew it wasn't worth pursuing.

"What is his name, Miss Wickens?"

Her desire to snub Joe grappled with the knowledge

that if she didn't tell Joe who the new teacher was, she'd be responsible for getting the message to him. That would mean stirring beyond the confines of her office. She didn't like leaving her desk, her territory. It meant she had to brush shoulders with students.

"Mr. Dolon. If he's not in the staffroom, he might have gone to the drama studio. He's covering for Mr. Phelps. Get that message to him right away."

"Yes, Miss Wickens."

Joe headed toward the drama studio. But once he'd disappeared from the Wickens' sightline, he doubled back to the science labs for his biology lesson. He wished he'd spoken to more people at school. As it was, he wasn't friendly with anyone who took drama apart from Ben, and he certainly wasn't going to talk to him about all this, so finding out more about Dolon the teacher was going to be a little tricky. But fortune smiled on him, because the biology teacher arranged everyone in groups of three to do a practical demonstrating osmosis using bananas.

Joe had to go with Raquel Waters and Sammi Jones. Normally, he'd have wilted faster than a bunch of tulips at the idea, but they were both drama types, rejoicing in any opportunity to exhibit themselves on the school stage, from the annual Pop Mime competition to the musical that Phelps used to do in the spring term. He was pretty sure they'd signed up for GCSE drama.

They completed the banana business quickly enough. They wrote up their notes and the girls started chatting about their plans for the weekend and who was the fittest boy in school. They ran through the year thirteens then moved onto the year twelves. Inevitably, Ben's name came up, but instead of bristling when Raquel said what a shame it was that he was gay, Joe laughed, making both girls gawp at him. They asked him to name the best-looking girl in the school. Joe shook his head. In his view, Nell was the best-looking girl he'd ever seen in the flesh, but that would be the wrong answer, so he named a girl in year twelve who was a local dance champion and swanned around the school as if it were her personal palace.

"Elissa? She's such a bitch. She's doing theater studies with Ben, isn't she?"

Joe nodded. Sammi continued. "They say they're all going to have real problems unless this guy who's taking over from Mr. Phelps is any good."

"I had him this morning. He's well fit—and really nice. I know it's sad about Mr. Phelps and the heart thing, but this Dolon guy is great." Raquel was clearly one of the type that Nell would describe as 'other girls'.

"How long's he going to stick around?" Sammi did all the work for Joe.

"Well, Mr. Phelps is off for the rest of term, so that's six weeks, isn't it? Then who knows? I reckon that he'll be signed off until Easter. It was a major heart attack. He's not even out of hospital yet."

This was bad news—six weeks of Eidolon hanging around school. On the other hand, it might buy enough time to think up a way to get rid of him permanently. But how much time was Eidolon going to spend in a school when he could be lounging in a Mediterranean villa or chopping people into little pieces or hunting wild animals? Whatever was coming would come soon. Besides which, Eidolon had the expertise of messing around with this dream stuff for centuries. He wouldn't chuck that advantage.

At the end of biology, Sammi and Raquel waited for Joe to walk with them to the canteen for lunch. Perhaps it was reflected glory, but it felt quite agreeable. Now that Smokey was no longer in the picture, Joe felt less defensive about talking to other people—and about doing some work. His quality of life might substantially improve…if he survived Eidolon.

Nell joined the lunch queue some minutes after Joe and his two new girlfriends. Although she was wearing a school uniform like everyone else, she looked different, as though the school uniform came from some swanky London shop.

Raquel and Sammi took the opportunity to slag her off, but when she stood looking for somewhere to sit, they waved at her to come over. She was about to go to another table when her gaze flicked back over Joe. Her raised eyebrows conveyed her astonishment at seeing Joe mix with females, but she came over anyway and sat by Joe, opposite the two other girls.

"Sammi and Raquel have been telling me all about Mr. Phelps. They've found a replacement for him already. A guy called Dolon."

"Dolon? Really." She gave him a sharp look but did not react further. The girls were ready to move onto some other subject, asking Nell if she wanted to see a horror spoof on Saturday night. Much to Joe's frustration, neither Sammi nor Raquel showed any signs of leaving him and Nell in peace. Then, blessedly, the bell rang, and like whippets after a hare, they sprang up and away.

"Dolon?" asked Nell, direct as always. "That's creepy. A supernatural sociopathic stalker. What are you going to do?" She had gathered up her books and started for the hallway to the classroom block.

"I don't know."

"You'd better think up something pretty soon, because he's definitely out to get you. Why else would he be here?"

"He's reformed and discovered a vocation for education?"

Nell grinned. "Sure, Joe, and De Beers is about to send me a free diamond necklace. Look. I'll meet you after school, and we can work something out."

"I'm collecting Liesel. We won't be able to talk once I've got her in tow."

"I'll come home with you, and we can talk about it then. It shouldn't take that long. I've got to be home before seven-thirty. Mum's got a date."

Joe agreed with relief. Nell was so matter-of-fact that she made Eidolon's appearance seem manageable. He would tell her his plan this evening, and she would make it even more effective. They'd work together and once they'd gotten rid of Joe's nemesis, he would take her on a long trip to some island paradise with no Smokey, no cocaine and no boars. They'd lie on a beach and drink stupid cocktails and maybe she'd let him kiss her.

This rapturous reverie occupied him through the rest of the afternoon, carrying him through another monotonous lesson. But he didn't fall asleep, which was a major breakthrough. The thought of Nell wearing a bikini and a warm look in her eye was more than enough to keep him awake.

Once they'd collected Liesel, they went to the bus stop.

One bus had come, but there were seven or eight stragglers, mostly year nine kids. Dusk was eroding the edges of the day, and the streetlights were beginning to fizz into artificial life. It seemed appreciably colder, perhaps because for the first time in days, the sky was cloudless. Nell looked up into the deepening blueness.

"There can't be a heaven. There's nothing else out there, just emptiness scattered with a few stars. Just darkness. At night, that's when you know there's nothing more. When we're turned away from the sun, we can't keep up the illusion that there is something more," Nell mused.

"That's a bit deep," said Liesel.

Joe grimaced. Speculation of this sort made Liesel uncomfortable. She preferred dealing with concrete realities like how to do a *pas de chat* and Sylvie Guillem's latest hair color. Joe suppressed the urge to snap at her. She was only a kid.

"How long till the next bus comes?" A prosaic question, but Joe was chilled and the thought of Dolon on the prowl made him jumpy.

"Ten minutes." Nell was wearing a thin coat and no gloves. She must be even colder than he was.

"We could walk to the next bus stop. There's time."

Despite Liesel's protests, they started off, Nell and Joe taking long strides, Liesel skipping to keep up with them, their bags banging against their backs.

Even though they were warming up, Joe regretted the impulse almost immediately. The next bus stop was down a street lined on one side by hedges and on the other by the ten-foot wall of a bakery, which channeled even the slightest breeze into a force ten gale. Local people avoided walking there if they could because thumping gusts of wind came from nowhere to buffet you as you walked or stood.

They reached the empty bus shelter and sat there miserably, gazing at the pavement. The bus would come any minute. It was too cold to talk much.

An asthmatic rumble from the road made Joe turn sharply. It was just a diesel lorry rattling past. As he looked back, he noticed that there were now five pairs of trainers grouped around the bus shelter. He raised his eyes. Five boys were wearing the shoes — and navy tracksuits and baseball caps and hoodies. Before he could react, one of the boys had yanked Liesel to her feet and was holding her by the ponytail, long and honey-brown, exposing her narrow neck. Joe thought it was a guy called Steve — *Steve Foster? Forrest?*

The boy standing behind Steve asked, "You want your sister?"

Joe might have known. Charlie Meek, but not in meek mode at all. Slowly, carefully, Charlie pulled a hunting knife out of his sleeve. Liesel whimpered. Nell was standing too, eyes narrowed into enraged slits, mouth tight, taut as a diver on the high board.

"Leave us alone, Charlie. Go home and leave us alone." Joe strove to keep his voice level.

"I don't think so. I want a piece of the Knightleys. Now which of you is going to give me a piece?" He held the knife against Liesel's neck. "Maybe a nick of the little ballerina's ear — or one of your fingers."

"Charlie, are you crackers? You can't expect Joe here to hold out his hand and let you cut a finger off." Nell could not conceal her contempt for their assailant. Charlie closed in on Liesel, and Joe saw that his eyes were dilated and his mind closed to reason. His four goons were also out of it. They wanted to do something nasty, and the opportunity had presented itself to them as unwittingly as a Christmas turkey allows itself to be slaughtered.

"Keep out of it, boffin girl. Go home and do your studying. Maybe you can learn how to be a surgeon and stitch up your friends here."

Nell and Joe exchanged glances. "Go, Nell. Go on." Their only chance was if Nell could get away and find help. Joe stood up. "Please, Nell, just keep out of this."

She bent down to pick up her bag. She twisted the handle around her hand then grasped it firmly. She straightened. Then she whirled and swung out, knocking two of Charlie's friends into each other. Their heads cracked together, but Joe did not wait. He hurtled at the guy nearest to him and nutted him, knowing that his right arm was still too weak to cause any damage. The guy holding Liesel loosened his grip.

Liesel reclaimed her hair and began hooting and screeching louder than the school fire alarm system. Nell was still swinging her book bag around her head like a warrior running amok. Joe got behind the boy who was now wrestling with Liesel and reached for his face, poking at eyes, ears, scrunching at his hair. He got one, then two fingers in the boy's nostrils and yanked. The boy let go of Liesel and yowled at the sudden and intense pain. The fifth boy took in the carnage and scarpered. Charlie, bemused, was still brandishing his knife as Nell yelled at him, "You want a piece of the Knightleys? How about a piece of me, Charlie? How about it, you cretin? Come and get me, Charlie."

Joe saw the two boys she had first felled staggering to their feet, one holding his mouth, the other his head, bleeding at the temple. He glimpsed Charlie's face, distorted into a demonic grimace.

"Nell, no. He's out of his head, stop taunting him." By the time Joe had finished his sentence, Charlie had lunged at Nell, and it was too late. Joe grabbed for his arm and deflected the second stab, but the first blow had driven deep and blood was welling at her neck. She had an utterly astounded expression on her face. Joe hauled at Charlie's arm, twisted him around and thumped him. Charlie crumpled to his knees, the knife still in his hand, and he retched, winded. Liesel was on the ground cradling her head. Nell was falling. She staggered against the bus shelter and put one hand out against the glass, the other at her neck. Joe went to Liesel.

"Give me your scarf, quick. You've got to be brave, Liesel. Nell's really badly hurt. Flag down a car. Get some help, please, I've got to look after Nell."

Liesel tried to stifle her sobs and watched with great shocked eyes as Joe took her pink fleece scarf and folded it up, then pressed it against Nell's neck. Nell leaned against him, and her knees gave way. She couldn't talk. Her mouth opened but no sound came. Joe held her and eased her down so that he was kneeling behind her, propping her up. Liesel went into the road. The bus finally arrived. When the driver saw the little girl, tear-streaked, frantic and saying someone was hurt, he switched on the hazard lights. A woman sitting near the front pulled Liesel on to the bus and tried to comfort her while the driver called for an ambulance.

The driver clambered out of his seat. Joe looked up at him, tears running down his face, then looked back at Nell. He didn't dare move. His fingers were wet and sticky. The scarf was crimson, but Nell's face was white. Her eyes were closed and her face was peaceful, as though she'd just fallen asleep.

Chapter Twenty-One

Aftermath

Sirens whooped in the distance. The ambulance arrived first, then the police car. The paramedics checked Nell's pulse. They tried to ease her out of Joe's arms, but he tightened his grip and they left him cradling her as they went to get a stretcher. The policewoman ushered Liesel off the bus and into the police car. The policeman got contact details for the passengers and the bus driver. The paramedics loosened Joe's grasp, lifted Nell out of his arms and laid her gently on the gurney. There was no urgency to their movements, just a steady calm with occasional comments to the policeman who'd come off the bus. They didn't zip her into a bag. Joe had been afraid they'd cover her face. The bus pulled away and more police cars arrived. There were men positioning striped tape, taking samples of things and muttering into their radios and mobiles. One came over to Joe and knelt beside him and the paramedics.

"Look, son, we need to get you to hospital, and we need to contact your mum or your dad. Can you stand up?"

Joe came to. He looked down and saw that his coat and hands had blood on them and that he was kneeling in blood.

The two men helped him to his feet.

"Liesel?"

"Your little sister?"

Joe nodded.

"She's already in the patrol vehicle with WPC Cartwright. They'll follow us. We'll go in another car. You need to be cleaned up, otherwise you might frighten your little sister even more. Okay?"

Joe continued nodding like a toy dog on the rear ledge of a car. His breathing was labored, and the tears kept coming. They eased him into the back seat of a small van where he sat, trying to stop his face crumpling and to suppress sobs. "I don't want her to be dead. She shouldn't be dead. Please don't make her be dead."

The policeman came round the other side. He strapped himself in and Joe remembered to do likewise. The mundane action helped him. He said softly, "It was Charlie Meek. He had four other guys with him, but he was the only one with a knife. I think they'd been taking something. He was mental."

"Thanks, son. Let me just get a team to track down this Charlie Meek. You're absolutely certain?"

"Yes. We're all at the same school."

"Lyndhurst?"

Joe nodded again.

"And what's your name?"

Joe told him, and explained who Nell was. The policeman forwarded the details to the station. When he'd finished talking on the phone, Joe asked, "Where are we going?"

"The hospital. We'll check you and your sister out there, then we'll have to take statements from both of you. Will you be able to cope, do you think? Both of you?"

Joe twitched his shoulders. "I suppose so."

"We'll get your mum there. We need her permission before we take any statements, and she can stay with you while you give your account of events."

Joe was convinced that he'd be examined by Dolon and spent the rest of the journey to the hospital trying to work out how to avoid being left alone with him. But of course, Dolon was nowhere to be seen once they reached the accident and emergency unit. It was quickly established that neither of the Knightley children was physically hurt, although a doctor did notice that Joe was bruised and stiff. They took away his coat and trousers and shirt and brought him some clothes that someone had borrowed from one of the male nurses. Before he was allowed to take a shower, a nurse took a DNA swab and a hair sample and a policeman fingerprinted him. They showed him a bathroom. He stood numb under the jet of water, watching as swirls of pinkening water sluiced away — the last he'd ever have of Nell. He closed his eyes tightly and pressed them with his palms to stop the tears, even though under the running water, it didn't matter.

Then he and Liesel were put in a small office along with the policewoman to await the duty psychiatrist.

Susan Knightley arrived before the doctor. The door to the office opened, and she was standing there, then hugging both Liesel and Joe to her as if she were glued to them. Liesel burst into tears of relief. She calmed down again and all three of them sat there under the gaze of the policewoman.

"What happened? All I was told was that there had been an incident at the bus stop and that you were here. What's been going on?"

"Mum, Nell Brennan... She's been stabbed."

Mrs. Knightley recoiled, her hand at her mouth. "But she's going to be all right? They're treating her now, are they?"

Joe shook his head. Finally, he gave way to the mounting pressure within him, and the tears came again. Hiccupping through the sobs, he managed to get out the words, "Mum, it was all my fault. If we hadn't gone to the other bus stop, she'd be alive. I said we should walk to get warm, but we'd have been safe if we'd stayed outside the school. Mum, what have I done?"

"Oh, Joe, you haven't done anything. You didn't stab her. You didn't attack her. You didn't do anything. It's not your fault, darling. It's not your fault." She took him in her arms and rocked him as though he were a toddler recovering from a fall, and the tears flowed down her cheeks as fast as his.

The policewoman held Liesel close. As Joe continued

to blame himself, she said quietly, "Your mum is right, you know. You didn't do this. You mustn't beat yourself up about it. You saw who did it. You'll be asked to give a statement, then you'll be able to go home."

"Who did do it, Joe?"

Joe explained about Charlie Meek and somehow, going over the whole appalling sequence of events calmed him down. When he'd finished explaining to his mother, he asked if Mrs. Brennan had been told. The policewoman wasn't sure.

The duty psychiatrist came in. He was a plump, matter-of-fact man with very little hair and pudgy fingers. He spoke directly to Joe and Liesel, almost seeming to ignore the policewoman and Mrs. Knightley. He acted as if traumatized teenagers who'd witnessed a murder were his daily bread and butter. He talked to the two of them about flashbacks and panic attacks, about recurring dreams and a sensation of numbness or detachment. Then he turned to Mrs. Knightley.

"May I have a word with you?" He held the door open for her. He left it ajar but took her across the corridor so that neither Joe nor Liesel could make out what he was saying. He spoke at some length to their mother, who was listening intently and nodding in response.

Then Mrs. Brennan came up. She said to Joe's mother, "Can I talk to him? I just need to know how it happened. That's all. I just have to know how it happened."

The psychiatrist reached out. "I'm not sure that's entirely wise."

But Joe saw Mrs. Knightley look into Mrs. Brennan's eyes. What she saw there made her nod and say, "If Joe doesn't mind."

So Joe found himself taking those same steps to the bus stop once more, sitting there with Liesel between Nell and him, seeing Charlie's shoes, Nell refusing to go home, swinging out with her bag, taunting Charlie, falling back, falling down, falling.

"So stupid. So, so stupid," Mrs. Brennan was murmuring.

Another policewoman came up and said, "Mrs. Brennan! I wondered where you'd got to." Then she took in what was happening and stopped.

"Niamh, what are you going to do now? Do you have somebody to stay with you? Who's going to look after you?" Mrs. Knightley couldn't bear the idea of this woman being left alone.

"My mother's there. She's got Kieran. She's looking after him. We'll manage. Thanks, Susan." Mrs. Brennan reached out for Joe, and he went to her and hugged her. "Thank you for telling me, Joe. Just so long as they get that monster. Just so long as they get him and lock him up once and for all." The policewoman accompanied her as she walked down the corridor.

Another policeman appeared with a laptop. He asked if Joe was ready to give his statement. Joe nodded. They sat, and the policeman typed as Joe spoke, unprompted, retelling the story for the third, or was it the fourth time? He'd lost track, but it didn't matter because the story was playing and replaying itself in his head over and over. There was no room for anything else in Joe's mind. Then the man asked to take Liesel's statement. She spoke slowly but definitely, and she named the boys who were with Charlie—Barry Hunter, Dean Dearborn—the two whose teeth and head had collided—Glen Carter, who'd run away and Steve Forest, whose nose Joe had yanked and who had been holding her when Charlie took his hunting knife out. She was clear about the length of the knife, and she was equally clear about how Charlie's face had creased with hatred before he went for Nell.

The policeman thanked the children and turned off his laptop. They were free to go now, but they should stay at home for the next few days, and they needed to be aware that there was likely to be media interest in the story. The press might be at their house already. These things had a way of getting out.

They should also know that Charlie was claiming that it was Joe who had stabbed Nell, a story that had so far been corroborated only by Steve Forest, who was receiving treatment for his nose.

"He needed stitches. I'd have done the same if it had been my sister, I tell you. But you stay at home. I mean it. Don't try to leave your house. Not for a few days. Once there's been a charge and a trial date set, things will calm down," said the family liaison officer.

"Will Charlie Meek get bail?" asked Mrs. Knightley, bristling at the thought.

"Absolutely not. He's staying on remand. The statements I've got here, and the state he's in are more than enough to ensure that he's regarded as a danger to the community. He'd taken methamphetamine. I reckon he's been a user for some time. Things are messed up in this world, but not so messed up that some story an addict has invented will stand up against statements that are as complete as these ones."

The policewoman added, "I'll probably be called as well. Joe's told a completely consistent story every time he's had to talk about this, and Liesel's statement verifies every word he's said. We all know what really happened, and that will come out in court. Believe me."

Mrs. Knightley said wryly, "I'm a solicitor. I know what can happen in a courtroom if he gets the best counsel going." Neither of the police knew what to say to that. They'd both seen enough cases where defense barristers had run rings around the prosecutor and got some lowlife off without any official stain on his character.

The Knightleys reached home around nine. Ben and Zahid were there. They'd cooked but no one felt like eating. Mrs. Knightley took Liesel to bed. Joe was slumped on the sofa. Zahid sat in an armchair, but Ben was restless and guilt-ridden.

"I shouldn't have made him look such a fool in front of the school. I'm sorry, Joe. I didn't think it would put you and Liesel at risk."

Joe shook his head. "Doesn't matter. He was out for me anyway. He thought I was tangled up with Smokey and trying to muscle in on his turf." He fell silent. If somebody picked him up and tapped him against a solid surface, he'd crack like a blown egg or one of those hollow chocolate Santas.

Ben went to the kitchen to tidy up. Zahid asked, "How come you couldn't dream your way out of this?"

Joe swallowed. He'd sat in the hospital asking himself the same thing. "I don't know. I suppose everything happened so quickly, and they had Liesel as well. When I got you out of that fight, I was holding on to you, and I had time to get my brain working in the right way. This time, Nell was up and at them before I could think. All I wanted was for her to get away, but she wouldn't run."

"If you can make dreams come true, why don't you just dream her alive again?"

That hadn't occurred to Joe. He breathed out and tension seemed to melt from him. He closed his eyes for a long moment. When he opened them, he was smiling. "I am so dumb. Why didn't I think of that?"

Zahid smiled. "Probably because having someone die in your arms isn't exactly conducive to clear thinking. Look. Get to bed, and you can deal tomorrow."

Joe could see that Zahid was trying to help. An unusual state of affairs. He'd always thought Zahid was a self-centered monster, but perhaps being saved from a beating had reformed him a little.

As he went upstairs, he met his mother coming out of Liesel's room. "She's asleep, thanks to these pills the doctor gave us." She went over to Joe, her lips clamped together and held him there on the landing, as tightly as she had when he was four or five, had taken a tumble and she could still kiss things better. Her voice was dense with tears, but she did not cry.

"I'm so glad you're safe, and I feel so bad because Nell

isn't. I just can't believe it. I remember her and you and Silas, all on the first day of primary school, all so excited and so sweet in your little uniforms. It's such a waste. Such a cruel, stupid waste."

Her arms tightened around Joe as if that would keep him safe forever, then she loosened her grip and brushed at her damp eyes. "The doctor said you should take something to help you sleep tonight too." She handed him two tablets. He gave her another hug and climbed up to his room.

Lying on his desk was the bag from Titan. He dumped his school bag. It was heavy with books and papers irrelevant to anything in his life. Exams and coursework were no longer of any importance to him. Sometime he'd have to overcome that feeling, but for now, he kicked the bag under his desk before sitting in his swivel chair and reaching for the book that he'd been given at the comic shop.

The cover had not changed, but there were new pictures — the dank, gray loading bay where he and Zahid had hidden, Karabashi's study then a picture of him and Zahid in a tangle on this very same bedroom floor. He hoped Ben wouldn't ever come across the book. For some reason, that frame looked incriminating. Then there were dark pages, dense with matte tints of gray, where the silhouette of a figure trying to haul himself out of dark places was faintly visible — a representation of those dreams he'd tried to avoid.

The rest of the book had empty boxes scattered across its pages. They were irregular in size and shape, some zagging diagonally halfway down a page, others dividing up the pages into several smaller boxes connected by arrows. Someone had already planned out the pace and structure of the future dreams Joe would have.

The questions mustered like infantry on a plain preparing for battle. *Am I the Dream Master? How does one become a Dream Master? Who had been the guy in America who had died? How had he died? How did the pictures get drawn?* Joe flipped back and surveyed the whole section where he'd been in

Eidolon's Elizabethan world. He reached for a magnifying glass and began to examine each picture, millimeter by millimeter, scrutinizing the draftsmanship and the coloring. The work was painstaking. He leaned back and checked again — then he saw it. The pictures were optical illusions. One was like the picture of a young woman who turns into an old lady if you alter your perspective slightly, but if you looked, first it was Eidolon then it became Joe, dressed in sixteenth century clothes. Another was like an Escher print of white and black birds crossing from night to day, showing the dawn coming over the horizon of Eidolon's manor house. A third was a portrait of Eidolon made up of fruits and vegetables, like an Arcimboldo painting. In the great blue bowl, the pattern of flowers and stems reformed to become readable script. It said, *He who dreams walks alone by ways no other men can roam.* The next picture showing the bowl was angled differently. Joe's eyes ached as he deciphered the miniscule script. *Sail away from the safe harbor. Catch the trade winds in your sails.* Then there was a third — *Dreaming is nursed in darkness.*

Joe was conscious of his rising irritation. It was maddening to find these cryptic aphorisms. They could be read in any way. If Eidolon had come across them already, he must have taken them as a sanction, providing him with a license to sow mayhem and reap lives wherever he chose.

He reached for a pen and began to jot down a list of things he wanted to do.

Dream Nell alive.

Dispose of Eidolon.

Discover the identity of the Dream Master.

Under each heading, he wrote down his options.

Dream leaving school again, but this time, stay at the bus stop outside school, then Charlie won't be able to isolate us.

Dream the attack again, but this time, get in front of Nell so that Charlie doesn't actually stab her.

Dream that I find her body in the hospital and see if I can wake her up.

The latter didn't appeal to Joe at all. He'd have to find her in the morgue, and he had some vague idea that she would be undergoing a postmortem and if he tried to rouse her, she'd be all opened up with her internal organs in basins and it would be messy and disgusting. It would make the dismembering of that boar look like a school outing.

Then he moved onto disposing of Eidolon.

Go into a dream as some incredible superhero and attack him there. But then he'll just jump through into some other dream.

Track him down in school and fight him there. No way... I'm not meant to be in school for at least a fortnight, and even if I do get him to attack me, he'd probably get me kicked out.

Find some way to talk to him and work out what his plans are. Did he manipulate Charlie into attacking us? Did he give him the whiz? Figure it out...how?

Offer him something to leave me alone. Offer him the Lamborghini. We can't report it as stolen because it's not technically a real Lamborghini. Mum would get the insurance money. It doesn't matter because I can't drive it anyway.

He had to get rid of Eidolon in this world. That was the only way to stop him from jumping around other worlds and trying to drag Joe into them.

As for discovering the identity of the Dream Master, the only way Joe could see of going about that was to dream more. Which might worry Mum, but if he claimed he was using the pills the doctor had given him and that was what was making him dopey, he might get away with sleeping much of the next fortnight away.

He glanced at the pills he'd dumped on his desk. He picked them up and went into the bathroom. He ran the water, filled a glass and drank it down. One pill would do. Then he crushed the pills to powder in the basin before running the water again and washing them away. Tonight, the last thing he wanted was to be doped out of his dreams. It was time to try to get Nell back.

Chapter Twenty-Two

Ostinato

He closed his eyes and he was back at the bus stop with Liesel and Nell, all three shivering and shrinking from the chill afternoon air, but he did not say anything about walking to the next bus stop. Liesel and Nell talked in a desultory fashion about teachers they both knew, and the shadows lengthened as the bus still failed to come.

"Let's go to the next bus stop," said Liesel. "I'm so cold and at least if we walk, we'll warm up a bit."

Joe objected but Liesel and Nell set off at a brisk trot and try as he might to get them to turn back, they would not, so he followed protesting, moaning, whining. At the next stop, they sat on the stiff reinforced plastic seats, the cold seeping back into their bones. Then Joe looked up and there was Charlie again, with his mates.

Joe forcibly dragged himself out of the dream and into wakefulness. If Nell died again, perhaps she would be doubly dead or there would be two Nells to save instead of one. Either way, the prospect of holding her again, watching helplessly as blood ebbed along with her breath, was unbearable. It had taken eleven minutes for her to die. The paramedics and police had worked it out. He remembered it was like looking through a rotating telescope. It seemed to have taken no time at all — or an eternity — depending on which end of the lens he was looking through.

He tried again.

This time, he found himself leaving school with Nell and walking up to the primary school to wait for Liesel. She came as before but this time, he tried to provoke her into a fight, then Nell butted in, smoothing things over so by the time they were back at the school bus stop, all was calm again and now, Nell suggested walking to the next stop.

Joe wrenched himself out of sleep again before they'd even set off again for the fifteen-minute walk.

The third time he went back to the peal of the bell and tried to lose Nell before she could accompany him over to Liesel's academy. But she tracked him down as he was striding toward the primary school. He turned in exasperation and said, "For God's sake, Nell, don't come with me. We're going to be attacked by Charlie Meek, and you're going to get killed."

"I know." She was serene and superior, her favorite attitude. "You can't change that, Joe. I am dead except for here in your dream. And I will die in your dream just as I did in life."

"That is no help at all." Joe dumped his bag. "I'm going to stop right here. Liesel will just have to wait at the school until you have gone."

"You can't change this, Joe. You can change other things, but you can't change this—not by dreaming it and not by living it."

"How do you know?"

"Because I'm dead. I know the things you aren't supposed to know yet."

"But you're going to tell me."

"I don't know. I don't know what I know. Joe. Where I am, there is absolutely nothing. I'm here because of you, but when you wake up, I'm not there. There's nowhere for me to go. But feel free to ask me anything you like, and I'll see if I can answer."

"Can I bring you back to life again?" It was the only question to which Joe really wanted an answer. Nothing else mattered.

"Only if you give up something you need. I don't understand what that means. I don't know what you have

215

to give up or how, but that's what you have to do. What I do know is that if you go and see Karabashi again, he'll help you." She shook her head as if clearing it. "It's weird. Maybe this is how computers are. You've fed me data, and I feed you an answer. I don't feel as if I have any control over what I say or do. My brain doesn't function anymore." She reached out and touched him. Her fingers were frozen and slightly blue. She sounded pleasantly amused. "I can't feel a thing. I wonder how long I'll stay like this. Maybe you shouldn't try to dream me back if this is the best you can do."

It was like having the real Nell but at her most irritating and, with added weirdness, transparent. It was like talking to a life-size Princess Leia hologram. "If I wake up now, you'll still be dead, even though I've left you alive."

"Yes, because I'm not alive. I'm dead. When you wake up, I won't exist anymore. When you dream about me again, I'll come back, but I'll be like this. Incorporeal. Insubstantial. Nothing. It's quite amusing for now, but I don't just want to be a projection of your image of me for the rest of eternity. How's my mum?"

"I can't talk about that, Nell. 'How's my mum?' is the sort of question that just requires an 'oh, doing fine' response and the last thing she's doing at the moment is fine. I have to get you back for real."

"If you don't do it before they cremate or bury me, I'll never be able to get back." She frowned. "That's so weird, having my tongue taken over like that. By the way, Dolon gave Charlie his ice. Charlie had been taking it before, but he'd stopped for a while. Then Dolon gave him some, and he went and shared it with his lovely pals."

"If I'd stopped him from taking it, then maybe he wouldn't have been there at the bus stop."

"Joe, you've got to get over the idea of stopping the actual chain of events that led to me getting stabbed. That won't work. I can't explain why it won't work. It's just something I know. I was stabbed. Get over it. Move on."

"Stop talking like some crappy soap, Nell. If you'd had somebody die in your arms, you wouldn't be saying 'get over it' the evening it actually happened. It was traumatic, you know."

"Well, yes, actually, I do know. I was certainly very traumatized, in fact I traumatized all over the pavement and Liesel's pink scarf. That's real trauma for you. You're the one who's alive, Joe. Now go and speak to that Karabashi guy and get the rest of the information you need."

Joe sighed. There was no arguing with Nell. Death had given her a hotline to the planet hyper-smug. He turned away and walked back into wakefulness.

He lay in the dark, digesting what Nell had told him. Nothingness appeared so irrevocable. Nell's words had seemed to surprise her, so they must have come from somewhere, but that might plausibly be Joe's own mind. He could be making her say what he wished to hear, filtered through her inimitable, irritating, gloating superiority. When he got her back, that was going to have to stop.

The dark seemed to intensify. He wanted to carry on remembering Nell a little longer, to think of her mobile face, her skin as pale as a white rose, her slanting eyes, the straight brown hair behind which she screened off the more aggravating aspects of her world, the lips that Joe had never actually kissed, although he had thought about being allowed to.

Before he went to Karabashi, he wanted something of Nell's. He got up, hauled out the golden carpet and lay back, his mind filling with the image of her room, fresh and full of her life, her books, her notebooks, her photographs, her perfume and lip gloss and the bangles she wore hidden under the cuffs of her school uniform.

Once he was there, he stood in the middle of the room as though getting too close to any actual object might jar him awake and back into reality. He turned his dark and heavy eyes on the world she had inhabited only this morning, clothes still dangling on the back of her chair, an unmatched pair of earrings on her dressing table adrift from their butterflies, a list of things to do over the weekend tacked above her desk in her firm, spiky handwriting, as precise and even as the ticking of a metronome, the book she had been reading still lying open, spine upward, pages splayed open on her rumpled bed.

On the bulletin board where she'd pinned her list were photographs of her with her mother and father before the split, with Kieran, with her best friend Emily, who had moved to London two years ago, with her grandmother in Ireland last summer. There was only one of her on her own, gazing across a sand-swept winter beach, breakers foaming in the distance, her hand shading her eyes and her hair whipping away from her face. He touched it, traced the outline of her face. He wanted it, but it would be missed. Mrs. Brennan and Kieran would want to keep that image of Nell near them, surrounded by wind and water, safe forever from stupid boys high on drugs.

He returned to the carpet and carried himself away before he took anything. Everything in the room had been heavy with Nell and to remove something would have been to dilute her. She had been sufficiently diluted for one day.

Besides, once he'd gotten her back, he'd never hear the end of it when she worked out that he'd taken something from her room.

* * * *

Arriving in Karabashi's world, he thumped into a starry night in the courtyard where they had last talked at length. He missed the rectangular pool by a handbreadth, but the fringes of the carpet were soaked and he leaped up to flick them out of the water. Karabashi was there on the same marble bench where they had last sat.

"I've been waiting for you. How inconvenient it is being unable to summon you." The scholar was nursing three books as if he feared a thief might run through the courtyard and wrest them away. He beckoned Joe to sit beside him. "I have found extraordinary things in these books—things I could never have imagined. And I have something you will need if you are to defeat this Eidolon."

Karabashi did not seem to be aware of Nell's death. Of course, he'd never known Nell, but since Nell had known about him, Joe had rather assumed that the scholar would know about her.

"I didn't come to you for that. I came because somebody suggested it to me. Someone who has died. She thought you might know of a way for me to get her back."

"Get her back?" repeated Karabashi. "From where?"

"From nowhere. From death. I have to bring her back to life, I really have to. It's essential."

"If she has died, it is too late."

"No. There is a way of dreaming her back to life, I am sure. I know it. It's more important than destroying Eidolon. I promise. Without her, I don't know if I'll be able to overcome him."

"She is a girl you love, and you say she is essential to you?"

"Yes." Joe's response was automatic and emphatic.

"You are no better than our sultan, a slave to his own concupiscence." Karabashi's fastidious tone betrayed his contempt for his ruler. He shrank in on himself, a cat curling into a protective ball.

"It's not like that. I... We... There's nothing like that between us. I've known her since I was four and if I lose her, I'll have lost part of who I am forever. She's like a sister—but less irritating. Except she can be really, really irritating. Anyway, that doesn't matter. I have to save her. Surely saving one person is better than trying to destroy another."

"That's the difficulty. Eidolon is not a person in the way that you and I are. His evil has unfolded for so long and has been so unchecked that he has become more and less than a human. He is more powerful and can wreak greater damage, and he is less because he has none of the compassion and love and pity that make us superior to rough beasts."

Joe considered this. "But you see, with her alive, I will be able to fight him more easily. She is nearly as wise as you are." He suspected that Nell was wiser but he wanted to flatter Karabashi into helping. He looked a little affronted that a female might be anywhere near as wise as he, but assented.

"I will have to read further to help you in this task. In the meantime, I want you to read this." He had marked one of the books with a ribbon of emerald silk. He opened it and passed it to Joe. As Joe first looked, he saw only the squiggles and sweeps of Arabic script, unintelligible. Then the inked text took on shape and meaning and he was pulled into the prose.

"Once, there was a man who was master of his dreams. When he dreamed, he could alter the world to fit his visions, and when he woke, the world would be made afresh, molded to the shape in which he had cast it..."

An image of the Dream Master comic strip flashed into Joe's mind. He read on. Karabashi was flicking through a second book, running a finger along the script and mumbling as he read. But soon, Joe forgot about everything, save what he was reading.

"The Dream Master was a boy of humble origins when he discovered his abilities. At first, he committed errors. He did not understand the great gift that had come upon him. But soon, with the gift of dreaming came the gift of wisdom. Naturally, so great a gift could not remain a secret and soon, this man came to the attention of generals and viziers, of mighty merchants, princes and potentates. He was wooed with promises of wealth. He was threatened with dire punishments. He was menaced with torture and his loved ones were endangered as all those who wished to take advantage of his powers sought to bring him under their sway. But he escaped his tormentors and took his dreams to serve the poor, the sick, the needy, those with sorrows too great to bear and those who likewise wished to assist their fellow man, not to subjugate him.

"When the time of his death approached — for though this man was gifted, he was like other men, mortal — the Dream Master sought a successor, but none could be found. He died and with him died his gift.

"Some years after his death, pilgrimages were made to his place of rest, and on one such journey, a boy, little more than a child, came with his father to plead for the life of his mother at the shrine which had arisen around the master's grave. When he came to the temple of the master, the boy was overtaken with strange sensations. He wished only to sleep, and for weeks afterward, when his father told him that it was time to rise and go about the business of the day, he would moan and roll in his bedding, giving up great lamentations. Then, one day after the father had left his son once again at their lodgings, he returned to find his son in so deep a sleep that he could not be awoken. Fearing that he was about to lose his son as well as his wife, the man beat his breast and cried out to his god for mercy. The boy rose, still deep in his sleep and spoke in a voice which was not his own, saying, 'Leave this child and return to your home. All will be well with your wife and with your son. But your son must remain here at the master's side to serve him and serve his ways.' In this way was the second Dream Master found.

"This boy served out his apprenticeship, also falling into errors and making grievous mistakes. Still, he reached manhood and when he was sere and worn, he knew more of how to choose his successor and what trials that successor must endure. He found a worthy follower who could undergo the necessary ordeals. And this third Dream Master was able to write down the rites by which one might attain mastery of the matters of the mind.

"These are the forms of examination — For the first, the dreamer must bring into existence his most coveted desire then destroy it. For the second, the dreamer must encounter in his dreams a strange beast and overcome it. For the third, the dreamer must bid farewell to his fondest wish and turn his back upon it. Having performed these three tasks, a boy is ready to become a man and a master of his dreams."

Joe looked up.

Karabashi's eyes were on him, steady and patient. "What do you make of this tale? Is it simply a story?"

Joe looked away. He had dreamed his greatest desire into existence. The Lamborghini was sitting in the garage, simply waiting for him. It would be painful to see it destroyed, but Joe knew that after today, the car meant almost nothing to him. It was no animate being who needed mourning, just a heap of steel and leather and rubber—a gorgeous, elegant, graceful heap, but ultimately, nothing more.

"In one dream, I was staying in a house owned by Eidolon. I was a prisoner, but I escaped. I had to go hunting. I had to kill a wild boar. Do you think that would count as overcoming a strange beast?"

"Is a wild pig a strange beast?" Karabashi sounded bemused.

"Yeah. Where I come from, they've been extinct for four hundred years, pretty much. That makes a wild boar strange in my book."

"Perhaps it will do."

"The thing is, what will happen if I complete these three missions? Will there be trumpets and a heavenly chorus? A round of applause? Or nothing? How would I know if I've completed them anyway?" Joe couldn't contain his sarcasm.

"If you completed these tasks, you would gain more control over what you dreamed, and this would tell you that you had become a Dream Master."

"That sounds really shaky to me."

Karabashi said nothing, but the tentative look on his face suggested that he felt much the same as Joe. They sat in silence awhile. Joe was thinking about the third task. "The thing is, my greatest wish is to make Nell breathe again.

Bring her back to life. And I can't turn my back on that."

"Would you forgo the chance to become a Dream Master?" asked Karabashi.

It would have been different if either he or Karabashi had had any idea what being a Dream Master involved. If it involved yachts and pretty girls and luxury hotels, Joe would be interested. But given what he'd read, it seemed to involve grief, aggro and responsibility, none of which particularly appealed to him. Giving them up hardly presented any difficulty. He had a feeling that saying this to Karabashi would not impress.

"If I knew what a Dream Master was, maybe not. But I don't. I won't miss what I've never had."

Karabashi's lips thinned as he suppressed the urge to argue. He simply handed over the second book to Joe. It was in Latin. It would certainly be a blow to give up this ability to read anything in any language, but Nell was more important.

"And there came into the country a man with such might that all laid down their weapons before him, although he was without men or arms or money. This man was a Dream Master, one who might translate those visions that came to him in the night into truth by daylight. He and his forbears were men of peace and wisdom who sought to soothe the troubles that afflict humankind. But there came against him another dreamer. This dreamer was a man whose only intent was to raise incubi and succubi and all the terrors that might torment a man. This creature was called Eidolon. Of the three trials that must be surmounted to become a master of dreams, Eidolon had passed two, but his chief desire was to become a master of dreams and to become a master, he must turn his back upon this desire. Instead he sought to steal the mastery by usurping the corporeal form of the Dream Master. In this he was defeated, but ever after he has wandered through existences, seeking out those children who show signs of becoming dreamers in the hope of entering their souls and usurping their powers. Thus far, he has been thwarted."

The notion of being a lure for Eidolon sickened Joe, but he brightened. "If I bring Nell back, then I can never become a Dream Master and Eidolon will leave me alone."

"No. You will be defenseless against the one who will dispose of you before he seeks out the next dreamer. You know more about him than any other in your world. He will not leave you alive, nor your family or your friends. He can follow you wherever you go, even here. You must, therefore, become the next master. If you decide to revive this dead girl, you will cast away your gift and will be unable to defend her against an enemy who has already brought one death to her."

Karabashi's logic seemed so watertight Joe snapped. "Why should I trust what you say? How do I know you aren't scheming to take over these powers?"

Disappointment and frustration shadowed the scholar's eyes.

"You need not believe me. Here. Let me show you." He handed over the third book. It was marked at a page that contained a simple instruction.

"The apprentice must go to the desert."

"What does this mean?"

"Exactly what it says. You must go to the desert."

Joe slammed the covers of the book together with a thud. He hurled the book at Karabashi and turned his back on the whole ridiculous business. But curiosity crept over him, and he addressed the older man once more. "How does this make you any more trustworthy?"

"If I could not to be trusted, I should not have given you any of this information. I should have kept it for myself, gone into the desert and taken the mantle of master myself. I might have betrayed you to Eidolon or to the palace guards. But here we are in a peaceful courtyard as the sun sinks because all I seek to do is pass on the knowledge you need."

"It's vague. What desert? How do I get there?"

This exasperated Karabashi. Waspishly, irritated out of his customary helpfulness, he snapped at Joe. "How should I know? Why don't you just dream yourself there? Go and harass some other poor fool into helping you when he has work of his own to do."

Joe made a contrite apology, but Karabashi remained offended.

"I really am sorry, you know. I mean it." It was hard to admit weakness. But a tense silence festered between them. Joe's discomfort increased. "It's hard. I don't want to give up on Nell. I can't. But I know you're right about Eidolon. I don't know what to do. Please help me."

Karabashi's umbrage dissolved. "Go to the desert. Dream your way there, and see what happens. You may not have to make any choice until you are there. Then things will be clearer for you."

Joe nodded. Karabashi reached behind him and passed over a parcel wrapped in dark-blue silk tied with a golden cord.

"Here. From what I have read in these books, this will help you."

Joe pulled at the cord and the parcel seemed to unfurl. Inside was a white cotton bundle, which he shook out. It was a shirt, simple in cut, quite vast and completely covered in geometric inscriptions, graphs and cryptograms. There were diamond patterns balanced in squares, heavily outlined in gilt paint, great trailing columns of Arabic script and, interlocking the whole, intricate trellises of tiny leaves and flowers. It was an extraordinary garment that must have taken months to decorate in precise, miniscule calligraphy.

"I've never seen anything like this. It's amazing."

"I hope that it lives up to its alleged powers. Astrologers, theologians and craftsmen have labored long hours to produce this shirt. It is said that it can withstand the deepest cut of the sharpest yatagan, ward off djinns and afreet and protect the wearer from his worst enemy. The sultan gave it to me as a token of respect. I am giving it to you. Put it on before you go to this desert. Use it wisely."

More than ever, Joe was mortified by his earlier petulance. He stammered his thanks. And when he said goodbye to Karabashi, tears filled his eyes, because this time he was convinced that he would never see the scholar again. There was no reason to suppose this would be true, but there was a different quality to their farewell, tinged perhaps by their disagreement. Joe returned to the carpet and dissolved back into his own room.

Halfway through the process, he was tugged by a desire to return to that calm sanctuary where water ran and the only other sound was the rustle of paper as books were read. But he quelled the urge and found himself lying on the floor of his room in total darkness, confronting his next great journey.

Chapter Twenty-Three

Tyche

Not knowing what he might come up against next, Joe dressed in combat trousers, T-shirt and a heavy jumper. He laced up his Timberland boots and put in his pockets a pen, a pencil, a notebook, some money, his MP3 player and his Maglite torch. Then he lay down again on the bed. In some dreams, he'd gone from wearing pajamas to wearing whatever was appropriate to the world of the dream — school uniform, that ridiculous doublet and hose getup — but there had been dreams where he'd turned up in what he was wearing. Whether he could control it, he wasn't sure, but it was worth trying. He didn't think he had a very effective bag of tricks, but it wasn't as if he had an arsenal of Gameboys that turned into GPS systems or CD players that turned into lasers. As he lay there, the list of things he might have taken lengthened — rope, matches, water, a mirror to signal for help, some energy bars, safety pins, a compass. Going to the desert with a Maglite torch and a notebook didn't seem to make him particularly prepared. But he had no idea what sort of desert he was going to or what he would find there. In fact, he had no idea about anything at all.

He waited. He tossed. He lay with his eyes open and with his eyes closed — on his side then on his front. He tried to name every country in Europe in alphabetical order. He listed his favorite bands in alphabetical order. He listed every teacher in school in alphabetical order. He listed superheroes and cartoon characters. He tried every conceivable way he could think of to bore himself to sleep. Then he thought of Nell and how she looked, but her features had become somehow blurred. With that realization, the tears came. With the tears came sleep.

The first thing Joe was conscious of was the sound of the wind. It ripped around him. He was lying on rock in the clothes he had chosen. He sat up. Above him, a row of five immense but headless statues sat impassively, facing some distant horizon. He turned to see what was before them and the breath was knocked from him. He was in the midst of a mountain range with no sign of human life. The peaks undulated away, wave upon wave of rock, glowing orange, copper and silver as the sun rose and strengthened. The sky above was cloudless and so intense a blue that it seemed outer space had invaded the atmosphere. He was on the top of the world. The cold was so dry he could feel his skin turning to parchment, the moisture in his lips and fingers shrinking from its intensity.

He walked to the edge of the plinth where he had been lying. Before him was a precipice of weathered limestone, cracked and slivered by wind and ice, as lined and worn as a man who has gazed for a lifetime into the sun. Behind the five statues was a smooth peak, an unnaturally even cone guarded by the seated figures and crisscrossed with several tracks.

Standing on the dais, Joe looked again at the statues.

Their heads had fallen and rolled from their shoulders and now lay between Joe and the statues like randomly tossed dice, their features smooth and unreadable with weathering, their eyes sightless. A stone lion sat on its haunches at one corner of the dais. And blending with the tearing, rending sound of the wind came the unmistakable rumble of a huge cat breathing. Joe walked toward the statues and climbed down the steps to the boulder-strewn ground. The lion was still, its eyes as blind as those of the gods it had guarded, but Joe was sure he still heard its purr.

An ear-rending shriek slashed the air, and Joe looked up.

An eagle was soaring high above, circling over the mountain, its shrill cry angry and mournful. He took a step and the parched shards of rock and pebble shifted beneath his feet with a rasping crunch.

He watched the eagle as it surfed the air currents, expressing its displeasure at the arrival of an interloper in its world. Its wingspan was immense and for a moment, Joe feared that it would swoop down and lift him up by its talons, only to drop him off the side of the mountain. But it glided past him, its yellow eyes penetrating, the wind ruffling at its dark feathers and pale head before gaining height once again and landing on the lap of one of the statues, where it seemed to have shrunk to the size of a baby. It glared down at Joe, frozen by its passage. Then it took flight again and he followed it. It led him around the mountain, which had been shaped long ago by human hands. On the southern face, he came to a terrace guarded by an immense pillar on which stood another eagle, this one carved from silvery stone, polished to a high sheen by the breeze. Joe found himself walking through a plantation of sculpted heads — a bearded man here, a young, clean-shaven king there. He stopped in front of a detached-looking woman with a garland of fruit and flowers wreathing her brow. The tilt of her head and her stern mouth reminded him of the way that girls would respond, "Whatever," when being ticked off by a teacher who they knew had no real power over them. Her eyes were widely spaced, the bridge of her nose flat, although she had lost most of the rest of it. When Joe stood beside her, he reached the bottom of her eyes.

Joe continued exploring. There was no sign of human habitation, no trace of human occupation of the mountains apart from this strange statuary. He had come to the desert, but what he was meant to do now, he had no idea. He traced relief carvings etched into solid rock and ran his fingers over the ridges and ripples of a maned lion surrounded by stars. There were four terraces carved out of the mountain's sides, one at each point of the compass, and with nothing else to do, as the sun rose, Joe began to sketch each of the terraces, choosing first an overview then a specific detail.

He ended up returning to draw the woman's head. She was the only female he had found there, and perhaps because she looked so petulant, he was drawn to her. At least there was some sort of emotion, some sign that the carvings had come from the human imagination.

Only gradually did he hear her humming. He had become so accustomed to the roar of the wind, the thrum of the lions and the whistling shrieks of the eagles that he scarcely noticed another sound among the noises reverberating around the mountain. At first, it was an occasional nasal drone, building gradually into a full-fledged melody, plaintive and swooping. It was catching. He'd completed a sketch of her whole head and was now trying to pin down a detail of her headdress when he registered that his movements were accompanying the meandering tune. He stopped.

"Continue," came a gravelly, rasping voice.

He searched for the source of the voice, and it was then that he noticed that where the statue he had been sketching had previously had sightless stone eyes, now, two dark liquid irises were focused on him. He tried to continue but he had lost the tune. She began to hum again, and he joined in as he was completing an outline of the garland.

"Show me."

Joe held up the pad before the statue.

"I've never seen a likeness of myself before. At least, not in this incarnation."

"You've had many incarnations?"

"I used to. And really, people never give up worshipping me, otherwise they would not gamble."

"What's your name?"

"I have many, but you will know me as Fortune, or Luck, or Chance. You may call me Tyche."

Perhaps this was a moment where a bow would be appropriate, but it seemed a little late for formality.

"Can you help me?"

"They all say that. You humans are very dull. I only have to mention who I am, and you bombard me with requests."

"I didn't mean it like that. I just wondered if you knew what I should do next. I was told to go to the desert because I'm an apprentice Dream Master. Is this the desert? Should I be doing something?"

"You're the next Dream Master! Why didn't you say so?"

Joe forbore to mention that he just had.

Tyche was much warmer now that she knew who he was. "You're in terrible danger. I suppose you know that."

Joe nodded. "I need to defeat this Eidolon guy."

"I can't help you there. That depends on your own ingenuity. Have you completed your three tasks?"

"Not yet. I wanted to ask about one before I went any further."

"Oh, here we go. You don't want to give up your heart's desire, I suppose. It hasn't occurred to you that once you've become a Dream Master, you can dream it back into existence with no difficulties at all."

"It had occurred to me, actually, but that isn't the point. Once I reach that stage, it won't be my heart's desire, will it?"

"You're one of the perceptive ones." There was a flicker of respect in the shining eyes of the goddess. "So what is the problem?"

"My fondest wish is to bring back to life someone who has died. Is that possible, or is there some catch?"

"Yes, of course there's a catch. That clause is irrevocable. It's not like the first one. The difference is that a heart's desire will change, but the fondest wish won't, so you can never go back to it and make it work. You lose the mastery if you do."

"So if I seemed to turn my back on it, then became the master and tried to make it happen, I'd stop being the master."

"Isn't that what I said?" The goddess rolled her eyes with

impatience. It looked as though they might fly out of their sockets.

"I'm just making absolutely sure that I understand this malarkey."

"Malarkey! You call ancient lore that has lasted thousands of years 'malarkey'? You're a cheeky so-and-so."

"You haven't answered the other question. Can I bring someone back from death?"

"You can. It'll take it out of you, and you won't be dreaming for quite a while if you play that sort of game, but you can weave that dream if you have to. You can't do it too often. Wrecks my plans a touch, I must confess."

"Do you plan?"

"Not in detail. Broad-brush stuff. Sometimes someone will take my fancy, and I'll give them a helping hand. The problem with you humans, though, is you think you can do without me. There's the one God business, for starters, then the ones who don't believe in a single god tend to think they can make their own luck. I used to get frankincense and virgin sacrifices. Now I'm lucky to get my face drawn by a spotty youth."

"I can't believe you really want frankincense. It's just smelly. And what can you do with a clutter of dead virgins messing up your altar? I bet I know what you really want." At that very moment, Joe had no idea what the statue really wanted, but he knew he needed her on his side.

"Oh yes? What do I really want?"

Joe sketched quickly. As his fingers flew over the page, he carried on talking. "I don't know how long it will last—I suppose that's up to you—but I think I can get you what you want, if you let me have a little rest." He finished sketching, tore the sheet out of his notebook and held it up for the goddess. She saw what was unmistakably her head, minus the fruit and veg topping, sitting on the shoulders of a pneumatic woman wearing dominatrix clothes—a tight black T-shirt, leather trousers, thigh-high boots with buckles and knife-skinny heels.

The dark eyes blinked to conceal their interest, but she said next, "So where am I, clever clogs?"

Joe drew frantically, positioning her in the middle of Piccadilly Circus, leaning casually against the fountain under Eros. All around her were men and women gazing hungrily at her magnificence.

"London, a summer's evening, loads of people falling for you, worshipping you."

"What do you want in return, little boy?"

If she was resorting to cheap jibes, it meant he had her. "While I'm Dream Master, you're on my side. Absolutely no chance for my enemies. Not an atom of luck. You don't even smile in their general direction."

She didn't much like it, but she was seduced by the vision of escape from the barren emptiness where she was trapped. After a little cajoling and flattery, she agreed.

"Done. Now how are you going to become Dream Master, little shrimp?" It wasn't a nice epithet, but the perspective of an eight-foot-high head was naturally a little different from the average human point of view.

"Get rid of my heart's desire and turn my back on my fondest wish. How will I know that I've become the Dream Master?"

"I suppose you want celestial choirs and brass bands. A fanfare. Bunting and a parade."

Joe could see she was going to ramble on. He didn't feel too confident interrupting a goddess in full flow, but it seemed important to correct her misconceptions. "No. I just want to know how the Dream Master deal works."

A little nonplussed, Tyche paused. "Haven't they told you?"

"Who are they? I've had one person help me out with some research and otherwise, I've been on my own. I don't know anything." Joe made sure his tone was clear that he was getting fed up with this state of affairs.

"I'd better start at the beginning. You'll know once you've become Dream Master. You won't really have to sleep to make dreams happen. They'll be much more vivid, and you'll have more control over what goes on in them. When I say more control, I suppose I mean total control. You will be master of your imaginings. The only thing is, you have to abide by the rules set by previous Dream Masters. Initially, I had a hand in drawing up a few guidelines, along with my relatives, but the Dream Masters began interfering. It became a death-bed prerogative, if you like."

"Who was the last Dream Master?"

"Some English milord, died in 1596. He didn't have time to appoint a successor. It was in a boar hunt organized by Eidolon. Our evil friend there had set up some youth to become the apprentice, but the youth disappeared. Unfortunately, Eidolon had set in motion the whole chain of events that led to the death of the master. Bit of a mess, really. He found this boar that had been killed. He dismounted to inspect the carcass, and its mate turned up, was a bit upset, charged him and the master didn't make it. Too quick."

"How do I find out about these rules?"

"I don't know. I should think they will tell you in a dream. Are you going to get on with freeing me or are you going to carry on asking questions forever? I'd quite like to get out of this head."

"Sure," said Joe and held the paper. He curled up on the ground and drifted away, to London, where he'd only been a handful of times, but at least those times had been memorable enough for him to get to Piccadilly Circus. He sat on the steps of the Eros fountain and looked around. Then she appeared, about six feet tall, her classical features obscured by white foundation and black eyeliner, her hair no longer bound, but instead a great teased black spikiness, her lips outlined in garnet lipstick. She wore black leather and had a kilt pin holding her coat together.

"Thank you, Joe Knightley. You'd better get back home. You don't want to hang around much longer on Nemrud. It's soooo boring."

She turned and walked away, and Joe experienced an uneasy qualm at having unleashed Tyche on an unsuspecting London.

He got back to the mountain she had called Nemrud and did more sketches, hoping this would help him plan for his return home. Once it was clear that he was simply postponing the inevitable, he returned to the plinth where he had woken and lay there, his eyes closed, his mind ranging free.

Which of the fancy gentlemen at Eidolon's Elizabethan home had been killed?

Before he knew it, he was standing over the boar he had killed. Blood spurted from its wounds and the dogs had fallen back. His horse had skittered away, and he could hear the drum of its hooves as it cantered into the distance. He stepped back too, then heard crashing in the undergrowth. Whether it was another beast or his fellow huntsmen, hanging about seemed unwise. There was a young horse chestnut tree nearby, its trunk forked at the sort of height that Joe could manage, and from there, he could climb higher into the boughs of one of the older trees in the forest. He swung himself upward and scrambled up first some five or six feet above the ground then a farther five or six feet upward into the shelter of an old oak shrouded in ivy. He pressed himself against the bark and hoped that no one would look skyward.

The arrogant young man appeared in the clearing. He dismounted and approached the boar. He looked for the beast's killer but saw only the dogs. He reached for the horn buckled to his belt and lifted it to his lips, blowing three long bursts, his cheeks full and his face reddening from the exertion.

It was then that the other boar broke cover, emerging from a hollow where it had been lurking in the browned bracken, its small red eyes gleaming with bloodlust, trotters shredding the earth as it hurtled toward the young man. Joe watched in horror as the boar thudded into him, its tusks slashing at his belly and groin, its powerful shoulders shivering with exertion as the man screamed in agony. Its snout and pelt splashed with blood, it turned and galloped away. Joe slipped down from the tree and went to the young man, kneeling at his side.

"I'll get help. I'm sorry. I didn't think it would be like this. She said that you were trying to dream it away but didn't have time. I never imagined it this way. It's all my fault, I shouldn't have killed the first one."

Blood was trickling from the man's lips and his eyes were frantic. "Doesn't matter. Last rule. Listen." He tried to take a deep breath but that made him writhe in agony. He blew out and flecks of blood misted the air then settled on his skin. Joe wanted to run. He'd had enough of violent, messy death. But the man clutched at his arm and said, "Last rule. Next master must destroy Eidolon. He must be destroyed. Go. Go now, Eidolon is coming, and he will finish me. Go."

Joe felt himself propelled away by a force emanating from the dying man until he was standing by a tree – then in the tree. As he was absorbed into its bark, Eidolon came running into the clearing.

"De Vere?" He stood over the dying man. "Lucifer and all his demons take you. You aren't meant to die now!" He looked around and cursed Joe fluently while the man on the ground twitched and twisted in pain. Eidolon drew his sword and said, "Since it's too late now, I suppose I should put you out of your misery." Then he plunged the blade into the man's belly again and again until there was no further sound or movement from the ragged, broken heap. Eidolon dropped to his knees beside the dead man. "I'll find that boy, and when I do, I'll make him mine and I shall be his master, no matter how you and all your kind try to thwart me."

Taking up an attitude of prostrated grief, Eidolon composed himself as an artist might pose a model for a painting. Joe shrank away and sought the sanctuary of his room.

Chapter Twenty-Four

Dealing with Dolon

Joe did not wake again until morning, his body finally rebelling against the destruction it had seen that day. He was lying on his stomach when he woke, his booted feet dangling over the edge of the bed. He peeled off his clothes then threw himself under the covers for more sleep. Again he sank into dreamless oblivion.

When he woke properly, it was after midday. Ben was sitting at Joe's desk in Joe's chair, hunched over a pile of books on the drawing board. Joe lifted his head and checked out the rest of his room. His clothes were strewn around the floor. The carpet was in a heap at the foot of his bed, and there was paper everywhere. That was Ben's, balled up and tossed aside as he'd struggled with his latest essay.

"How long have you been here?"

"Mum sent me up around ten. She doesn't want you going downstairs in your usual Saturday morning state. The house is mobbed."

"Who's mobbing us?"

"You're a tragic hero for all the red tops from the *Burton Enquirer* to the *Sun* and the *Mirror*. Boy cradles dying teenager as her lifeblood drains away. The police did warn us, but Mum hadn't expected it to happen quite so quickly. They've got photographers with zoom lenses out there ready to capture the slightest sign of life at the front and the back of the house." Ben's tone was sour.

Joe levered himself upright and wandered through to the bathroom. Ben packed up his books and left, calling to their mother that Joe had shown signs of life, so could they have lunch now?

Liesel was sent up to accompany Joe directly to the kitchen without going into the front room or anywhere near the front door. She behaved like a burglar, sneaking down the stairs and shushing Joe if he made a step creak. They sat down to soup and toast. Mrs. Knightley broke the silence.

"I've emailed Dad. I don't know if he'll be able to get away, but of course, he had to know. I'm amazed the phone didn't wake you, Joe. It's been ringing off the hook all morning."

"I couldn't get to sleep at first, then those pills must have kicked in."

"Oh yes."

Silence fell as they sipped their soup. Cream of tomato, what Mum always made in times of sickness—only no one was really sick.

"What happens when we want to go out, Mum?" asked Joe.

"I don't know. We've got plenty of food, and I can put in an order over the Internet for more on Monday or Tuesday. I'll go to work, but I don't want any of you at school for the moment. The police rang this morning. It was that woman who was with us last night. She's been appointed as our liaison officer. She suggested issuing a statement through the police. I've drafted a couple of paragraphs, but maybe you want to add something. I don't know. You can take a look after lunch, then I'll email it to her if you think it's okay."

"Will that make any difference? They're going to be camping out there for days." Ben did not sound at all pleased at the prospect.

"Until the next big story comes along," said Joe, "which will be in a couple of days' time."

"Bang goes the weekend."

"Ben!" Mrs. Knightley rounded on her eldest son. "Someone died yesterday afternoon, someone you've known since she was a tiny kid and all you can think of is missing a date? I never thought you'd be so callous."

"That's not what I meant, Mum."

"Isn't it? It certainly sounded like it. Now eat your soup and focus on that essay. You might as well use your time productively."

Once again, the Knightleys stopped talking. Joe stared into the soup as if it might reveal some great secret. He couldn't swallow any more. He'd been able to deal with his own thoughts about Nell's death because he knew he could recover her. But hearing Mum talk about her as a tiny kid took him back to the days when Nell had refused to come to school unless she was wearing her cowboy boots, the day when she'd squirted paint all over their first teacher, Mrs. Nelligan, who'd thought it was on purpose, and the day when Nell had biffed him with her Cry More Tears peeing dolly. Memories of Nell seeped and slithered through his mind, eclipsing everything else. When it occurred to him that there could be no more memories, he was overwhelmed by a sensation of nausea so powerful that before he could quell it, Joe was throwing up what tomato soup he had drunk. He had managed to get to the sink in time.

"Great. A weekend cooped up with Mr. Vomit."

"Go to your room, Ben, and don't come out until you can be civil."

Ben squared up to his mother, but when it came to outstaring her, his eyes dropped, and he slunk off.

Mrs. Knightley went over and stroked Joe's back as he rinsed out the sink and his mouth with cold water. "There, there." She didn't say it would be all right. Nothing could make anything all right at the moment. Even if they managed to get Charlie Meek locked up in a truly horrible juvenile detention center, Nell was gone.

Wrung out and shabby, Joe shambled over to the couch in front of the television. He switched it on and it was time for the news at one. Nell's death was the second item after a car bomb in the Middle East, not a million miles away from where Dad was working. First they had a photo of Nell in her school uniform, giving a faint smile as enigmatic as the Mona Lisa and far prettier, then a series of shots of the bus stop, with blue-and-white police tape everywhere and a dark patch where she'd bled. After that, they announced the arrest of five minors and finally, they had some talking-head bloke pontificating on the evil youth of today and their hoodie-wearing culture of pointless and random violence.

"Where do they find these pompous gits? Boys have been going on the rampage since cavemen got together and decided it would be a good idea to mangle a mammoth." Mrs. Knightley went over to the television. "Do you want to watch any more or can I turn off this drivel?"

"Turn it off, unless Liesel wants to watch something."

Liesel *did* want to watch something—one of her interminable ballet videos. Joe went back upstairs and tidied his room. As he went through the mechanical process of picking up, folding, stowing, hanging, sorting and chucking, he thought about the Lamborghini. It had to be destroyed. There must be hundreds of ways to. It could be scrapped or crashed or sent over a cliff. But how was he going to get it to a scrapyard? Or out onto the road? To do any of those things, he needed to be able to drive. But how would he get out of the car in time for it to be destroyed? The whole car business had emphatically put him off any acquisitive longings. Whatever else he'd learned from this dream business, he grasped that wishing for things then getting them simply caused trouble, whether it was boring, besuited company men hassling his mother or crazed time travelers intent on destruction.

He'd been nursing the kernel of an idea for some days now, though. The only difficulty was that it required the house to be empty of Knightleys.

Once his room was tidy, Joe sat at his desk and began sketching. There was a knock, and his mother immediately put her head around the door.

"I've got that statement for you to check. Do you want to look at it now?"

Joe nodded and took the piece of paper his mother had printed. It sounded stilted and formulaic, but it would do. It would at least be some meat for the ravening hyenas sitting on their doorstep, and soon enough someone else would do something to draw them away from the Knightleys' extremely dull comings and goings.

Although Liesel stuck to her mother, still unnerved by the attack and its aftermath, Ben and Joe preferred to spend their confinement in their own rooms. They met up for mealtimes, which were uncomfortable, although Ben had exchanged resentment for a complete suppression of his personality. This did not bother Joe, but Liesel, in her characteristically tactless fashion, was quick to pick up on why.

"You're jealous of Joe. Normally you get all the attention, but all the exciting stuff has been happening to Joe. He got that car. Then there's all these reporters saying he's a hero."

Their mother didn't say anything, but she gave her eldest son an inquiring look and he blushed. He did settle down after that, and they all managed a reasonably amicable game of Monopoly after supper.

By Monday morning, the door steppers had faded away. There'd been a big coach crash involving local people and there was some corruption scandal emerging from the county town. Besides which it was clear that the Knightleys weren't going to issue anything more than the bland statement they'd given over the weekend, and since the murderer and his accomplices had been picked up, there was no great mystery. After some negotiation, Mrs. Knightley agreed that Ben and Liesel could go to their dance classes as normal that Monday afternoon.

Joe had used the time in his room to draw a series of images. As soon as Liesel and Ben had left the house at half past three, he lay down and waited for sleep.

The doorbell rang. He went down to his parents' room, which overlooked the street. There were no reporters around and an unfamiliar car was parked in the road, just in front of the house—a small hatchback, a real teacher's car. Perhaps his plan was working. The bell rang again, this time for longer. He went downstairs and checked the peephole. It was Eidolon, dressed as the drama teacher, wearing a secondhand Harris tweed overcoat and a long, knitted scarf of maroon and gold. Joe opened the door.

"Good afternoon, Joe."

"Hello." Joe leaned against the frame of the door, not sure whether to let Eidolon in or to keep him waiting on the stoop.

"It was rude of you to run out on me like that, after I'd gone to so much trouble to get you into my dream."

"I apologize."

"How formal. Are you going to let me in? Or have I come at an inconvenient time?"

"I think you can probably say whatever you need to right here. I don't imagine it will take long."

"It might, actually. I was going to make a suggestion, but it is a little complicated. It would be more comfortable for us both if we could sit down and discuss it, perhaps over a nice cup of tea."

There was such a disconnect between this mild-mannered man who looked so innocuous and the loony tunes psycho-killer that Joe nearly succumbed to the voice of reason. But he paused and looked closely at Eidolon and saw the pulse throbbing at his temple, the tense, clamped jaw and the gloved fists clenched tight in black leather.

"I don't trust you. You're a dealer and a nutter, and I'm not letting you into our house. I'll meet you somewhere."

"Burton Hill," muttered Eidolon, baring his teeth like a wolf under threat. "Sure I can't give you a lift?"

Joe smiled and shook his head. He closed the door.

On his bed, he stirred and turned over. Now he had to get to Burton Hill. It was their local landmark, a gently rising slope on one side then a cliff, as if a giant had taken a cleaver to the other half and scooped away the earth and rock and vegetation in a single sweep. It was about four hundred feet high, a pleasant afternoon's scramble. Periodically there was talk of fencing off the vertiginous drop, but accidents were rare, and those people who threw themselves off the edge, it was argued, would have found a way to do so regardless of fences and barbed wire. There were melancholy spots where decayed bouquets had been left to wither and weather away, their stilted messages to long-gone loved ones blotched with rain. There was a car park halfway up the slope for ramblers and dog walkers.

There Joe appeared, leaning against the Lamborghini. It looked even more out of place than it had in the Knightley garage, surrounded by the detritus of family life—unused power tools, a luridly plastic lawn mower, piles of clothes that Mrs. Knightley meant to sort and give to charity. Here, on the uneven dirt path, sitting under a leaden November sky, it looked as alien as a supermodel in Sainsbury's.

He watched as Eidolon's little car puttered up the lane and into the car park, where it pulled up on the opposite side to the Lamborghini.

"My, we have been busy. Does it drive well?"

"Mmm."

Eidolon yawned and stretched his arms, then rolled his head and his shoulders as if he were warming up for a run. Joe half expected him to do some quadriceps stretches or a couple of lunges. Then he linked his fingers and cracked all the little bones like a pianist preparing to play.

"My suggestion is that we become partners. At the moment, your dreams keep interfering with mine. But if we could dream together, if we could combine forces, we could work very effectively together and I could stop…um, eliminating people you care about. What do you think?"

What Joe thought was that Eidolon had made an admission of defeat. But it wouldn't be polite to point this out.

"What's in it for me?"

Eidolon turned. He scanned the hillside and walked over to the fence surrounding the car park. He leaned casually on it then held his palm outward. Joe waited. Nothing appeared to be happening. Then one of the bare oaks on the lower slopes of the hill began to smolder. Smoke billowed from its bark, and its branches began to crackle. Twigs flared up and flames began licking from deep within the tree until it became a pillar of fire. There had been no visible cause of the conflagration, no fiery beam from Eidolon's palm, but that was clearly the source of the flames. It was hard to sustain his pose of adolescent world-weariness, but Joe managed.

"Is that a dream thing or some other trick you've picked up over the last half-century?"

"It's a dream thing. I'm surprised you haven't found out about your arsenal yet." Eidolon's smile conveyed smug relief.

"You mean this arsenal?" Joe closed his eyes. When he opened them again, the great porcelain bowl from Eidolon's mansion was hovering fifteen feet up in the air above Eidolon's car. Joe released the bowl and in slow motion, it crashed down on the car roof. On impact, its shards glided across the car park while a dent molded itself into the roof of Eidolon's runabout, and the window struts gave way, shattering the front and rear windscreens. The car bounced once then settled.

"You're not making this easy," said Eidolon. "If we carry on like this, I'll have to hurt you. I really don't want to. It always gets so out of hand when I start hurting people."

"Enough with the cheesy villain talk. Who was the last person you hurt? You directly, I mean. You get other people to do the hurting—pathetic tossers like Charlie Meek, desperate for a fix."

"I was executioner for a sultan."

"Yeah, and you stabbed De Vere when he was already dying. I bet that was the last time you got your hands dirty with the nitty-gritty of death. Four hundred years ago."

"Why should I mess around with murder when I can find so many willing people to commit it for me? Oh, and before I forget, just how many people have you killed?"

Joe wanted Eidolon to shut up. For a supervillain, his voice was whiny and this particular incarnation—the impoverished teacher in his faded chinos and his stupid scarf and jumble-sale coat—diminished him further. Joe peered at the ground around Eidolon's feet. It began to crumble and slip.

Eidolon glanced down and saw that he was sinking. He lifted up his hand again.

"Is that your fallback?" Joe was genuinely curious. He could feel the heat approaching. He gazed directly at Eidolon's palm. He directed the heat back, and as the earth continued to suck Eidolon down, his fingers then his arm sprouted flames—at first small, delicate little lickings at the flesh and sinews and tendons, then a fiercer, bolder heat that made the skin glow and the flesh melt. Eidolon started screaming.

Joe had to decide how the creature should be extinguished, because the earth would stifle the fire if Eidolon sank any further. But the agonized squeals and the terrible smell were awful, so ice seemed like a good option. At first, Eidolon looked relieved to feel the cold, but then, as his breath formed crystals, his skin took on a blue tinge and his limbs solidified, his cries were stifled and his eyes were enormous with pain and terror.

It was then Joe understood that he was toying with this creature, which was cruel and unnecessary, making him no better than Eidolon. He turned his gaze on the Lamborghini. He could operate it like a giant remote-controlled toy. He maneuvered it until its engine was backed up against Eidolon, thrumming. Joe turned his full attention to the car and the sound of the engine deepened and darkened. The smooth, golden paint began to blister and smoke billowed from under the boot. Petrol spilled from the tanks and ignited. Joe ran for cover—ran faster than he ever had before—and dived as the fireball erupted.

He woke up at home, lying on his bed. His hand hurt. It was clenched tightly shut, blood oozing between his fingers.

He unfolded his fingers and found that he was holding a broken shard of blue-and-white porcelain, its edges sharp. He held the fragment under the cold tap and watched as blood swirled around the white sink.

The house was still silent and empty. He went into the garage. Apart from the usual detritus of family life, there was nothing. The Lamborghini had vanished.

Chapter Twenty-Five

Sleeping Venus

The next thing that Joe knew, his mum was shaking him awake.

"Where's the car?" she demanded.

"What?" Joe was befuddled with sleep.

"The extremely expensive car that you won has disappeared. Where is it?"

"How should I know? I've been up here all afternoon." He sat up, rubbing his eyes and trying to unkink his neck.

Mrs' Knightley's hands were on her hips, her eyes hard, her shoulders tense. "Do you know how much money I've forked out to have that car legally registered in our name, and all you can say when it vanishes is 'How should I know?' You lie there sleeping while some burglar comes into the house and makes off with it, even though it sounds like a snoring buffalo, even in low gear?"

"I was at the top of the house. You know I can't hear anything up there. You put me up there on purpose so nothing would interfere with darling Ben's practicing and darling Ben's work and darling Ben's life in general, then you blame me when I can't hear anything? I didn't ask to be exiled at the top of the house." He paused for a breath. "Anyway, what does it matter? It's just a car. Nell died yesterday, and you want me to fuss over some stupid car?"

"First of all, it's not any old car. It's *your* car, your massively expensive, valuable car, and secondly, of course Nell's death matters, but this has nothing to do with it. And finally, you weren't exiled at the top of the house. We asked you first which room you wanted, and Dad did it up especially for you. So don't try sidetracking me with shabby little tantrums." She glared at Joe.

He glared back, then his rage melted. "I'm sorry, Mum."

She blinked, disarmed.

He took the next step. "I'm sorry about the 'darling Ben' crack, but I really have no idea what's happened to the car. Maybe you'd better call the police." He suppressed his guilt about lying to his mother. The truth was so implausible that it would probably make her head twist around and explode.

With resignation, she nodded. By the time Joe had joined the others in the kitchen, the police were on their way. The radio was blaring. It was tuned to the local station because Liesel had met one of the DJs at a road show over the summer and developed a massive crush on him.

Whenever Liesel could get away with it, she retuned the radio away from Radio Four to Central Southern. The pips for the six o'clock news bleeped. Nell's murder was supplanted as the number one news story by a fresh item about a massive explosion on Burton Hill. Two cars had been destroyed, and there was one confirmed but unidentified casualty. Then Dave Tanqueray came back on air, and Liesel sat enraptured at the table, her chin cradled in her hands, a goofy smile on her lips.

A couple of uniformed men came to take Mrs. Knightley's statement about the car. She had to show them around the garage, and they spotted that the lock had been melted away by what looked like a high-intensity welding machine. An unusual, but effective, way to breach the garage and snatch the car.

Joe didn't remember dreaming that, but he was relieved there were physical signs that the garage had been forced.

It meant that the insurance might pay up, although probably not up to the full value of a new Lamborghini, given the doubts about the car's provenance. He didn't much care about the money, but it would make up to Mum for the hassle caused by the car's arrival.

Once the police had gone, he was left pondering his next conundrum. Defeating Eidolon had not been as gratifying as he'd expected. He could not forget that he had effectively tortured Dolon before destroying him, and the forces he had unleashed in doing so terrified him. Sitting upstairs at his desk, he fingered the shard of porcelain. He began flicking through *Dream Master*. This time, in addition to frames from Joe's perspective, the artists had included thought bubbles showing what Eidolon had been considering. It was no comfort to discover that Joe had been quite right not to let the man into the house, where he had planned to make a complete mess involving Joe's eyeballs, guts and skin before getting started on the rest of the family. Even the knowledge that Eidolon had been the sickest of beings could not ease Joe's consternation at his relish in tormenting him. In less than a month, he had gone from a normal — well, normal-ish — teenager to havoc-wreaker, and he didn't like it. He wanted to be normal again, to ditch this dream stuff once and for all. But first, he had to recover Nell.

He wanted her back more than ever. He missed her common sense and her calm competence, the way she talked to him as if he were an idiot. Most of all he missed knowing that whether he was with her not, she was there, somewhere on earth, thinking, doing, being. He would gladly give up on the Dream Master gig if it only meant he could make her live.

But first he had to demonstrate that he had relinquished her. It was his hardest dream, harder by far than combusting Eidolon, an act that had not required deliberation.

He was in a boat on a river, without oars, without a rudder, without any means of propulsion, carried by a current that accelerated into a mist out of which shapes loomed then dissolved. He huddled deep into the warmth of his dark woolen cloak. The current gentled until the boat came to a stop in an expanse of black water so still that it seemed oily in its density. The water sucked at the sides of the boat. He sat. About fifteen feet in front of the boat, a column eased from the water. Gradually, the column took shape and Joe saw that it was Nell, slender, gray as the mist, the slash down the left side of her neck raw and oozing darkly, stickily. She started speaking and sinking simultaneously.

"Rescue me, Joe. Come and get me. Don't leave me here. Please don't leave me here. You have to help me, Joe. Please help me."

But something was wrong with her eyes and the supplication of her hands, which seemed to reach the very edge of his boat.

"I can't help you, Nell. It's too late to help you." Her fingers now clung to the side, her hair slicked back, her eyes still wide and crazed, her face the chalky white of a portrait of the aged Elizabeth, Virgin Queen, her mouth gaping and black as her voice echoed in the hollow mist, pleading, begging for him to save her.

He recoiled and he gazed at the water. The first wave swelled beneath the vessel, causing Nell to lose her grip. The second wave swept the boat around. The third wave carried it away from her. He heard a piteous wail, but he did not look back. He did not turn. He sat firm, his hands gripping at the bench so hard that he could feel the grain of the wood impressed into his skin, knots and whorls and all. The boat picked up speed, rushing over the waves, but from across the stream, he could still hear his name, a woeful, elongated moan.

As the boat eased through the water, the mist cleared.

Joe was traveling through a steep-sided valley, thick with trees and shrubs, uninhabited territory. As he gazed at the landscape, the boat shuddered and slowed. He stood and looked around him. Holding out a hand, he traced a line along a contour of the land. Instantly, the trees and shrubs along that line were erased and a barren strip of earth appeared. Stunned, Joe quickly reversed his action. It was like watching a film played backward. Mature trees and lush undergrowth sprang back into position. It wasn't bunting and brass bands, but it was an incredibly powerful sensation, more than enough to leave him in no doubt that he'd achieved the promotion. Joe longed to have Eidolon alive to witness this.

Then he remembered what he had done to Nell and his innards shriveled like a slug on the receiving end of a shower of salt. He had to get home and discover how to fetch her from nowhere, from nothing.

Back in his room, he checked *Dream Master* again. It was even harder to read about rejecting Nell. In the boat, he had turned away, but here, looking at the images of her, he could not mistake the appeal in her eyes. He shut the book, sat at his drawing table and sketched her over and over again, wishing he had taken a photo from her room so that he could be sure of the details of her face. He did not want to look at the book again, but it did have other pictures of Nell. The only thing it didn't have was her actual death in the bus stop. That hadn't been a dream.

By the time he looked at the clock and saw he should have gone to bed two hours before, he had filled sheets of paper from which Nell gazed ironically, irritably, peacefully, cynically, happily. Every time he remembered another expression, he had drawn another picture, cramming the pages with hundreds of angles of her face.

He shoved them under his pillow and went to bed, convinced that it would not be as simple as this to bring her back. His assumption proved correct. When he went down for breakfast, his mother was in her dressing gown, finishing her toast.

"Why aren't you at work, Mum?"

"I've taken the rest of this week off. I don't care that much about the car. Well, I do care about the car, but what with Nell and the car, I just don't feel easy being away from you lot. Bad things happen in threes. If anything else is going to happen, I want to know about it immediately, not hear about it over the phone or when I walk through the door at the end of the day." She took her dishes to the sink and asked if Joe wanted anything.

"It's okay. I'll make it."

The phone rang. Joe was so hungry that he barely registered what his mother was saying. He did notice that she'd put on her soothing voice, the one she used when clients at the end of their tether had winkled her home phone number out of the receptionist and were determined to list every flaw of the spouse they so wanted to ditch, despite knowing that this was billable time. He'd finished his second bowl of cereal by the time she put the phone down. She reached for a tissue, blew her nose with ferocity and dabbed away the traces of tears.

"That was Niamh Brennan. She was just telling me that Nell's body is being released to the undertaker today, so she's going ahead with plans for a funeral on Saturday."

"Nell's still dead?" blurted Joe.

His mother hugged him. "Oh, sweetheart, did you think you'd wake up and everything would be all right?"

"No." He submitted to his mother's embrace for a moment, then shook her off. "I don't know why. I'd just sort of hoped. Stupid, I know."

He wanted to pummel himself for his stupidity. He'd drawn Nell, but he hadn't actually dreamed about her. The drawings were not enough, no matter how masterful he'd become. It was frustrating. He had until Saturday to recover her. Once Nell was buried, it would be too late to get her back from anywhere, let alone nowhere.

But for the first time since that first fishy dream, Joe hit a wall. He could not dream. He spent all Tuesday trying to dream of anything at all, but every time he nodded off, there was nothing—just blank, dark emptiness.

He went to bed early, straight after supper. Ben and Liesel exchanged weirded-out looks. Still nothing happened. He plunged into sleep and stayed there, eclipsed by exhaustion. When he surfaced on Wednesday morning, it was nearly midday. He got up, sloped downstairs where he found his mother sitting at the computer. He had a go at her.

"Why didn't you wake me up? I've wasted the whole

morning. You should have woken me up. You're always hassling me to get up, and the one time I want to get up, you leave me in bed until the whole bloody day has gone."

Mrs. Knightley was startled by Joe's vehement outburst. "You need to rest, Joe. The psychiatrist told us you might sleep more than normal. Do you remember? It's a reaction to shock. It's not unusual. Anyway, why do you want to get up? You don't have school. You don't have any work, because I made it quite clear to Mrs. Elphick that you can catch up with coursework when you get back to school and not before. So where's the fire?"

Joe agreed there was no fire. He went back to bed.

This time he stayed in the dark. He reached out and touched it. He found he could grasp it. It felt velvety and emollient on his skin. Cool. Soothing. He pictured himself surrounded by the dark. When he was smaller, he'd gone to a party where the going-home present was a rubber ball with a little plastic figure suspended inside. Some kids had dinosaurs, others had cars or fish. He'd been given a shark. He imagined himself like that shark, in a rubber ball of darkness, bouncing around a huge, light space. He gazed at the trajectory the shrinking ball of blackness was making, smacking against the whiteness like a squash ball against the walls of a squash court. Finally, he managed to suck the blackness deep within himself and now he was standing within the great vacuum, and still it was blank.

He concentrated harder and steadily created a door in the wall opposite him.

It opened into a narrow alley, running between two immense stone buildings and topped by a sliver of distant night sky, occasional stars dotting the way like the strip of guide lights running down an airplane aisle.

He felt his way down the passage. At times he could touch both walls, then one of the buildings would retreat a little and he was left tracking the right-hand side of the passage.

There was no sodium glow of streetlights. He could feel himself descending, but the buildings on either side did not seem to get any higher. On and on he walked, increasingly uneasy. He looked back and immediately behind him found the doorway he had come through, although it should have been hundreds of meters behind him by now. More disquieting still, there was no handle, no means of retreating through it. As he walked farther into the darkness, he felt like a letter on a page along which the cursor was traveling in delete mode.

Then he heard the panting. Some distance away, several dogs were huffing and puffing. They sounded pleased, as if they had done good work for their master, reminding Joe of the dogs that had accompanied the hunt. One bayed, its howl reverberating along the passageway, sending shivers up Joe's spine. He half expected a mad, red-eyed slavering monster to bound toward him. There was the sound of paws bouncing about, claws clicking against some solid surface. Joe kept on walking. But as the sound faded, he grew impatient, no longer content to remain in the dark. Once again, he was in a section of path where he could touch both walls at the same time. He stood, stretched out into a star shape and began pushing the walls apart. His body elongated, his arms and legs grew in length and size, and the walls slowly began to ease away from each other. He turned to the right-hand wall and leaned hard against it until it folded into itself, then repeated the action with the left-hand wall. Before him now was a huge expanse of night sky, like being in a planetarium. But there was nothing else there. Once again, the dogs started up, panting and snuffling for some scent. Then he saw it. It wasn't very dignified, but it was large and it had three heads, which was why it made so much noise.

One head was mastiff-like, majestic, heavy and drooling. The second belonged to a more elegant hound, an Afghan or saluki with a neat snout and eyebrows that looked bemused. The final head belonged to a Doberman, teeth bared and eyes cruel. As Joe approached, all three heads snapped up. There was teeth baring and growling. Joe stopped to look at the creature. It resembled a radioactive mutation, but it was there, and it was nearly a meter high at the shoulders. The very substantial shoulders needed to hold up and govern three different heads.

The dog attacked. Joe created an impenetrable barrier of air and it—or they, he was not sure which—became more and more wound up, frenziedly barking and leaping up and down, jaws agape. He manipulated the air around it, encircling the beast in a sphere in which it ran and tumbled like clothes in a dryer.

A crescent moon rose and lit a courtyard surrounded on three sides by classical temples, colonnaded, decorated with marble friezes, caryatids and balustrades with tiled roofs. The courtyard was paved with marble tiles and in its center where one might expect a fountain was a chaise longue of gilded wood and wine-dark velvet. On it reclined a woman wearing a dress of the same wine-colored velvet. She lay on her back, one leg swinging off the edge of the chaise longue, her head pillowed on her folded arms. Her feet were bare and her hair was swept back from her face.

It was Nell.

Joe ran to her side. He checked her neck. The skin was unbroken and unblemished. He could discern no breath, no rise and fall of the chest, none of the twitches or shifts of sleep. But she was solid and real. He leaned forward and kissed her. Her lips were still and cold.

He stood again and readied himself to carry her out of this place. He gathered her to him. The dress bunched and nearly tripped him up as he turned, and he was so busy shifting Nell's weight and collecting up the material that he did not notice that he had been surrounded by a platoon of skeletons. It was the fragility of their bones which first struck Joe. Then he saw they all had their right arms lifted across their chests, as if covering the hearts, which no longer beat beneath their ribs. As he moved toward them, they parted ranks and made a passageway of bones through which he walked. However mild they seemed, they unnerved Joe and he wanted to escape them. With a rattle, they lifted up their arms to form a bridge, and in the distance, he heard children's voices singing Oranges and Lemons. The sky remained crepuscular as Joe passed the three-headed dog, still trapped in its bubble.

The slope seemed steeper as he went up it. At first, Nell's weight seemed manageable, but his arms tired and his breath came quicker and quicker. The children's voices faded away. He leaned against a wall to get his breath back, not daring to put Nell down. The distance he covered between each rest diminished until he was taking only a few steps before halting.

Finally, he absolutely had to put her down. He sat beside her, his elbows resting on his knees, his upper arms burning from the exertion. He looked at her face, and he saw that where her skin had been uniformly white, now there was color in her lips and cheeks, and her eyelashes and eyebrows seemed darker, more clearly defined. There was still no breath. He stood up, clenched his fists then released his fingers as though flicking water off his hands. Then he sculpted the air, creating an opening and found himself in Nell's room. He picked her up and carried her back into his world.

Chapter Twenty-Six

Back to Reality

As he had planned, the opening he had created led Joe straight into Nell's bedroom. It was dark and he nearly stumbled and dropped her, but he managed to right himself and lower her onto the bed. He fumbled for the bedside light. To his relief, her chest now rose and fell. She breathed. He knew he ought to leave, but he wanted to look at her. He eased her over toward the wall and lay on one side, his head on his arm, his other arm resting on her diaphragm so he could feel her steady, comforting inhalations and exhalations. He breathed in her leafy scent, like the damp of a warm garden after a rainy night. Even as he told himself he ought to be getting up and going, the ache of his arms and legs and shoulders eased away, leaving only a delicious looseness, like his limbs were liquefying.

When he woke, he was lying on the floor of his own room, still stretched out on his side as though Nell were next to him. It was dark, which meant it could be anywhere between four in the afternoon and eight in the morning. The clock glowed, showing that it was quarter to six in the morning. He climbed back into bed.

* * * *

The next thing he knew, Ben was shaking him awake. "Come on, we're going to be late. Didn't you set the alarm last night?"

"Late for what?"

"School, dimwit. School. Remember, where we go every day?"

Joe gazed at Ben as if his brother had grown an extra limb. "But we're not going to school just now. What about the press? And Mum's staying at home too."

"On what planet?" Ben sounded exasperated. Joe saw that Ben believed his lame little brother had lost all grasp of reality. "It's the middle of term, Joe. We've got six more weeks of school before the Christmas holidays."

"Six? The last time I looked it was only four." Joe got out of bed and rummaged in his desk. He found his diary. He remembered writing down three major pieces of coursework over the past two weeks, but the diary was blank.

"What day is it, Ben?"

"Wednesday."

"No, I mean date."

"The seventh of November."

"Shit." This finally galvanized Joe into action, and Ben left him to get ready.

There was just time to check the garage before he left for school. The Lamborghini was lurking there like a docile cat. At school, Smokey was eager as ever to discuss being turned into a fish and Joe's curious absence from classes the day before. Frustrated by Joe's stonewalling, Smokey whined, "It's like you don't trust me, man."

He looked Smokey in the eye and said, "Not as far as I can throw you."

Smokey recoiled as if Joe had slapped him. "What do you mean?"

"Look, Smokey, we've got nothing in common. You want to get wasted or laid or both, and I want to get some GCSEs and get out of this place. I like graphic novels, you hate them. You like getting hammered, I hate it. I could carry on, but why bother?"

"You're so gay."

"No, that would be my brother," Joe said evenly.

Smokey stepped back. Until now, Joe had had a sense of

humor bypass where his brother was concerned. Normally, Joe would have really lost his rag, but now he seemed mellow. Confident. "What have you been taking? You're not like you."

Joe smiled. It was true. He wasn't like himself, but it didn't matter. He had been a Dream Master and even if he never had another dream, nothing could take that away.

"Maybe I'm more like me than I've ever been before. See you around, Smokey."

Turning his back on Smokey, he headed off for his form room. He liked this time loop business, even if it did mean that Charlie Meek was going to be unbearable. Except that now, he had plans for Charlie Meek, whether he could manipulate his dreams or not.

For the first time, Joe was more than an observer at school. At lunch, he went over to where Sammi and Raquel were sitting. They were deep in conversation when he stood by their table.

"Can I sit with you?"

The girls exchanged startled glances, then nodded. Joe sat. He unwrapped his sandwich and listened as they chatted idly. He'd wanted to know about their drama teacher but they were evaluating rock bands. When Raquel proclaimed a newfound passion for Johnny Borrell from Razorlight, Sammi appealed to Joe.

"They're pants, aren't they?'

"I don't know. I quite like them. I wouldn't pay to see them but their videos are okay. A bit same old, same old."

"That drama guy who replaced Phelps, he liked them," said Raquel, pouting.

"He was a tosser, Raquel. He came here for one lesson and now he's disappeared, so we're lumped with that prick Thomas."

Sammi waved at someone in the queue, and Raquel turned to see who it was. Joe swallowed. Nell came over and sat next to Sammi. She somehow made a school uniform look like haute couture and was practicing her withering look.

"You all right, Nell?" he asked.

"Why wouldn't I be?"

"No reason. You didn't say much in maths. That's not like you."

"Perhaps I was just astounded by the pearls of wisdom you were uttering. Most unlike you, Joe."

Joe grinned. He could hardly confess that this was the second time he'd sat through that particular lesson. His face lit up and all three girls reappraised him as if perhaps this Knightley was going to be just as gorgeous as his sadly unavailable older brother.

* * * *

As he was leaving school that afternoon, he heard his name. It was Mrs. Elphick, watching the students streaming away from the premises.

"Joe Knightley, I want a word with you."

He went to her.

"Did your American houseguest get home safely, Joe?"

"Yes, he did. Thank you, Mrs. Elphick."

"I hope we won't have any further disruptions of that nature on school premises."

"Absolutely not, Mrs. Elphick."

Her tone was shrewd. "I'm sure it's not the last time you'll be at the bottom of some bizarre incident or other."

"I'll try to make sure it won't happen again, Mrs. Elphick."

She arched one sculpted eyebrow then dismissed him.

Joe ran to catch the bus and just made it. The key thing was to find out if he still had powers, if he still had Karabashi's carpet, if he still had the *Dream Master* book.

When he got in the house, he gathered up the post and swept upstairs. His room was a pit—the duvet tumbling off the bed, papers everywhere, clothes dumped on the floor, a pile of CDs tumbled all over the rug. In his cupboard he found Karabashi's carpet. It felt lighter, silkier than before. He sorted his papers. All the pictures of Nell were there still. Underneath them was the book.

The final picture was of Nell on her bed, wearing her burgundy dress with him laying alongside, their eyes closed. The likelihood of getting that close to Nell ever again was remote, but at least he had this picture.

One question remained. Was he still a Dream Master?

The only thing to do was to have a dream and see what happened. He cleared a space on the floor and laid out Karabashi's carpet. But when he tried to travel back to the scholar, nothing happened. Maybe having some form of proof that Eidolon had been destroyed would help. He folded up the carpet and imagined himself back on Burton Hill, in the car park.

He managed to hover above it, watching as police tape flapped around the burned out remains of a car. Only one car.

Not the Lamborghini, but the Japanese runabout that Eidolon had been driving. There was also a striped tent of the sort that repair men from utility companies use to cover their holes in the road. A policeman was standing sentinel. Hovering around was irritating because he couldn't get close enough to hear what was happening. However, he could hardly have strolled past the policeman into the tent. He did want to know what was left of Dolon, which was when it occurred to him. Dropping to the ground, he closed his eyes and concentrated. First, his eyes changed. Then he looked down and saw that his hands had become paws and that fur was covering them in great ginger clumps. He turned, trying to examine the tail that had grown from his spine and the legs that had shifted position and alignment. Having no arms and four legs felt different. The policeman looked at the cat and laughed.

"Here, puss. Here." And he made those funny kissing sounds that are supposed to attract cats, although Joe couldn't see why. "Come on, kitty." Joe looked at this man dubiously. Why would anyone want to stroke a mangy ginger stray? But this guy was so bored that he probably welcomed any distraction from standing around outside the tent. Joe circled the policeman's legs, smearing against them like butter on toast, and he purred. It was fun purring, a sound that simply wasn't accessible to humans, which was a shame. It was also great being stroked, feeling a solid, warm hand rubbing his fur. It was also pretty intimate, more so than Joe had ever been since he was a toddler prone to hugging anything static or moving.

Then the transmitter on the policeman's shoulder crackled into life and Joe had his opportunity. He sidled into the tent and looked. There was a mound of charred cinders. There were some lumps. And beneath the ashes, there were four bones protruding from the earth. Two pairs of fibula and tibia. He remembered them from the human body software Mum and Dad had given Ben for Christmas the year of his GCSEs. It was stupid, the memories that flashed into the mind when one was confronted with something that didn't really bear thinking about. He batted at one of the bones with his paw in the hope that it would come out, and he could take it home.

The policeman poked his head into the tent and shooed the cat out. Joe was glad to go. He trotted off, remembering the purpose that most cats seemed to carry with them. Once he was out of sight, he sat down and transformed back into a human.

Just as well no one had walked into the room while he was feline, else he might have ended up with cat's paws or a tail as a hangover from the dream. He checked the book, but this time, there were no additional pages. Not knowing if this had been simply a dream or one of the dreams that had come true, Joe gave up and went to bed.

* * * *

Things were quiet over the next few days. Everything was drearily normal until the following week when finally, Joe chanced on Charlie Meek. It happened in the boys' toilets at school, a place he tried to avoid because it reeked, because there was always stupid graffiti, plus it was the kind of location that thugs like Charlie Meek used for their daily business of intimidating other kids, safe from adult intervention, for what teacher would ever go near the boys' loo?

He was washing his hands when the door burst open and a year eight kid rocketed in and fell over. Joe went over to help him up. By the time the kid was standing, Charlie Meek was trying to loom over them but failing because Joe was considerably taller than Charlie.

Two other boys followed. Charlie's latest acolytes, Sean Stanton and Ryan Vernon. Two of the boys who had helped him at the bus stop. Joe dusted down the year eight lad.

"Get out of here right now," he said and pushed the boy past Charlie and his two friends. There were probably a couple more idiots waiting outside, but the boy might yet escape. And if he did, he might have the sense to find a teacher. There had to be some around. They usually patrolled the corridors during lunch.

"What you doin' interferin' in my business, Knightley?"

"I can't stand around while you mash up some little kid. What were you after? His lunch money? Or were you just trying to nick some crisps off him? You are so petty, Charlie." Perhaps it would get him into trouble, but he'd had enough of staying out of Charlie's way.

"Watch your step, Knightley."

"You and your mates gonna take me?" Joe knew they wouldn't. But he wanted to provoke Charlie, get him out in the open and get him caught so that once and for all, he was kicked out of school instead of having detentions which he skipped, temporary exclusions which he thought were just holidays and internal exclusions which meant that he just sat in a room in school watched by teachers and did bugger all for three days.

"We can take you, no problem, but we ain't gonna. You ain't worth it."

Joe looked hard into his eyes. He didn't think Charlie had taken any drugs yet today, but he wanted to be sure. If Charlie was on amphetamines, he'd be unstoppable. He carried on staring at Charlie, who looked away. All three thugs stepped back. Joe looked solid, so substantial that beating him to a pulp must have seemed a tricky prospect.

Joe closed his eyes and forced himself to dream.

The kilo of coke Smokey had stolen was now in Charlie's backpack. So was the knife he'd used on Nell. The corridor was no longer empty, because Tucker and Crosbie were walking down it. They were mates because they'd both started teaching at Cosham High the same year, somewhere around the time that the triceratops had become extinct. Tucker was swearing blind that he hadn't imagined young Joe Knightley being sucked into a wall. A year eight was running toward them, scarcely looking ahead because he kept glancing behind him, totally unnerved. He collided with Crosbie's substantial stomach.

"Steve Upshaw! What are you doing here?"

The child gabbled something about Charlie Meek and the boys' toilet. Crosbie and Tucker slumped a little. They knew they had to investigate. They had to go in there.

Eeeeuuuughhh!

Charlie pulled out his knife. The door opened abruptly. Instead of backup, Charlie found himself looking at Crosbie and Tucker. Joe opened his eyes. The teachers saw the knife. Tucker reached for his mobile then dialed reception. The receptionist said that Mr. Dunwoody, the principal, would be there immediately.

"Immediately isn't soon enough," said Tucker. Then he called the police. When the police saw the stash of cocaine, they nodded, muttering about secure training centers. Charlie wouldn't be coming back to Lyndhurst once he was released.

Once again, Joe couldn't decide whether he'd been responsible for the dream or if the events that it had unleashed would have happened anyway. Either way, he wasn't bothered. It was good not to fall asleep any more during classes. It was good not to be swept away into unfamiliar worlds, and it was good having a life. Because perhaps for the first time since he was six, Joe felt like he did have a life. Smokey left him alone. Liesel was preoccupied with her Christmas dance extravaganza, Ben saw a lot of Zahid and Mum was still in thrall to the Lamborghini, counting down the days until Dad got home for Christmas and they could go roaring around in their new toy.

Not everything was going Joe's way. Nell was colder than a katabatic wind. That sweet, brief time where they had been friends again had ended, and her blasts of disapproval chilled Joe to the soul. He was always on his best behavior. He played none of the goonish tricks that had so irritated her, but it was too late for any rapprochement. Other girls talked to him now, and not just because he was Ben's little brother.

Nonetheless, Nell remained aloof.

* * * *

At the end of term, once Liesel's performance was over and in the few days before David Knightley returned home, the family went up to London. Liesel had asked if they could see a West End musical for their Christmas treat. She really, *really* wanted to see *Billy Elliott*, and somehow, they had found tickets. Mrs. Knightley was relieved when Joe opted out of the theater trip, saying he'd prefer to go to the movies and the Forbidden Planet store. They arranged to meet up at a café just off Leicester Square after the *Billy Elliott* matinée for a quick bite before catching the train home.

The play began about forty minutes before Joe's movie. He reassured his mother that he would not talk to strangers or get lost, and as soon as Ben, Liesel and his mother had passed the theater ushers, Joe made for Piccadilly Circus. The streets were thick with bodies bouncing off one another, armed with carrier bags and ready for further sorties into the shops selling scarves, beads, bags, music, books, DVDs, scented potions for bath and body, shoddy T-shirts and mugs with Union Jack flags, plastic policeman's helmets and postcards — still — of Princess Diana and — more recently — Prince William. Though it was just after two, the lights were already on and the huge neon billboards rolled through familiar brand names — Coke, Nike, Sony, Nokia.

Sitting on the Eros steps was a statuesque punk with spiked black hair, red lipstick and heavy kohl around the eyes. She wore a black leather jacket and red tartan trousers. Joe wasn't quite sure how to approach her, but she made it easy, coming forward to embrace him and kiss him on both cheeks.

"Joe, so good to see you."

"Tyche."

She stepped back and inspected him. "You look well. Different. Less feeble, somehow. Got the girls chatting you up then?"

He looked down and smiled, muttering, "A bit. You know."

"I think I do, Joe."

"I was hoping we'd meet again."

"We're going to be meeting pretty regularly, Joe. It's part of the territory."

"What territory?"

"Dream Master stuff. Most of you humans don't make it, but when you do, we have to work together. Work things out. I like how you handled the Meek business, very neat. Got your friend Smokey out of a bit of bother too. As for finishing off Eidolon, very slick. He certainly underestimated you." She looped an arm around his and led him toward Leicester Square through the tumult of last-minute shoppers.

"But—"

Tyche overrode Joe's interruption. "You're going to be big. I can tell. Bigger than we've had for some time — vision and a touch of flair."

"Hang on." Joe stopped dead. "I'm not meant to be Dream Master. Do you remember? I got Nell back, much good it's done me."

"That wasn't your fondest wish, dumb-ass."

"It wasn't?"

She led him into an ice-cream parlor. He didn't particularly want ice cream on one of the coldest days this winter, but he wasn't about to contradict a goddess. She sent him off for a triple sundae with scoops of tiramisu, Bailey's and Belgian chocolate with butterscotch and sprinkles. He got himself a coffee. While she waited for him, she examined her nail polish, black and chipped, and nibbled her cuticles. It wasn't very goddessy, but he didn't think it tactful to point that out.

"So, Tyche, if getting Nell back wasn't my fondest wish, what was?"

"You don't know?"

Talking with Tyche was so frustrating that Joe wanted to slam the table, but he merely put his coffee cup down and said, "No. If I knew, I wouldn't be asking you."

"I suppose not. It's worked out quite neatly really. Your fondest wish was not to be a Dream Master. Eidolon wanted to be Dream Master so much that it was never going to happen. And you didn't want anything to do with the whole—what did you call it up there on Nemrud?—malarkey. So you get to be Dream Master. That's how fate and wishes and so forth always work. It's a rule we gods have."

"In that case, why can't I get Nell to like me?"

"You haven't been paying attention. The Dream Master deal doesn't allow for personal wishes. It's a global thing. You have to think big. Your job is to make other people's dreams come true. What you want is really...well, pretty irrelevant to the grand scheme of things." She licked her spoon then pinged it into the empty glass dish. "Thanks for that, Joe. Absolutely delicious. And thanks also for the transformation. I've been having a great time since you got me out of that stone-cladding costume." She stood, dropped a kiss on his nose and sashayed out of the ice-cream parlor, the gobsmacked eyes of several weary, shopped-out fathers following her.

Joe sipped the last of his coffee and called the waitress. It was weird, being on his own, spending money, deciding he really didn't want to go and see another shoot-'em-up movie and making his way through the crowds to the place he did want to be.

At Forbidden Planet, he was soon lost in other worlds as he browsed through the stocks of new and used comics.

They had magazines, books, models, posters, key rings, T-shirts—everything a comics addict could desire. Then he came upon the book. It was black, with silver writing embossed on the front, the font familiar to him. He opened the book and the first frame was a ginger cat curling around the legs of a policeman. He snapped the book shut and took it to the counter. The guy there couldn't find the barcode and called the manager. A small, neat man with a mass of curly graying hair and thick glasses with round black frames came out. He looked the book over then he checked Joe out.

"It's yours. No charge."

The young guy at the till, astonished at this largesse, slipped the book into a bag. Joe picked it up then left. It was nearly time to face his family.

About the Author

A.Z.A Clarke

A.Z.A Clarke has worked as an English teacher and journalist in Beijing, Brighton, Brussels and the Isle of Man.

A.Z.A Clarke loves to hear from readers. You can find contact information, website details and an author profile page at https://www.finch-books.com/

.